LEGEND HUNTER
IRISH MYSTIC LEGENDS BOOK ONE

JENNIFER ROSE MCMAHON

For all those who love a good Irish legend.
Finscéal Maith Éireannach

BOOK ONE

LEGEND HUNTER

by Jennifer Rose McMahon

CHAPTER 1

I t was somewhere right around here that I lost sight of her as she was pulled away into the howling mist.

Kicking at loose chunks of gravel, I rubbed my unbelieving eyes to clear the crushing reality of the event. It had been mere seconds since she disappeared, but it already weighed on me like a tortured eternity.

The thick, whirling fog had come out of nowhere and strong gusts blinded me for the few short moments before it took her. I crouched down, fearing it had come for me too. But when I opened my eyes, the assailing wind dissipated, creeping through the grass and out to sea… and she was gone.

Blinking into the bright light of mid-day, I watched the blurred greens and blues of the rolling hills and the Irish sea separating into their own vivid dimensions. I shook my head, clearing the dream-like quality from the historical surroundings of the ancient castle ruin before me.

My face dropped into my hands as my knotted stomach churned. It was the curse—the haunting visions that lurked in every shadow. I'd always feared them, but now their danger was more real to me.

Maeve was gone. Vanished into thin air. And I could be next.

My eyes squeezed shut as I pictured my classmates back at school, sitting in uniform rows with glazed stares plastered across their faces. That was where I was supposed to be, where my grandmother wanted me to be. And yet again, because of these crazy visions, I was here at the ruins of Doona Castle instead.

As my clouded senses cleared and returned to sharper focus, I turned with squinted eyes, searching for the others who were with me. Had they seen the same thing--the disappearance? Or was it an abduction? Their reactions would prove to me what was real and what was maybe a dream.

It was only when the distorted ringing in my ears had died down that I heard their painful cries. They searched for her in every direction and their incessant calling of her name shattered me with terror. I pressed my hands over my ears to stop the tormented sound and crouched down to protect myself from the chaos.

Rocking, tight as a ball, I isolated myself while the shocking wails faded out beyond me. Pictures of lush green fields and meandering stone walls filled my mind as I tried to lull myself into tranquility. The vibrating hum of my voice reverberated through my skull though, rising to an unsettling moan as my voice grew louder in my throat.

"Noooo. No. No!" The pounding words shot out of me, tightening my clamp around my head. How could she have been taken away? The irrational thought of her disappearing terrified me.

Helplessness washed through me, draining my inner strength, and then my shoulder shook as I was yanked up to standing.

"Get up, Izzy! Ya need to get out of here." Declan commanded me, lifting me like a weightless doll. "Isobel!"

Pulling me away from the crumbled castle walls, we stumbled along the uneven ground, racing toward the car. Michelle followed, with a hand on his elbow as she kept her eyes fixed on the desperate scene behind us. She was Maeve's best friend but judging by the lost gaze on her mystified face, she had no idea what was happening.

The other two in our group stayed behind, searching the castle ruin with faraway stares, voices hoarse from calling her name again and again. The one in a black leather jacket barreled around the corner of what was left of its stony walls, scouting every direction with wide-eyed bewilderment. His voice broke through the salty breeze and carried a sharp ring of shock laced with stinging guilt. His fists pounded at the open air, cursing as if it had betrayed him.

But the other—the more refined of the two, the professor—his response was different. He remained frozen in the same original spot as his scratching voice called her name over and over in shattered disbelief. The desperate sound of misery haunted me. His shoulders slumped with the weight of centuries and his eyes scanned the horizon in broken anguish.

I pulled against Declan. "We can't leave them!"

"We have to. It's not safe for you here!" His grip tightened on my arm as he hurried me to the car. "Do you want to be next?"

My eyes caught Michelle's and within them I found the same despair that coursed through me. Her unblinking stare of loss shot her terror into me and I sent the same back to her. In our eye-lock, we confirmed the truth of the events that had unfolded—and my silent promise to her to one day make it right.

That day haunted me like a train wreck I couldn't turn away from. It defined my every waking moment, leaving me without direction, thinking I could disappear and be whisked away at any turn. Maeve had had visions, just like I did, and they'd been the end of her. What happened that day could happen to *me*, without warning, and the uncertainty of my safety ate away at me every minute. My ragged cuticles and chewed nails were clear proof of it.

So I kept returning to this location at Doona Castle, in hopes of finding clues to where she went or maybe even finding *her*. Anything to bring balance back to my upside-down life. My own visions were growing worse now, reminding me of everything that didn't fit right in my life. The not knowing if they would take me, too, was enough to drive me mad.

A breeze tickled across my face making me flinch. My eyes widened and I looked all around me. Only I would have such a paranoid response to a little wind. My eyes narrowed then as I looked at Doona and its familiar looming shadow.

My regular visits to the castle had accumulated to the point where I could measure my growth against the sidewall of the stronghold. I had been nearly twelve when Maeve disappeared and now six years later, the top of my head reached the arch of the gothic-framed entry-way. Though I was still petite in comparison to my peers, I could at least see in through the windows now.

But it was the steadily growing pile of flowers, dry stems, and tattered ribbons hidden in the clearing high above that I measured the true passage of time with. Its mystery intrigued me as much as the mystical qualities of the clearing itself.

I moved along the stony wall of the castle, running my hand across the cold, rough exterior. A shiver ran up my arm, heightening my senses, attuning them to the details around me. My clear recollection of that frightful day remembered a crumbling ruin—broken from battle and time, only the corner remaining of a once glorious strong-hold. But that was no longer true. The castle remains stood strong and proud now, all walls intact, defying time's crushing blows.

I rubbed my eyes to ward off the migraine that always came when I tried to rationalize how at one moment, the castle had been a devas-tated ruin, and the next, it stood in its full form. Something shifted when Maeve went away. Something changed. And only *we* knew—those who were there that day.

I glanced up the green slopes of the surrounding hills, tempted to make the trek up to the clearing. My head turned back toward Gram's vintage BMW, calling for me to hop in and drive home to safety, but the pull from the clearing was even stronger. And more insistent. Every time.

Salty mist pulled through my hair and I looked up the hillside. Echoes filled the gusts that moved past me, causing my arm hairs to bris-tle. I could swear I heard tin whistles, and sounds of an ancient language laced throughout the undulations of the breeze. My imagination played with me again as I surveyed all around, chewing the inside of my cheek.

My lips pressed to the side as I thought of the stagnant classroom I was supposed to be confined in versus the dangers that might lurk ahead of me. I always felt like a criminal when I skipped school, but the urge to come back to this place was stronger than the pull to my final year of monotonous high school classes. Plus, the judgmental stares from my peers, and the incessant whispering, it was to the point of being unbearable.

Not only did I look different, with my slight frame and wispy white-blonde hair—like an imp my brother Declan always said—but the visions...they made me weird in their eyes. They'd caught me in my trance-like state enough times to actually be afraid of me. And fear of the unknown or the unusual always led to brutal exclusion.

I'd rather be here anyway, in the open air by the sea and rolling green hills. They called to me in every salty breeze, like there was something bigger for me, something waiting...waiting for me to take the next step. And it hid just out of my reach.

My body turned, as if by habit, and I climbed the steep incline toward the clearing. With each step, the wind grew stronger, sometimes pushing me along, other times brushing me off my course or slowing me. It carried a warning, though, something that unhinged my joints and quickened my heart rate.

Smells of molten iron and steaming deer stew had filled Maeve's tales of her visions, and sounds of trilling tin whistles and echoing drums completed the five-hundred-year-old legends. But it was the forceful energy of clan resistance against the crown that consumed my senses now as determined gusts tracked my every move.

I stared up toward the clearing and took a deep breath. It was crazy to go there alone. Strange things had happened there before, unexplainable things, and the incessant gusts in my face slapped me with repeated warning—which I ignored. My feet moved me forward with a mind of their own while my eyes remained fixed on the car behind me, attempting to pull me back to its safety.

Answers. I needed answers.

Gram said I had to ignore the visions and get on with my life but I knew I never could. I needed to learn the ways of the visions if I was to ever stop cowering and hiding from my own existence.

I climbed higher, looking over my shoulder as the wild Atlantic view expanded all around me. My gaze travelled out to sea to the high peak on Clare Island, then all around across the vast green landscape. The wind continued to swipe at me from all directions, reminding me of its awareness of my curious presence. I welcomed its companionship and continued to follow the familiar carved path of the trickling stream that led me toward the clearing once again.

Damp mist coated my face as rain threatened to come. It always did. But the tingle I felt in my bones as I got closer to the mystical clearing proved something else was coming too.

Something strange and unnerving.

CHAPTER 2

E very nerve in my body twitched as I entered the hallowed space. My eyes fell while I fought back the notion that, on the contrary, it was damned. And *I* carried its curse—one that spanned time and fused within my every breath.

A dark shroud of mystery blanketed the silent clearing as it dangled an ancient secret from its medieval past just out of my reach. My eyes moved around the circle of huge boulders that surrounded it and I envisioned Maeve's stories of the whipping post that once stood in the center and the unfortunate prisoners held by rival clans. But now, I hoped the spot held different possibilities for me.

Maeve never realized how much I had absorbed of her myths and her side conversations with Paul, her Celtic history professor. But he had been more than that to her. They had a mystical connection that spanned hundreds of years. It was like they were meant to be. Destined. And their stories wove magic through every word.

I walked to the middle of the clearing, remembering her larger-than-life tales of the pirate queen and her rescued lover as a warm smile turned up the edges of my mouth. A new, fresh breeze tickled my hair across my face and I turned to it, allowing it to sweep my hair behind me.

At the edge, along the base of one of the boulders, a yellow ribbon flickered in the airflow, dancing to its own mystical rhythm. The bright contrast of color drew me in and I moved closer to its inviting flutter.

I reached down to touch it and its silky sheen tempted me to tug. I pulled on the ribbon and it resisted, holding tight to its dried stems, wedged far into a dark gap between two boulders. I tugged and jimmied the dead bouquet from its crevice and watched the crisp, brown petals crumble and blow away on the wind. I looked back into the space between the boulders. It overflowed with stacked piles of dry bouquets.

My eyes widened as I gasped at the sheer volume, stepping away from the strange hiding place of someone's obsession. The wind picked up and blew me further from the spot as I continued to stare into the darkness of the hidden space.

Someone had been coming here, leaving flowers.

Time and time again.

For years.

And I couldn't help but feel the wind surrounding this place was protective of the hoard, somehow. Sheltering its secrets. Or enticing me closer.

Ignoring the nagging flight response that twitched in my muscles, I reached into the crevice without hesitation like a moth to a flame, and pulled on another bunch. This one still held color in its drying green leaves and the pale shades of pink hidden within the wilted edges of the rose petals. The white ribbon was gray and blotched from water stains and mildew. Only a knot remained on what once must have been a lovely bow.

As I ran my fingertips along the length of the fabric, my spine straightened and my eyes shot wide open. A low hum filled my ears and rose to a high pitched buzz within seconds. I knew the sensation well. The wind had been warning me, and I resented not listening to it. Before I could snap myself out of it, my peripheral vision darkened as my pupils constricted to pin pricks, focusing on a single point in front of me.

My vision.

It had turned.

Turned to my alternate sight, the one that saw things that weren't there. Things that confused me and scared me, from times that had passed or maybe even events yet to come. My breath stopped short as my hands curled into tight fists and I prepared for the frightening disturbance that was about to unravel me.

The wind continued its dizzying dance, blurring my vision while my foot tapped, willing it to go away. All of my energy focused on hanging onto reality, keeping in touch with the moment. My stomach turned as I feared losing myself to my visions again and I fought harder to stay alert and grounded.

The dream-like trances never seemed to last long, but I wished for it to hurry and pass anyway. I wasn't safe here in the clearing. Alone. And I just wanted it to be over with already.

Scrunching my eyes closed, I willed it away and shook with resistance. Then, before I spent another second fruitlessly trying to stop the onset, I disconnected from myself and weightlessness took me over.

Hurdling through a blur of sound and color, my jaw clenched as terror filled me. With no idea of where I might land or what I might see, I gasped for air that was impossible to breath. Then, in a shocking instant, my senses shifted to fresh focus and I gazed around me.

I followed my line of vision along a cold, lonely road and stepped forward. A black lake ran alongside me as I travelled down the dark lane. With each step, the scenery passed by me quicker and quicker, like I was moving at the speed of a car although remaining on foot.

The bleak roadway turned away from the lake and moved into a secluded area sheltered by heavy tree growth. My eyes darted around me, looking for anything recognizable, when a break in the trees opened up a landscape of sculpted shrubs and manicured lawn.

A sprawling manor stood proud with its floor-to-ceiling windows and ivy-covered stonework. My eyes pulled to the one object out of place. It didn't belong on the grounds of such a regal estate, just off to the side of the majestic stairs that led to the enormous front entry. A massive black pot, like a caldron the size of a hot tub, sat on the terrace waiting for its next use.

A famine pot.

I'd seen one before and knew its purpose in an instant. Starving people at the time of the Great Famine would line up with their cup or bowl, desperate for a scoop of life-giving sustenance.

My gaze travelled up to the stately front door, intimidating to any commoner, and my head tipped in recognition. I'd been here before, as a kid. But it wasn't alive like this. It had stopped breathing. When I last visited, it was untouchable, for viewing only. It was a museum of Irish history called Westport House.

As I stood blinking through the freeze-frames of my memories, my attention shot to a low, vibrating sound growing behind me. I spun around and scanned the wooded perimeter of the grounds, trailing my vision down the road that led me to the estate. The unsettling sound came from the narrow drive. A wave of shuffling and dragging along the dirt and gravel stiffened my spine.

But it was the eerie moaning that made my hair stand up on end—several voices united in collective despair, resonating through my brain, forcing me to run and hide. I jumped behind the famine pot and held on to the rim as I crouched and peeked around its bulging side for a better look.

I pinched my leg to gage reality as I realized I was reacting within my vision. I'd never actually responded in one before. I had only observed from afar, but this time, I was here, living it. Terror widened my eyes as my heart rate tripled.

Haunting groans and desperate wails grew louder as the rhythm of staggering footsteps sent a chill into my heart, stopping my breathing like ice. I held my breath and stared at the road, anticipating whatever it was that would appear from around the bend.

Then, like slow motion, a band of ragged, skeletal people moved into view. At first twenty, then forty, then a hundred. Stumbling and dragging their own weight, they pushed themselves onward toward whatever it was they sought. Tattered and worn, their clothing hung from them. Their drawn faces held no color or life, only grief.

Without slowing, they continued to move closer and I inched away from my hiding spot, looking behind me for a place to run. I stumbled on wobbly knees, stiff from crouching for so long, and scrambled back behind the caldron. But it was too late.

The movement got their attention and all eyes shot in my direction. With hollow stares, their gazes locked on me as if I were really there. I'd never been seen before within a vision so it made no sense, but their eyes met mine with clear desperation. My breath sucked in as their pace quickened and they moved directly for me. Their moans grew to a higher pitch, one of hope for salvation, as they hobbled and limped with focus and determination.

I stepped backward, again and again, shaking my head in fear as they came closer with arms stretched out toward me—ripped fabric hanging from skin and bones. Death itself was coming for me.

I turned on my heels and ran up the wide expanse of granite stairs to the estate. Smashing into the huge white door, I pushed and pulled on it, banging with all my might. My fists pounded onto the door in panic, pulling paint and splinters off and tearing bits of my skin.

"Let me in! Help me!" I screamed.

I turned back to look over my shoulder and my heart rate went into overdrive, beating in my ears as I watched the tattered, broken people moving up the lawn to the terrace.

I tore along the front of the manor to the corner and pulled myself around the side. Searching for another way in, I peered back at the endless wave of walking dead and exhaled the air I'd been holding since first seeing them.

They'd stopped their pursuit of me.

Instead, they swarmed around the caldron, reaching into its vast emptiness, and their wails broke out into cries that shattered my mind and my soul.

Several of the hopeless fell to their knees. Others laid on their backs staring into the sky, waiting to be taken from their misery. Some collapsed and died before they hit the ground.

My hands flew up to my open mouth and then pulled back through my hair. As my head shook in denial of what I was seeing, my feet carried me backward, away from the horrific scene.

I turned and ran without stopping, without looking back.

I ran across the open lawn behind the manor and went straight for the thick of the trees. I flew into the cover of the forest and tripped over roots and rocks. The more I stumbled, the slower I moved.

Looking down at my tripping feet, I screamed out in shock as I stumbled across burial mound after burial mound. Mud sucked at my feet as I tramped over countless fresh, unmarked graves that surrounded an elaborate family cemetery of masterfully carved crypts and decorated plots of ornate stonework. The mess of hurried, shallow graves all around the cemetery filled my sight everywhere I looked and the terror of being trapped amongst the dead nearly dropped me to my knees.

In a final gasping attempt at escape, I turned and threw myself out of the thick cover of the woods, back onto the massive, open lawn. And I ran.

Fists pounding, hair flying behind me, I ran faster than I'd ever run. My lungs burned for more air as my feet fumbled and squished through the boggy ground and I tore around the far side of the estate. Tears streamed from my eyes, blurring my vision, and my ankles twisted on the uneven terrain. Stumbling down a hill, I slowed my pace and wiped at my eyes for clarity.

Holding my breath, I looked behind me and all around, to be sure they weren't coming after me, the living or the dead. But all I saw was vast, rolling green hills leading out to a blissful sea. My air released from my lungs in a huff as I blinked into my new, safe surroundings.

Doona stood proudly by the sea. My gaze moved back up the landscape toward the clearing. I'd left it far behind in my panicked run and my eyes scrunched, trying to understand what just happened.

It was my vision.

It had found me again and its familiar haunting still twitched in my muscles.

And this one was more powerful than any I'd ever had. I'd never actually run from anyone in them before, or been chased. I would always just watch as the vision unfolded, like a bystander, but this time...this time they saw me and they came for me.

A shudder ran through my soul and shook my bones. Something had shifted, expanded. I looked behind me one more time to be sure the tattered people hadn't followed me back here. Back to the present. Because something else was different now. My vision had actually taken me to a different time, rather than just showing me a scene to watch.

My hands ran through my hair as my eyes grew wide. Then my face twinged and I squinted in pain. I pulled my hands out from my hair but they snagged in it, causing jabs of sharp burning as the hairs caught on jagged bits in my skin. As I scanned the outer edges of my palms, my jaw fell open. I stared at the splinters and deep scratches that covered them. I picked the larger slivers of wood out of my skin and winced in pain. Cracked white paint covered each piece and my shallow breathing shot to rapid panting in an instant.

My desperate pounding on the enormous front door. It had torn at my fists, causing them to bruise and bleed. But that was in my vision. I stared at my damaged, jittering palms again, and held my breath in wide-eyed panic.

Shaking my head, I picked up my pace and hurried to the car. I had to get the hell out of there.

It was real. Somehow it had all become too real.

The sound of my feet crunching through gravel filled my ears as I raced to the car, looking back over my shoulder every other step. Off in the distance, somewhere on the wind, the dragging and shuffling of the ragged people in my vision filled the spaces between the grinding of the stones under my feet. Swatting at my ears, I couldn't stop the haunting sound. They were still close, somehow.

Throwing open the car door, I dove in and dug for the keys feeling like I was being tracked by the mob of undead. My heart pounded out of my chest as my voice squeaked out of me. "Jesus, Izzy. Get a grip." I looked up to be sure the car hadn't been surrounded by flesh-hungry zombies. "I'm losing my mind now, for real."

The keys fell out of my jacket pocket after I shook it and my head reeled back in utter relief as the engine roared to life. Shooting gravel in two powerful streams behind me, I tore down the dirt road like I'd seen a ghost.

And I had.

Hundreds of them.

And now it was different.

I pulled at small splinters in my hands with my teeth as I drove.

It was a new feeling this time. One that terrified me.

"Be careful what you wish for," Gram always said. And now, her words rang true as I drove away from my threatening vision. The one where, this time, I had control within it. Control I had been searching for and dreaming of for years.

But now, all I wanted to do was run.

CHAPTER 3

I needed help. And there was only one place I could hope to find it. My heart beat continued to pound in my ears, heightening my internal alarm. Instead of running straight home to Gram's and hiding under my bed, I flew through the roundabout on two wheels toward NUIG to find Declan and Michelle.

I had no doubt they'd be at the university in their usual spot drinking coffee and researching the paranormal. My eyes rolled at my judgmental thoughts about their graduate work. I mean, I was sure their dissertations would be great, but their perspective was padded and safe. I, on the other hand, was *living* this crap. I only *wished* I could write about it from their cozy place in the college library, instead of running from it all time.

I parked and flew past the gothic spires of the ivy-covered university quadrangle, then trailed along the walkways toward the library. My lips moved as I mumbled to myself, shaking my head and processing what I had just witnessed.

A couple college girls passed me and stared with raised eyebrows, then chuckled as they looked back for one more glance. Shit. No matter how I tried, I always looked like the awkward freak, standing out like a sore thumb.

But this was college. I stood a little taller as I shook off their rude behavior. Somehow, it was safer than secondary school and I could let things roll off me more easily. I'd always felt at ease here, like I belonged—unlike my own school where the kids shunned me. I'd been labeled 'untouchable' to the point where if anyone sat with me or spoke with me, they would jeopardize their own social standing and would fall in rank. It was foolish, the rules of high school, but it was also desperately painful.

I returned my focus to my own mission. I had to remain focused on me, not them. *I* was what mattered and they, well, they would disappear from my life after graduation. I ground my molars at the fact that I was still even thinking about them.

"Ugh!" My head fell back. "Grrrrrrr..." I allowed my growl to lead me away from thoughts of my school tormentors to the people who really mattered in my life. My big brother, Declan, and his awesome American fiancé, Michelle.

I leapt up the steps of the library and flew inside, allowing the door to slam behind me, leaving behind my fears—the real ones of dying people stalking me and the unreal ones of insidious social collateral and pecking order.

I hesitated as I considered my concepts of what was real versus unreal and my eyebrows scrunched together.

The smell of old books and the calming, hushed tones of murmuring voices blanketed me and my shoulders fell from my ears as I welcomed the comfort. I snaked through the maze of computer stations and bookshelves to their favorite spot by the corner windows overlooking the Corrib River.

I plopped into an armchair next to them and released my tense muscles, allowing myself to be absorbed into the fabric of the chair. Declan and Michelle looked up at the same time and their studious faces turned ashen.

"What the fook happened to ya?" Declan's voice fell out of him as he leaned toward me from the edge of his chair. "Jazus."

"What?" I pulled back in offense and ran my fingers through my hair to try to comb it down.

Michelle fumbled with her phone and reversed the camera. She held it out and passed it to me.

I peered into the phone at my image and nearly died. I'd forgotten about the heavy black eyeliner I put on this morning and my futile attempt at mascara, both of which were streaming down my face like I was a goth-zombie.

"Shit!" I blurted out while licking my finger and wiping at the black smears that trailed all over my face. "Well that's the last time I make any attempt at the cat-eye thing."

Michelle burst out laughing in a blast of air and spit. Her loud guffaws and vibrating snorts always released her built-up stress, making it obvious when she was uncomfortable. It was one of my favorite things about her, aside from her Boston accent, but this time not so much, considering *I* was the source of her discomfort.

"Izzy, what the hell happened to you?" she gasped. "You look like you've been to hell."

"Yeah. Kinda," I replied in a whisper. "I think I have, actually."

Declan straightened in his chair and smacked his laptop closed. "What did you do, Izzy?" His judgmental tone disciplined me before he even heard my explanation.

The moment my story hit the part where I was alone in the clearing, having a vision, Declan stood, gathering his things. Michelle's eyes followed his every choppy move as he shoved his computer into his bag.

"Does Gram even know you took her car? And you're supposed to be in school. How many days is that now? They probably won't even let you graduate at this rate." His lecture shut me down and I looked to Michelle for relief.

He was right though. From his perspective, I was the wayward sister who had fallen off her path. He worried about me all the time. But in my heart, it felt like I had finally fallen *onto* my path, allowing myself to be who I was meant to be and to embrace my visions somehow. I needed him to know this.

Michelle took Declan's arm and pulled his attention off me for a minute.

"Come on, Declan," she said. "Let's just get Izzy home and figure things out there. No one got hurt, so let's just—"

"She could've got hurt though," he interrupted, then shot a glare at me. "You need to be more careful. Don't, don't invite these things, these visions, into your life. You're just looking for trouble," he snapped.

I couldn't blame him, I guess. He had taken on the parent role for me long ago. I mean, Gram was my actual guardian since my parents passed, but she was, well, old and clueless. She loved us and took care of our every need, but old-school was an understatement. She basically followed the church ladies around, hanging on their every word and helping them with every new project.

Declan wasn't home much anymore though. He lived with Michelle now like they were an old married couple, so most of Gram's focus was now on me. Which was fabulous.

They followed me along the coast road in Michelle's car and as I passed my school, a twitch of guilt tightened my stomach. It was too late to go in now and I crouched low in my seat as I turned onto Gram's road.

My eyes followed the semi-attached townhouses, one by one, all of them identical, yet I knew each one individually like the back of my hand. I'd walked past these houses my entire life. We pulled the cars into Gram's short driveway and hopped out. I prayed she hadn't noticed her car missing. Again.

The front door was open before we reached the stoop and Gram greeted us with open arms.

"A sight for sore eyes. In wit' ya." She hugged us all and pulled us into the foyer. "I've just taken the scones out ta cool and the kettle's on."

She looked back out at the car, wiping her hands on her apron. Her squinting eyes proved things weren't adding up for her but she closed the door anyway and walked to the kitchen with us.

The smell of the house filled my senses and brought a comforting smile to my face. My eyes trailed up the stairs along the old-fashioned carpeting and absorbed the ostentatious floral pattern of the wallpaper that clashed with the design on the steps. The musty smell of antiques laced the air, mixed with fresh-baked scones and newly dried laundry. It was home.

We sat in the dining room on orange-cushioned seats and my arms rested on the seasoned wood table, barely propping me up.

Gram poured the tea and placed marmalade and butter on the lazy-Susan. Starving, I grabbed a scone and covered it in both and shoved it into my mouth. The emptiness in my stomach ached as a desperation to fill it consumed me.

"Easy, lassie, ya'll choke on the crumbs." Gram rested her hand on my shoulder and smiled.

But she was right.

The crumbs lodged in my throat as it constricted with emotion, tightening with guilt while I thought of the starved souls in my vision. I coughed and crumbs flew from my mouth.

My eyes locked on the images in my head and I stared into space. Visions of the dying people filled my sight and I reeled back in horror. Another cough. More crumbs. More pictures of starving, ragged villagers coming for me with outstretched arms.

I shook with terror and my shoulders jolted. Then, like waking from a dream, I blinked back to Gram's table as Michelle and Declan stared at me, jaws dropped. Gram continued to shake my shoulders and then pounded a heavy thud onto my back.

I coughed more crumbs out and gasped for a life-saving breath of air as all eyes pierced through me, searching for an explanation.

I stared back at everyone as embarrassment washed over me. I watched Gram take a step back. Her face transformed from happy homemaker to concerned guardian.

"It's happening again?" she asked in a low tone.

I nodded slowly.

It had never stopped actually, but I'd been able to hide my visions from Gram for the most part. I wanted to protect her from worry, but more so, I needed to protect myself from her aggressive interventions.

Gram had taken me to see every specialist, every esteemed shrink, and even had me sectioned—twice. The emergency psych ward was the worst. I'd been taken by ambulance for immediate evaluation and easily convinced them I was sane, but Gram rattled on about psychosis. I squeezed the rest of my scone to crumbs from the awful memories.

I was determined that would never happen again. Ever.

I was old enough now to push back as well, though I didn't want to have to do that to Gram. But there was no way I'd go to a hospital again. They were filled with meds that made me comatose and caused me to lose days of memory, the staff trying to make me believe I was insane. No way.

But I saw the familiar look in Gram's eye. It held fear and desperation.

Maybe if I explained things for her, maybe she would understand better.

I looked to Declan and Michelle for help. They could usually temper things so Gram wouldn't overreact.

"Gram, please don't panic. This is just a part of me. It's who I am." I started with caution. "I have these strange visions but it doesn't mean I'm insane or certifiable or anything like that. Please stop trying to get me hospitalized and just listen." My trembling voice pleaded with her.

Her lips pressed into a white line and the plates in her hands rattled.

"I have visions of the famine. The Great Hunger. Always have." I kept my tone steady and gentle to keep her from becoming too upset. "They're just getting..." I hesitated, filtering the word 'worse' out, "... more real now."

I looked down at my wringing hands to avoid the truth in all of their eyes. They must have thought I was nuts.

Gram dropped the plates onto the table with a crash, making everyone flinch.

"What'cha mean, more real? What am I supposed ta think of that?" Her voice rose three octaves.

Michelle and Declan squirmed in their seats, speechless.

Gram continued, "I won't sit around and watch yer life fall apart like this, Isobel. Yer vulnerable. Fragile. It's time I do something about it. Once and for all." She paced from the kitchen to the dining room and back again.

My chin pulled in and I grabbed onto the rising angst in my gut. The one that said "fight," not "flight."

"I am *not* fragile!" I shouted in defense at her low blow.

But she was right. I was weak. I was frightened.

I took another breath. "I'll figure this out. I don't need your help. I can do this by myself."

"Oh," Gram interrupted. "Like yer friend, Maeve?"

The words punched me in the gut. She'd never spoken her name before and her tone was like a slap to my face.

Declan stood in an instant.

"Stop, Gram." His voice left no margin for challenge. "Not another word."

Gram's face fell, like she knew she had gone too far. But it hardened again in a tight grimace as she looked back at me.

"I won't have ya go missin', Isobel. I wouldn't be able to live with m'self." Her voice cracked and she spun to hide her face. Her trembling shoulders betrayed her though. She was crying.

I looked to Declan and Michelle for help but they both held deep worry in their eyes too. It was their sympathy, oozing out all over me, that pissed me off though. My hands lifted to my face and rubbed it in exasperation.

Gram turned back to me before I'd realized she'd stopped crying. Now her face flushed crimson with determination and focus.

"Yer comin' with me. Now." She turned down the hall and opened the closet. In a blink, she had her coat on and her purse slung over her shoulder. She dug through the bag with impatience. "Where are me keys?"

I reached for my pocket and felt them there. I turned my gaze from her for fear of her reading my mind.

Too late.

She stood next to me, tapping her foot, extending her hand to me.

I dropped the keys into her palm.

"Up," she commanded. "We're going."

~

My mind scrambled through escape plans as I pictured pulling into the Emergency parking lot of the hospital and jumping out of the car, running. Gram couldn't catch me. I had that in my favor.

But where would I go?

My head shook in defeat as my eyes dropped to my lap. After leaving Declan and Michelle back at the house, Gram drove me without speaking a word. But she didn't need to say anything. I knew exactly what was going through her mind and it had everything to do with her granddaughter being unruly and out of control.

As we pulled out onto the coast road, my body anticipated the left swing of the roundabout, toward the hospital, but my body knocked in the opposite direction as Gram turned right, toward the Spiddal road.

I strained to see the oncoming road signs in case Gram planned on taking a different way.

"Where are we going?" My tone rose with my anxiety.

She glanced at me quickly, then returned her gaze to the road.

"Ta see Mother Maureen," she stated. Her flat tone hinted at her uncertainty with the decision.

Mother Maureen?

Gram had spoken of her before in what seemed more like bedtime stories or fairy tales. She described her as a mystic, for special effect and added intrigue, I always thought. But she was also a dear friend to Gram. She was actually Gram's longest-known friend, whom she'd met in the early years of school and kept in touch with since then.

Strangely enough, though, I'd never met Maureen. Gram had

somehow dodged any overlap between us for all these years. I picked at my cuticles, thinking maybe Gram was trying to keep me a secret.

My shoulders relaxed from their high, defensive perch at my ears as I absorbed the fact that I wasn't being admitted to the psych ward. Instead, I gazed forward at the open road that travelled along the jagged coast of the wild Atlantic and considered what Gram thought Maureen might be able to do to help.

One thing for sure though, I was not going to say a word to her. Gram was out of her mind if she thought I was going to discuss this situation over tea with an old biddy friend of hers. My eyes nearly rolled into the back of my head at the thought of it.

If I played it right, I'd convince them both that I was just having weird dreams. I'd change my diet. Drink less coffee. Attend school on a regular basis. All the crap they'd want to hear. Then I could get home and think about what really mattered. My visions, and figuring out why they'd changed.

I chewed on my lip with impatience as we entered the quaint village of Spiddal, passing a couple pubs nestled in between small shops and brightly painted store fronts. Gram turned down a narrow, hidden road toward the coast. The car bumped and jerked along the uneven lane with only two lines of dirt for the tires and a row of lush grass running down the middle.

In the thick overgrowth of brambles and nettles, a stone wall emerged, surrounding a humble cottage within its private confine. Smoke plumed in swirls out of the chimney that rose from the thatched roof, sending the scent of burning sod through the briny air.

Gram pulled the car to the side of the country road into a grassy patch by the wall. Before we could even get out of the car, the front door of the cottage flew open, spilling welcoming light out into the misty gray day.

Maureen was at the car in a flash, greeting Gram with hugs and welcomes that stretched for miles. I crept out my side, hoping to go unnoticed for as long as possible.

Which was all of about two seconds.

"My stars, Eileen, how she's grown. Barely just eighteen." She spoke like I wasn't even there. "Such a beauty, Loov, sure I can't take me eyes off her."

She walked to me and reached for my face, like she knew me. Her warm eyes settled my rising angst and I allowed her touch.

"Deary, I've known you yer entire life and I've waited fer this day each an' every moment of it." She spoke to the depths of my soul with her heavy, country dialect, and I let her in without guard. "Come. Inside. Let's get ta know one another, shall we?"

She led me up the path to the cottage as Gram followed. Gram's eyes shone relief through their relaxed lids as if she believed she made the right choice bringing me here.

Entering the cottage, Maureen turned to me and said, "You're very welcome here, Isobel." She led me through the warm, open space of the cottage to the table by the fire. The kettle was boiled and she placed a pot of tea next to the small milk jug and sat across from me. She glanced at Gram while filling my cup and then leaned in toward me, gazing into my eyes.

"They call me Mother Maureen. I'm a seer. I've the gift of second sight. And Eileen here, your Gran, she tells me you might have the same."

The hairs on my arms stood up.

There was a name for it.

Second sight.

I was a seer.

CHAPTER 4

M y back straightened and the cup in my hand sloshed tea over
its rim. I looked to Gram for a reaction but she remained
unaffected by Mother Maureen's words. I settled my cup onto the
table and stared back into Maureen's face.

"It's a gift, dear, that's passed down in some families," she started.
"Most every generation has one or two and it's somethin' most don't
understand, or sometimes ignore." She poured more tea into my cup.
"The gifts can vary, ya see, depending, but I see it in you clear as day.
The gift of the sight."

I pressed my back into my chair to create distance between us. Her
intense gaze made me squirm and I lowered my eyes.

I had no idea what she was talking about but she spoke like she
had full understanding. And what about Gram? This kind of talk was
sure to send her over the edge. I glanced at her for a micro-second,
wondering what she knew of this.

"Ach, I'm sorry. I don't mean to shock ya like that. I can't keep me
mouth shut when I get excited." Maureen passed Gram the milk jug.

I pulled my eyes up again and looked at Maureen. "It's okay. I just,
I've just never really spoken about it to someone new, or in front of
Gram." My gaze moved to Gram as my lips pulled back, showing my

teeth in apology. But at the same time, the knot in my stomach suggested betrayal or anger for her not telling me what she knew too.

Gram nodded. "I didn't want to believe it meself, Isobel. Didn't think it possible, really. But sure, I've avoided the truth long enough. For years." She looked to Maureen and then into her cup. "I've waited too long, really, and I'm sorry fer that. I just, I never thought it could happen to me own granddaughter. And I figured if I found another explanation, it would be better for everyone." She lifted her gaze halfway up to almost meet mine. "I've been a fool to avoid the truth. And it caused you harm. I must live with that now as my one true regret."

Her words of remorse jabbed me in the heart. I always knew she tried desperately to help me. To save me. But I had no idea she was trying to save me from my true self. All of her modern techniques had failed. And now, it was clear she had realized she needed to look deeper–in a place she had sheltered me from for my entire life. But why?

Gram moved her gaze from me to Maureen and back again. "Ah, sure, I'll leave the two of ye so for a chance to chat. I'll take a stroll down to the sea and get some air."

"Wait now, Eileen, lemme see if Ryan can go wit'ya. No need to have me worryin' about ya slippin' on the rocks and breakin' a hip." Maureen chuckled into her tea cup. "Ryyyannnnn..." She sang out.

"Ah, go on now, I'm no invalid Mo." Gram resisted at first. "Sure, a chaperone needn't be necessary, but mind you, I won't say no to the chance to catch up a bit with Master Ryan."

Maureen shuffled to the front door and peered out. "Ryyyannn," she trilled again.

"What is it, Shanny?" His fresh, youthful voice travelled across the yard from the inside of the shed.

"Can ya take a minute from yer tinkerin' and take Eileen here for a quick stroll to the sea?"

"Gimme a sec. I've just gotta..." his voice trailed into the wind as Gram went out to greet him by the shed.

"Now," Maureen sat back down across from me, "that's better. We'll have a chance now ta speak freely. Get to know one another, like." Her warm smile lit up her face as she lifted her tea cup for a long sip.

My eyes moved to the door, following the path Gram took when she left. I couldn't believe she actually just left me here. With Mother Maureen. Whom I'd just met. I mean, lifelong family friend and all, but still.

I reconsidered my escape plan for a moment as I questioned the unusual situation I'd been dropped into. But something about it rang true deep within me and I believed I should at least listen to what Maureen had to say.

I glanced around the cottage, soaking in the old-fashioned details of the stonework around the hearth and the lumpy, white plaster walls. Dried herbs and flowers hung from hooks in tied bundles, just above a variety of mortars and pestles. Antique trinkets covered the shelves, and, moving my eyes back to Maureen, I realized these items weren't from vintage shops but from her own life activities. She saved everything. And by the looks of it, used everything.

I sipped my tea as Mother Maureen told me about her family and all the generations who lived in the cottage before her. They were a well-known family with a history of gifted ones. Local villagers and travelers from afar came to visit them in hopes of information or healing.

"Ach, sure, I musta been around ten or eleven when it came known I had the gift," she said. "'Twas when I noticed the pregnant women at mass. Every now and again, I'd look upon a woman and see she had become a mother. Before she even knew it. And I'd tell her she was having a girl. Or a boy. Depending. And I was always right." She smirked. "Word spread and next I knew, I was dragged and pulled around to various houses and even some churches in a guarded manner. People just wanted answers to all their questions. They didn't bother wondering how I could do it, at the time."

"Did you have the answers for them?" I lingered on her words, anticipating what she'd say next.

"Mostly." She poured milk into her tea to cool it. "It was the questions about the lost loved ones that sent me into hiding though."

"What do you mean?" My head tipped.

"It was too much for me. I was so very young. Grieving people would want answers so badly. It frightened me. And they were prepared to believe whatever passed from my lips. The responsibility was too great."

I nodded as I took a deep breath. I'd never considered what it would be like if word of my visions got out and people wanted a piece of it.

"Ya see, once they know about yer gift, it's all you are to them." She leaned in closer. "And when they don't get what they want, they turn against ya. And then the persecution begins. Name callin' and accusations of immoral conduct." She took her last sip of tea and smacked the cup back down on the table. "So, I went into hiding for a while. Let things die down a bit. I'm sure this is why yer Gran has brought you ta me. She must see now that you are at a turning point. Becoming all consuming. The point of persecution." She raised her eyebrows at me in question. "She can no longer keep it hidden."

I nodded my head. "Yes. It's getting bigger now. More complicated. More...real."

Maureen reached across the table and squeezed my hand. "I'll tell ya everythin' I know, if ya feel ready fer it. You must know the power within you so you can be sure ta keep it under control. Ta not let it consume you." Her eyes grew wide. "Are ya ready, Isobel?"

Her words haunted me, as if my response might change the course of my life. And I wasn't sure if I was ready for that.

But Mother Maureen's gift was different from mine. She saw the future, in a way. She made prophecies and predictions that never failed. But my visions weren't straightforward like that. Mine were frightening, with images of dead or dying people from the famine. And they were getting worse. I glanced at my sore, damaged palms and rubbed them.

I always thought it would be easier to suppress my visions or to just keep ignoring them like they meant nothing. They'd already caused me to be an outcast. But now that I was able to react within the vision, and get hurt even, it was different. It had become dangerous. But intriguing, as well. It was like I'd already taken the next step. One that brought me closer to the truth.

I had to decide if I was ready. Mother Maureen waited for my answer. Was I going to hide from my visions and be tormented my entire life by them? Or was I going to face them and discover their meaning, even if it meant putting myself in danger? Grave danger, even.

My eyes closed as I thought of Maeve. She'd been brave and faced her visions. And she was gone now.

My head shook in my silent conflict. I wanted my life back. I wanted to be the one in control of it. I pushed my chair back from the table, realizing there *was* no conflict. It was clear what I had to do.

"I'm ready." I stared into Maureen's eyes. "I'm ready to confront all of this." I paused and looked down. "At least, I think I am." My insecurity forced its way out through my words, and I grimaced at their bad taste.

Maureen smiled and nodded.

I continued, "But I think my visions are different from what you've described." I picked at the tiny splinters in my palms. "My visions are of the past, not the future. And I don't just see things." I peered up through my lashes. "I'm actually there. I can *do* things."

Maureen's hand rubbed her mouth as her eyes narrowed. "How do ya mean?"

"I see people and now they can see me too. It's like I'm active in a dream, but it's more real than that." I scanned the room, unable to explain myself better, then added more. "My friend, Maeve. She was the same. She was able to travel back in time and do things. Change things."

I fumbled with my words, knowing I made no sense. But all my whirling thoughts kept coming back to one point of clarity: figuring out what happened to Maeve, to be sure the same didn't happen to me. But the nagging detail in it all was, she changed things. Doona

Castle was no longer a ruin. It stood proud and strong after Maeve disappeared. I would always hold onto that knowledge, knowing she had something to do with it.

"I want to learn how to control my visions," I stated.

"Yes. I can help you to temper them, to make them more tolerable." Maureen nodded in assurance.

"No, that's not it. I want to *control* them so I can use them. To travel through time." I gazed into her eyes, unblinking, proving to her my determination and surprising myself with the revelation at the same time. "People are starving. They're dying. And Maeve is trapped somewhere there too, somewhere in the past. Or maybe just lost in the abyss. I need to go and help. I need to do something. And I'm beginning to believe I can."

My words flew out of me and I made no attempt to filter them. I was done hiding. And if anyone was going to understand any of this, it would be Maureen. She'd lived it.

Maureen sat back in her chair and her lips parted, preparing to say something. But she remained silent and only stared.

A flicker of insecurity hid behind her eyes, like she was seeing something bigger than expected. Something she knew nothing about.

"Shanny," Ryan's voice burst through the front door. "Shan, come see what Eileen found."

His eyes met mine for a moment but moved away with what appeared to be rude disinterest.

But my eyes remained welded to him. His warm, tanned skin surprised me in comparison to the fair, pale skin of practically everyone else around this place. Sunshine was a commodity not often seen in the west of Ireland and most people remained indoors, or so it seemed anyway. But him, it was clear he spent his time outdoors, likely engaged in hard labor judging by his strong, lean build.

Maureen and I jumped to standing in response to his enthusiasm and followed him outside.

Gram paced at the shed, looking with bright eyes at a metal rod propped against the sidewall. Ryan stood near her with his hands on his knees, bending in for a closer look at the relic. He turned with a flash of excitement in his gaze, and waved for us to come see.

As we approached, Ryan lifted the long piece of steel and balanced it out across his two hands.

"She pulled it out from the space between the two boulders, at the pyramid of rocks, like it was no big deal, sure." He glanced at Gram like she was a genius. "It must be hundreds of years old, judgin' from the ironwork." He ran his hand along the length of what I now could see was the blade of an old, corroded sword.

I stepped closer, not taking my eyes from the fantastic artifact.

"Whoa." I reached to touch it and moved my fingers along the rough surface of the blade. "That's amazing." My wide eyes lifted to Gram's in awe of her discovery. "I can't believe you found that, Gram. It's incredible." My heart nearly stopped at the miracle of such a find.

My eyes moved back and caught Ryan's as he stared at me in frozen disbelief.

"You like medieval relics?" His voice held a judgmental tone, condescending even, and I was sure my being a girl had something to do with it which sent my blood boiling. No way was he going to be rude twice within a matter of seconds, and him having never even met me before.

"And that surprises you why?" My head tilted with the lift in my voice, waiting for his response as I stared at him, unblinking.

Maureen stepped closer before another snarky word could be spoken. "Ryan, dear, this is Isobel. I'm not sure ya've ever met. She's Eileen's granddaughter from Salthill." She turned to me. "Isobel, this is my grandson, Ryan. He meant nothin' by his tone. Isn't that right, Ryan?" Maureen eyeballed him.

"Mm." He tipped his head and looked back to me. "Pleased ta meet'cha, Isobel."

"Likewise." I peered at him with a sideways glance, still annoyed by his arrogance.

Then I looked back down at the sword. Excitement returned and my questions flew before I could censor them.

"What will you do with it?" My hand continued to run along the length of the sword. "It has to be..." My voice stopped short as I watched Ryan's fingers squeeze around the blade until his knuckles turned white. My eyes jumped to his only to find him staring at me with a hollow glare, like he saw right through me.

A gasp escaped me. His penetrating stare unsettled me and I fidgeted under his silent, intense scrutiny.

I turned to Gram to see if she noticed his strange reaction to me and her awkward fidgeting proved she did. My gaze shot to Mother Maureen and the moment I caught her bewitched eyes, my heart stopped.

Terror shone from Mother Maureen's eyes, straight into mine, as she stared deep into my soul. It was like she was reading me and saw something that frightened her. Looking back to Ryan, I watched his trembling hands clench harder on the sword and his tight jaw caused his reddening face to shudder.

As the first drop of blood appeared through his fingers from his palm, cut by the rough metal of the sword, I twisted around on my heels and ran.

~

I ran as fast as my racing heart would allow. Getting far away from them was my only focus as fear from being seen too clearly filled me with terror. And I had no idea what it was they saw in me anyway. But at that moment, I didn't care to know.

"Isobel!" Gram's voice called to me, but I didn't look back. She had placed me in the middle of all of this crazy and I wanted nothing to do with it.

I sprinted onto the narrow, grassy road and sailed in the direction of the village. These people were freaking me out with all the talk of gifts and seers, and now the sword and the blood. It was too weird and unexpected. All I wanted was to get away from them. Escape from them. And find my own normal again.

My heart pounded as my breath shot in and out of me, small sounds of fear leaving my throat. It was as if they had seen a ghost when they looked at me. But Ryan, that was even worse. It was like he had seen my entire life, and more. I'd been stripped of all my armor in their eyes. Especially his.

A shudder ran through me, sharpening my senses further, alerting me to the sound of thunderous footsteps pounding behind me. My eyes flew wide open and I forced myself to look back over my shoulder. Before I could stifle it, a small scream escaped my lips as I saw Ryan barreling toward me with sharp focus in his eyes.

I set my gaze ahead of me again as my fear and adrenaline shot unbelievable speed into my legs. But it was useless. No matter how fast I ran, he was much faster.

His crushing steps and heavy breath were upon me as he caught up to me in a matter of seconds. His arms wrapped around my shoulders, weighing me down and stopping me.

"Get off me!" I wriggled to escape his stronghold. "Leave me alone!" I jabbed at his ribs with my elbow and stomped back onto his foot with my heel.

"Oof." He grunted after my elbow connected with his side. "Wait. You don't understand. Please." His hold around my arms tightened to protect himself from further hits and I yanked harder to get free. "Just listen. For a second, Isobel!"

"You're scaring me. Let go!" My voice tightened in my throat and squeaked out of me, threatening that tears would be next. With one final pull, I broke from his hold.

His grip had loosened but he still reached for me. "I'm sorry. I just needed to stop you."

A line of red blood ran along his pinky finger and dripped onto the ground. He tightened his hand into a fist and shoved it into his pocket.

I stepped back from him as my eyes searched for Gram, who remained standing back by the shed with Maureen, staring at us. I looked behind me to see how much farther it was to the main road.

"Please, don't leave. We need to talk. I might be able to help you." He dropped his other hand by his side.

"I don't even know you. What makes you think you can just, just..."
I pointed around us. "This!"

A slight smirk lifted the side of his mouth and he let out a huff.
"Yeah, sorry. Your gram sent me to catch you." He paused. "Things can
go from very calm to very crazy around here, rather quickly." He
pulled my eyes up to his. "But we have a lot in common and it, well, it
would be cool if you'd stay a little longer." He moved up next to me
and turned toward the direction of the cottage. "I didn't mean to scare
you. I was caught off guard. I'm sorry. Will you come back?"

My eyebrows pulled together in annoyance.

"First, you totally ignore me. Then you stare at me while squeezing
a sword, like you're about to attack me. What the hell?"

He took a step toward the cottage and my feet followed his lead.
We took a few more steps and then he stopped and turned to me.

"I didn't mean to be rude at first. I apologize." He looked to his feet.
"Mother Maureen has talked about you my entire life. It was just a
little weird to finally see you in person. To say the least."

I thought of his injured hand in his pocket. He couldn't be trusted.
There was something strange about him and my wits remained on
high alert.

"But the blade. You—" I looked to his pocket with a cautious glare.

His eyes fell in shame.

"I know." He scuffed the gravel under his feet. "That happens sometimes. I can't really control what I do when I...see things."

My air sucked in.

"No, no," he interjected. "I never hurt anyone. Just, sometimes,
argh..." His hand shot up to his head in frustration.

"Are you a seer too? Like Mother Maureen?" I watched him closely
for his response.

He lifted his gaze to meet mine and shrugged. "Something
like that."

CHAPTER 5

I followed Ryan back to the shed, hoping for an explanation about what he meant by, "Something like that." The evasive response made me think that his visions, or whatever it was he saw, was worse than mine.

Staying a step behind, I stared at his back, watching for any false moves. I still wasn't sure if he was to be trusted. We approached Gram and Maureen and a sense of safety returned to me. They'd placed the sword inside the door of the shed, out of view, maybe hoping the awkward incident would be forgotten. I chuckled to myself at their failed attempt.

"Come on. Back in fer tea, shall we." Maureen tipped her head toward the cottage, acting as if nothing peculiar had happened at all.

My knees went rigid at the thought of us all sitting in there sipping our tea, discussing our common oddities. I cringed and dropped my eyes to the ground, planning my next great escape.

"We'll be in in a sec, Shanny. I just want to show Isobel something. Kay?" He nodded at Maureen, leaving her little wiggle room.

My eyes lifted to him, questioning what he had in mind.

Gram stepped closer to me to check if I was comfortable staying back with him. She certainly seemed to trust him and wasn't rattled much by his injury, or the cause of it.

I lifted one shoulder to let her know it was okay, I guessed.

"Ach, sure, Ryan. If it suits 'er," Maureen replied. "Ya mighta given her a fright though, ya see. She mightn't have much time fer such carryon." Maureen jabbed an elbow at me and I smiled back with a nod to let her know I was okay. "Fine." She turned with Gram and they walked toward the cottage, looking back at us every few steps.

"Thought ya might like ta see my shed?" His shoulders lifted to his ears. "I dunno. It's got some cool stuff in it. And, sure, anything's better than gettin' trapped at the table with those two once they get started." He smirked.

My eyes narrowed as I sized him up and wondered how many times he sat and listened to Gram and Maureen. He probably knew more about me than he let on which was actually annoying, but he seemed good-natured anyway. Maybe even kind-hearted. I could tell by how he treated his grandmother. And by how he was able to convince me to come back. Somehow.

I rubbed my lower lip and pressed on it.

"Wow. Apparently I've made a bad first impression." He huffed. "Not the first time. I kinda do that. Yeah." He dropped his hand from the doorknob of the shed.

"No, I just...You're not..." I shook my head. "I mean, you need a bandage." I looked at his injured hand, still well aware of how the injury got there.

"I know. I actually have a first aid kit in there." He looked toward the door of the shed again.

My eyebrows scrunched together. "What else do you keep in there?"

I pictured machetes and chain saws, other devices of torture, and had second thoughts about going in with him. But Maureen and Gram had given the green light and I trusted in that.

There was more to it though or I would have kept running back there, never stopping until I was well under my bed. I wanted something. That was obvious. And what else was obvious was that Ryan seemed to know some stuff that might actually be useful to me.

I looked at the shed and then at Ryan. There must be something interesting in there, particularly if he needed to keep a first aid kit handy.

"It's my workshop. I make stuff. Out of metal." He lifted the latch and opened the heavy wooden door, which let out a slow, burdened creak. "Wanna see?"

I did want to see. I wondered what he made from metal. And how he made it. I wondered about how he spent his time.

My head tipped as I tried to peer in around him.

"Come on in." He stepped inside and propped the door open for me.

He plugged in the light and it buzzed to life just as my eyes focused on the ancient sword lying across his work bench. The white glow of the fluorescent bulb brought the medieval details to life and I moved straight for it.

My curious fingers reached for the relic and trailed along the corroded hilt. I leaned in for a better look and then turned back to Ryan with wide eyes. "It's amazing."

He watched me with a gentle smile and wiped a rag along the end of the blade. "Yeah. It is." He stared at me with a warm gaze of curiosity.

"What?" I fidgeted under his watch.

He shifted his weight and leaned back on his heels. "It's just weird to finally meet you. He pushed his hands into his pockets. "You're not at all what I expected."

I wondered what that could mean. He wasn't what I expected either. I didn't even know he existed. And he was actually so close this entire time. I couldn't help but think about why Gram kept me from these people for so many years.

"Is that bad?" Insecurity crept through me as I fell into his gaze. But then I shook my head to release myself from his stare. I hardly knew him and his opinion shouldn't matter. But my ears strained to hear his response nevertheless.

He let out a slight huff as a half-smile lifted one side of his face. "No, it's surprisingly good, actually." He laid the rag across the sword. "I wonder why we've never met before. That seems kinda strange doesn't it?"

He stepped closer and my heart skipped a beat as I questioned my sensibility in being in this confined space with him. As my breath caught in my throat, he moved to my side for a better look at the hilt of the sword. My relieved exhale ran for miles as I blasted myself in my mind for being so weak around him. But he was just so...interesting.

Ugh. What was wrong with me? I'd only just met him. And well, he was a freak.

Like me.

~

I pulled my curious eyes off him and instead looked at the variety of weapons—or at least, that was what they looked like to me—hanging on the walls. My gaze moved around the shed, soaking in the array of metal pokers, anvils, hammers, and a leather apron hanging from a peg, then looked back at Ryan. He watched me in silence as I studied the details of his personal workshop.

I stepped closer to the heavy anvil in the corner. A small bowl of ash sat on a stand next to it and I peered in. Ryan came closer and then reached into the ash and fished around the charcoal bits with his fingers, pulling out a small nugget of left-over melted iron that had cooled in a geometric shape.

"Why do you make all this stuff? I didn't know people still did this." I watched him roll the nugget between his fingers and examine it.

"It's a hobby, I guess. Maybe a distraction, too. Like, I'm fascinated by these old artifacts, so I like to try to recreate them." He looked back at the sword for a second. "Crazy timing, you know, your Grand-mother finding that today. I mean, the storm must have stirred it up, but still."

My head nodded. "Yeah, crazy timing." I peeked up at him through my lashes, wondering if I could talk to him about...stuff.

"What?" He shifted his weight again.

"I want to learn more about my, my gift, as Maureen calls it." I reached for the apron and rubbed the leather.

"More like a curse, you mean." He dropped the metal nugget back into the bowl of ash with a clang.

"Call it what you like, but I'm sick of being terrorized by it. I want to learn how to control it. How to use it." I stared into the bowl of ash.

His forehead scrunched tight as his spine went rigid. "Not me." He took a step back. "I try to get on with my life and ignore it. Feckin' pain in the arse, it is."

"I know, that's how I felt too, for a long time. But, I, I don't know." I reached into the bowl fishing for the nugget. "I feel like I need to use it now. Or at least figure out how...I don't know, like how to get stronger with it, instead of feeling weak all the time."

He stepped back from me like I'd turned into a troll or something. Had I said too much? Crap. It seemed like it was okay to talk about this stuff here but I had to remember I really had no idea who these people were.

"Are ya daft? Have you any idea the pain you'd bring on yerself? People don't take too kindly to witches around here. Never have."

"I'm not a witch." My voice cracked in response to being called one for the first time in my life. And by him. "You're just scared. But that doesn't mean I shouldn't learn more about this. It's who I am."

His hands balled into tight fists. "I'm not scared. Jasuz. Ya come in here talkin' of tampering with your, your situation, and when I tell ya it's dangerous, ya go callin' me weak. What the hell is that about?" He glared at me with contempt, but behind the shield, I saw his curious vulnerability. I'd tapped into something.

Blood oozed between his fingers from the pressure of his fist and I moved to him and took his wrist. "Come on, where's that first aid kit?"

His fist loosened and he stood without moving, staring into my face as I held him. My chin pulled back from his close scrutiny.

"Where is it?" I pressed, attempting to break his intense gaze.

But he didn't falter. He continued to stare at me with a look of lost wonder. I allowed myself to fall straight into his eyes and was pulled into the deep blue depths of his soul.

Suspended in time, I floated in his eyes and travelled through his memories—his insecurities from being gifted, his intense focus on his craft, his hopeful dreams for his future—until he blinked, breaking the ethereal moment like a flash.

He stepped back from me and pulled his wrist from my hand. My mouth opened to speak but I found no words. Words were too trivial after having a glimpse into someone's soul without their permission. And I'd never even known such a thing was possible.

His jarring response, pulling his wrist from me, was unnerving and I jolted from the separation.

He dropped his gaze to the floor.

"When I touch someone, or am touched, I see things." He rubbed his wrist as if he still felt my hold. "Even indirectly, like when you touched the sword as I held it, earlier."

My eyes grew to saucers as my breath sucked in. That was his gift. He could see things when he was touched.

"What kind of things do you see?" I bent my head to catch his eyes again.

He swallowed hard. "Things about them. Their life. Their past." He hesitated. "Their future." He turned away from me. "It's a curse. No two ways about it. I'm better off staying isolated here." He moved to the opposite side of the shed, likely to create as much space between us as possible.

"You can see things about the person you touch?" I held my breath waiting for his answer.

He nodded. "Yup."

"Okaaaaaayyy. So are you going to tell me what you saw about me?" I lifted the rag off the sword and snapped it at him. "Please."

Holy crap. What could he have seen?

Wait. When we were touching, I was drawn into *him* as well. It was more like a feeling than anything else, but it was still something.

Then I thought back to when we were holding the sword together. He had looked at me with what appeared to be rage.

He lifted a metal spiral from the floor and hung it on the wall. "It doesn't matter. I try to ignore it. There's no other way to have a normal life, otherwise."

I exhaled in frustration and looked around the shed for the first aid kit. I noticed a white box behind him, covered in soot and black streaks, but the red cross in the center made its purpose clear. I stepped closer to him and stretched around for the kit.

Gauze, creams, bandages, it had everything.

I sat on a stool and reached for his wrist again. His brows scrunched together as if I hadn't heard a single word he said. I wiggled my fingers for him to lift his hand to me.

"I don't mind if you see things about me when we touch." I watched his confusion line his forehead. "Come on, we can't pretend our gifts don't exist. What kind of life would that be? Constantly hiding or running. Gimme your hand."

He lifted it slowly and I grabbed onto it. Opening his palm, I spread his fingers, exposing the angry slice. It wasn't too deep but would require tape strips to hold it together for proper healing.

I took a water bottle from his work bench and poured fresh water over the wound, then took care of the next steps with gentle precision —just as Gram always did for me.

A strange euphoria filled my mind as I worked on him. It was almost like he roamed in my head having a gentle look around. It was strange that I didn't seem to mind. I think I kind of liked it, having someone know what was actually going on in there.

As I finished wrapping the gauze around his hand, he looked up and his wide eyes spilled his bafflement all over me. And then he spoke.

"You want to learn how to use your visions to travel through time?"

∼

I pulled my hand from his with a gasp, as if it had burned me. He *did* see everything. Including my developing plans on how to use my gift of second sight. His eyes narrowed, penetrating me with what felt like sharp judgment.

"You *are* crazy." He shook his bandaged hand.

"I'm not! You're the crazy one, turning your back on your own strength!"

"You mean weakness!" His voice quaked throughout the shed.

My breath stopped short. Oh my god. He believed his gift was a weakness. I guess I had believed the same about mine all this time, too. No wonder he hid here, out in the country, this small village, this tiny shed. I'd been hiding too, in my own head.

We were both afraid.

"Wait, do you ever leave this place?" I watched the four walls closing in.

His shoulders sank as I unfolded the layers of his private hell. Sickness rose from my stomach, one borne of sadness, while his face revealed his loneliness and disappointment with his sentence.

"Ryan!" a husky voice boomed from outside the shed, making us both jump out of our skin.

A nervous giggle left my lips and Ryan chuckled at our abrupt return to the outside world.

"It's my buddy, James." He moved to the shed door and looked back at me. "I *do* have a life, ya know." And he smirked with exaggerated arrogance.

James burst through door of the shed, filling it with his large stature and broad grin.

"Where the fook ya been? I got this pile of shit in the boot a' me car, clangin' away at every bump." His louder-than-life voice shook the shed but then fell silent as he caught a glimpse of me behind Ryan.

James looked at me, then at Ryan. "Who's that?" His voice had lost its zeal and took on a heavy, serious tone.

Ryan stepped to the side and said, "This is Isobel. An old family friend." He looked at me with a new discomfort in his gaze. "Isobel, this is James, my—"

"Wow. Nice to meet ya. It's not every day I see such a pretty girl in Ryan's shed." He gawked at Ryan like he was a hero. "Ryan? Ya got some explaining ta do?"

"Shut up, asshole." He turned to me. "Sorry, Isobel. I meant to tell you he was a dick."

"Sorry. Sorry," James retorted. "I accept that, I can be a bit of a dick. My apologies. Ya just caught me off guard, like." James took it down a few notches but continued to stare at me any chance he got.

"Go on, get outta here, James. I'll catch up with ya later." Ryan encouraged him to leave.

"Hell, no. I'm unloadin' this crap first. Scrap metal is not a draw for the ladies." He looked at me again. "Or, shit, maybe it is."

With that, Ryan barreled toward James and shoved him out of the doorway and onto the lawn. "What's the matter with you? Jazus." He kept pushing James as he stumbled closer to his car. "Come on. Gimme the pieces and get out of here." Ryan's voice reprimanded James for his bad behavior but I also heard his low rumblings. "Don't fuckin' mess this up fer me man. I like her. Asshole."

A silent gasp escaped my mouth as a strange tingling sensation ran through my veins. I wasn't sure what it was, but his words had started it and it made me nervous. No one had ever spoken about me that way before, at least not that I was aware of, and I didn't know what to do.

As they looked into the boot of James' car, I snuck out of the shed and hurried over to the cottage. It was all too overwhelming and I needed air.

Looking back, I caught Ryan's eyes as he watched me leaving. A shadow of disappointment crossed his face and then shifted to tight jawed anger as he turned back to James. I was sure he was going to punch him right in the face.

Inside the cottage, Gram and Maureen cleared the table, lost in endless chatter.

"Gram, can we go now, please?" My voice sounded breathless as I made my demand, bouncing in my shoes.

"Sure, Izzy. Everythin' okay?" Gram asked.

"Yes, I'm just ready to get home. Now. Please."

Maureen dropped her damp tea towel onto the table and moved to the window to look for Ryan. Once she saw James, she turned back to us, nodding.

"Ah, sure, ye must come again soon. Really. We've so much to talk about still. Will ya, Isobel?" Her bright eyes held hope and welcome.

"Yeah, okay." I moved to the door to encourage Gram to make her exit faster.

I needed time to think. Too much was happening too fast. These people, it was like they knew me so well, it was scary. I just needed some space for a minute.

And Ryan. The way he looked at me sent butterflies through my core. But then he was so irritating at the same time. And the things he saw. Things he knew. It frightened me. But it elated me at the same time.

Gram reversed the car into an opening at the side of the narrow lane and turned around with quick effort. It was clear to her I was in a hurry, she just didn't know why. As she pulled out, I heard Ryan's voice call out from the yard.

"Isobel!"

And then it was lost to the roar of the engine and grinding gravel beneath the tires.

CHAPTER 6

He'd called out for me. The sound of my name in Ryan's voice distracted my every thought. I'd wanted to get out of there, more than anything. But now that I was back home, alone, I couldn't stop thinking about him.

It was annoying. He was weird and judgmental. He was, well, he was nice, too. And supportive, in an obnoxious way. He was gifted. And he was a freak. And he called me a witch.

But still, he was the only one, besides Mother Maureen, who could help me. Or at least, understand me. I would need to go back to him. There was no way around it.

I'd spent the past week thinking about Ryan, but it was just too embarrassing to go back there. I kind of ran away from him, and I was ashamed of my immature behavior. And he scared me. His intensity was too much and I felt so exposed around him. I guess because I was. He could see everything about me when he touched me. It was intimidating.

My hands ran through my hair as my mind wove through the tangled mess of Ryan. He'd twisted my thoughts into a rat's nest that mixed up my emotions.

But I couldn't help thinking that we could combine forces and somehow come up with a way to figure out how to control our 'gifts' better. At least we weren't alone.

A huff left my mouth as I considered the absurdity. "*Oh, hi, Ryan, so want to help me go into a trance and like, you know, travel back in time with me and stuff?*"

He *was* cute, too--which I should not allow to distract me.

My mind had wandered too far, taking this to a whole new level that likely didn't exist in Ryan's world *at all*. He was a loner. And seemed happy that way.

"Izzy!" Michelle's voice broke my ridiculous daydreaming.

"Yeah, what?" I dropped my pencil and stared at the abyss of my homework. It was so irrelevant compared to what was really going on. Just a sick form of torture for the young. Meant to break our spirit, like we were wild horses. And it seemed to work like a charm...on most of us.

"Get down here!" she belted out.

Michelle and Declan had come over for dinner and now Gram was cozy in her reading chair, half asleep. The kitchen was tidied and they were hanging out in the sitting room by the fire.

I bounced down the stairs, drawn to any excuse of a distraction from my torture.

"Hey, girl. What's this Gram says about a visit to Mother Maureen's last weekend? Sounded like an interesting trip," Michelle probed.

"Oh, huh. Yeah. I guess it was kind of an unexpected thing." I plopped on the couch and stared at the glowing coals in the fire.

Declan's head stuck in his laptop and his fingers tapped away on the keyboard.

I lowered my tone with Michelle. "I would have told you, but I didn't really want Declan to know. You know how over-protective he gets," I mumbled.

"Yeah, I get it. I wondered why you would keep something that juicy away from me. But makes sense. I hear Mother Maureen's a freak." Her eyebrows lifted in hopes of details.

The word 'freak' shook me. It seemed to be the go-to term for all of us. But I let it go, knowing Michelle meant nothing, well, didn't mean it. I moved on and told her about the cottage and Ryan's shed, the sword, and Maureen's trinkets. Then I mentioned their gifts and that was when Michelle leaned in further.

"They're seers," I whispered. "Maureen calls it the gift of second sight. And she believes I have it as well."

"What does that mean? Like, they have freaky visions too?" Michelle's eyebrows pulled together.

I took a steady breath. "Sort of. Different from mine. But, yeah, they see things too." I shrugged one shoulder. Then I pulled my legs in and knelt on the couch, leaning closer to her, and whispered, "I think they might be able to help me find out what happened to Maeve. You, know, like, *what happened.*"

If I could say that out loud to anyone, I figured it would be Michelle. There was no way she'd given up on Maeve either.

"What!" Michelle's voice broke the calm in the room and Declan's eyes darted up.

"What?" Declan looked at each of us.

"Nothing," we said in unison and went back to hushed whispers.

"What are you talking about?" Michelle nearly fell out of her seat. "What about Maeve?"

"Don't get excited. I'm just saying. Maeve disappeared and I haven't forgotten a moment of that day. It haunts my every breath. It could come for me too. At any moment. I can't live like this, Michelle. Not knowing." I paused, then added, "And Maeve might need our help, you know, to get back."

My words faded as I watched the shock in her eyes grow.

"Izzy. Maeve is gone. It's been almost six years now," Michelle stated in a steady, flat tone.

Her words made me reel back like she'd stung me. I never expected her to be so matter-of-fact and, well, cold about it. I couldn't believe she'd given up on her like that. They were best friends. My head shook, trying to clear it of the bitter words.

But I had to remember, none of this made any sense to Michelle.

She'd go crazy if she didn't release it and move on. The detachment had to be her coping method.

I didn't have that luxury though. My visions were a constant reminder of what happened to Maeve and what lurked around every corner for me. For six years.

"Time doesn't matter, Michelle. If anything, it's helped. I'm older now. I can actually do something about it. Finally." I held her eyes to convince her of my truth. "But I need you to believe it too. That it could be possible."

She inhaled for what felt like hours. Held it. Then blew it out in a slow stream of judgment, analysis, and regret.

"Fine. Whatever." She rolled her eyes. "Talk about ripping the Band-Aid off." Her voice slapped me. "But honestly, I knew this wasn't over. Not by a long shot." Her gaze stared off as sadness seeped out of her.

But then something shifted, and she looked back at me with a sinister smile I hadn't seen in ages, and I knew I had her.

I reached over and wrapped my arms around her for a huge hug. I needed her support more than anything and I'd had no idea until that moment. It was like I needed a witness, someone to keep record of what I was doing, or at least someone to know about it.

A shudder ran through my bones as I remembered going to Doona to see Maeve connect with her vision the day she disappeared. I was the witness. I didn't realize it at the time, but it was clear to me now. And this, all of this was why. Without a witness, it would all have been forgotten.

I took a deep breath and decided my next move.

"Will you take me to him?" I asked.

"To who?" Her eyebrows lifted.

"Ryan."

The thought of going to see Ryan again turned my knees weak. Now that I'd made the decision to go back to see him, I had to figure out my actual purpose. It had all seemed so clear to me when I told Michelle, but now, my nerves had shot all rationality to hell.

Having contact with other gifted seers was exactly what I had needed. It proved I wasn't crazy for starters, but opened new possibilities to me as well. New information. Saturday morning couldn't come fast enough.

Michelle had promised to take me back to Spiddal to Ryan's cottage—well, Mother Maureen's cottage. I was ready to face him again. He was all I'd thought about all week, so I knew seeing him again had to happen.

I just didn't know how he'd react to my visit. I hoped well.

With two hot coffees in the cup holders, she picked me up in her hundred-year-old Mini Cooper. It might have shown its age on the outside, but the thing drove like a new race car. I fastened my seat belt and braced myself for Michelle's heart stopping driving—her never-ending joy ride.

"So, is he expecting you?" She watched *me* more than the road.

I avoided her eye contact so we wouldn't end up in a field surrounded by a bunch of curious sheep. "No. There's no way to contact him. Or Maureen. They're completely off the grid, technology-wise anyway."

"Okay, sooooooo, hopefully this will go well?" Her lip curled up on the side.

"Stop. You're making me nervous. It'll be fine." My eyes moved out the side window as I second-guessed my unannounced visit.

Michelle set her playlist to the Saw Doctors and laughed as the adventure-themed music echoed out of her phone. I splatted my hand to my forehead as I rolled my eyes at her constant attempts at bringing fun into everything.

As we entered the quaint village of Spiddal, I pressed my hand into the air to slow her as I searched for the hidden coast road. After the short row of pubs and shops, I found the secluded turn-off, concealed by overgrowth, leading to the cottage.

"Holy crap. This is a road? There's grass going straight down the middle!" she complained as the Cooper rattled down the narrow, bumpy passageway.

"I know. Shut up." I laughed, seeing the absurdity through her American eyes.

The private lane was familiar and welcoming to me this time though, like I'd always known the place it led to. It must have been the way Ryan and Maureen had treated me, like a life-long friend or family, even. There was no awkward getting-to-know-you crap, even though there had been plenty of spats and uncertainty already. They just allowed me into their world without question.

So, I felt like it was okay to just show up like this. I hoped.

A sweet smell of burning metal hit my senses first as the stone wall around the cottage came into view.

"Park here." I pointed to the spot where Gram had left her car before.

From the Cooper, I followed the trail of smoke to Ryan's shed and watched bright orange flames dancing in a bowl on a stand by the door. In that same moment, the shed door pushed open and Ryan stepped out holding a long rod of steel. He stuck the end of it into the fire and poked it around, searching for the perfect spot, then left it in the flames.

"Holy shit! Is that him?" Michelle's jaw fell open. "He's gorgeous." Her head swung to me like I'd left her out of a big secret. "You didn't tell me he was freakin' gorgeous!" Her eyes bugged out of her head as she stared at him.

Oh my god. She was right.

Looking at him from a distance, removed from the emotional tension of our past conversations, I saw him like she did. And I couldn't. I had to look away or I wouldn't be able to function around him.

"He's fine. No big deal." I looked down at my hands wringing in my lap. "I just need his help."

"Yeah, right. Gotcha. His help. Ooookayyyyy..." Her voice trailed off behind me as I climbed out and slammed my door.

Ryan's head shot up and he spotted me as I walked toward him.

His eyes brightened and a smile spread across his lips. The butter-flies in my stomach took full flight and I returned his smile. But then his enthusiasm faded as I got closer and his gaze became more guarded and suspicious, causing my gut to clamp down on the flutters.

"Hi." My voice squeaked out of me.

"Hi." His eyes searched me. "What are you doing here?"

His blunt question sucked the wind out of my sails. Like my visit made no sense to him or something. Had I created a false memory of our last meeting, like it meant something, when in fact it meant noth-ing? My plummeting pulse drained from my head straight to my feet.

"What? Oh, um, I was hoping to be able to talk with you a little more about, you know…" My voice trailed off into insecure-ville as he pulled the iron rod out of the fire to inspect it. He pressed it back into the coals and his eyes darted all around, as if he felt we were being watched by more than just Michelle.

He was weird. I had to remind myself of that. He was unusual and probably lacked some social graces, considering he'd removed himself from society altogether. Okay, that might explain it. But it wasn't enough because right now he was actually just being rude.

"Um, is this a bad time? I didn't mean to interrupt." I bent my head to get his attention back.

"Actually, it is, a bit. I'm sorry." He avoided eye contact.

Oh my god. Kill me now.

Did he have another girl in there? Was that it? My palms broke out in sweat and I took a step back, mentally measuring the distance back to the car, knowing I'd never make it before falling apart.

"Okay, no worries. I'll stop by another time then. See ya."

I turned on my heels and hurried back toward the car, faltering on every clumsy step in the uneven grass. Swearing in a low voice, I distracted myself with self-soothing words that 'another time' would never happen. Not as long as I lived.

Michelle's wide eyes met mine and she lifted her hands in confu-sion. She looked back toward the shed and then dropped her head on the wheel, banging it, over and over. Her response mirrored exactly how I felt inside and broke my weakened wall of defense, sending my tears spilling over.

I ran the last few steps to get to the car before I could embarrass myself any further. I whipped the door open and fell into the seat, leaning over to hide my face from public humiliation.

"Go! Let's get out of here," I begged. "Quick."

She fumbled with the gears, grinding them as she turned the car in an emotional panic. It must have been at least a fifteen-point turn before she got the Cooper ready for its dramatic peel-out.

I grabbed the top of her hand on the stick shift, trying to help in any way and frustrated from her making it more difficult than it needed to be. And then I saw Ryan from the corner of my eye. His muscles strained as he ran toward us with his eyes locked on me.

"Go! Go! Go!" I commanded.

He was nearly on us and there was no way I was going to let him see my embarrassing tears of rejection.

I swiped at my face as I kept focus on the road ahead of us, refusing to look back at him.

Just as Michelle moved the stick into gear to blast us out of there, Ryan's hands splatted on my window, banging on it.

"Stop. Wait. Isobel!" His palms held the car as if he had the power to stop it. But it was the drawn, desperate look in his eyes that did the real job.

"Wait, Michelle. Hang on." I reached for her hand on the stick shift again and she let up her tight grip on it.

I looked out the window into his anxious face as the gray mist of the day turned to gentle rain beading on his skin. He dropped his hands from the window and stepped back, taking deep breaths while holding my eyes with his.

I broke from his gaze and turned to Michelle, speechless.

"Go!" She shoved my knee. "Get out. Are you nuts?" She pushed on me again and I looked back at Ryan.

His hands rubbed his face and moved back through his hair as he shifted his weight from one foot to the other, waiting for my next move.

As I took a deep inhale, preparing to face him, Michelle gave a final shove that knocked me against my door, causing it to fly open. I nearly fell out and Ryan jumped back.

I stumbled out of the car, glaring daggers back at Michelle, as she chuckled into her steering wheel. Ryan looked in at her, likely to check on her sanity, and grinned at her antics.

"Shit. I'm sorry," he said. "You took me by surprise back there. I'm an idiot." He kicked at the gravel.

I needed more though. His detached response still stung deep.

He fidgeted under my silent stare and swallowed hard. "I can explain. I didn't mean to make you feel unwelcome. Shit." He ran his hands through his hair again. "It's just not safe for us. Here." He looked around as if feeling like he was being watched, then glanced back at his shed.

"It's okay. I'll go. I didn't mean to…"

He interrupted me. "No, stay. Please." He stepped further from the car as if to entice me away from it.

I looked back at Michelle and she nodded for me to go, revving the engine.

Ryan bent down to see her better and waved his hand at her. "I can get her back to town."

Michelle nodded and looked back to me for my agreement, and I bit my lip. That was all she needed, and she pulled away without a second glance.

"What did you mean that it wasn't safe?" I looked around for any obvious signs of danger.

He chuckled. "You're fine. Don't worry." He turned and took a step toward the yard, raising his eyebrows to encourage me along.

I followed him in silence, allowing him plenty of room to explain himself.

He took my obvious cue and started.

"The townsfolk are threatening us," he said. "Superstitious fools. They want us off this land. They say they'll send my Shanny to a home. That she's not fit to be livin' here." He spoke into the open air without looking at me for my response. "I just don't want to give them anything more to latch on to, you know. To stir things up again. I didn't mean to—"

"No, it's okay," I interrupted. "I shouldn't have stopped by uninvited. I didn't realize."

I closed my eyes to shield myself from his vulnerability and blinked away the light drizzle. I had no idea my visit could have caused any trouble.

"They know of Maureen's gift from stories over the years," he continued. "And they suspect mine. Some of them call her a witch." He hesitated, likely remembering calling me the same. "Who knows what they call *me*. You know, they just don't get it."

He spoke toward the cottage, knowing I was following. Listening.

"They tend to blame any misfortunes on her." He huffed. "They want us gone. And visitors tend to make them take more notice."

"I had no idea. I'm sorry." I slowed my pace.

He turned to me and nodded his head toward the shed. "Come on. It took me a little too long, but I've decided, fuck 'em, I can't stay holed up here for the rest of my life."

"Do you really think they have any power over you and Maureen?" I chewed my nail, surprised that people could treat others like that these days.

Superstition. It spooked even the most level-headed of people.

"Nah. It's the developers too. They're in on it. Looking for any excuse to evict us." He picked up one of his tools from the grass. "The land's a gold mine apparently." He threw the tool toward a pile of wood by the shed.

I watched his movements realizing the unsteady balance of his life here with Maureen was teetering on his young shoulders.

"Well, I shouldn't be here," I said. "I don't want to the one who gets you guys in any trouble." I reached for my phone.

"No, please. You're here now. I'd really like it if you stayed." He searched my eyes.

I looked back to where Michelle's car once was. My escape route, gone.

Shit. What did I want? I was completely lost at this point. The complications were growing and it made sense that they could affect me too.

Gram had avoided bringing me here for years, and now I began to understand why. Being gifted was a curse in some ways and she had gone to extensive means to shelter me from its truth.

"I can get ya back to town later. Not a worry." He followed my gaze to where Michelle's car had been.

"Yeah, okay." I nodded and watched his chest fall in relief.

He swung his head and led me toward the shed.

"What's that iron rod for?" I asked, pointing to the glowing flames.

"Come on. I'll show you."

He went into the shed and came out tying his leather apron with thick gloves covering his hands. He handed me what looked like full-sized headphones and told me to put them on. All went silent around me as soon as they snugged around my ears. He pulled his own set on as well.

As he pulled the iron rod out of the fire, it glowed bright red and steamed with muted sizzling hisses as it met the moisture in the air. Ryan jerked his head to encourage me to follow him into the shed with it.

He moved to the large anvil in the corner and took a massive hammer from the side table. Again and again, he struck the molten metal with the hammer as he moved the rod along the anvil, turning it at different angles. Each hit molded the iron the way he wanted and the effort of each strike took his entire strength.

Once it was hammered to the shape he wanted, he secured the rod in a vice with the hot end sticking up. He took a strong pair of pliers and latched onto the tip. He twisted the metal around and around as it created a beautiful spiral effect down the length of it, until it wouldn't give in to him any further.

He released it from the vice and held it up for my viewing.

"Voila. A hearth-fire poker to sell at the market. They pay the bills 'round here." He smiled at his creation.

"That's really good, Ryan. I'm impressed." My eyes moved around the walls of the shed as I noticed other metal work. All of it was made by his hands. "I can't believe you can get the metal hot enough to do that to it."

"It's part of the craft. Makin' a hot fire. I start with wood but end with coal. The coal burns hotter and longer." He half-smiled. "So, yeah."

I moved to his work bench and sat on the stool by it.

"How's your hand? Is it healing well?" I remembered every detail of bandaging it.

He lifted his hand into his view and opened and closed his fist. Dirty tape wrapped its way around the palm. "Yup. It's good. Nearly all better. Thanks."

Silence fell around us as we struggled with what to say next.

Then he broke the silence.

"So, you wanted to see me again?"

CHAPTER 7

Heat rose in my neck as embarrassment washed over me. My face surely turned beet red right before his eyes, and seriously, when my face burned red, against my light blonde hair and pale skin, it was super obvious. I could die.

I wasn't sure why his blunt question created such a rise in me. He was only inquiring about my wanting to see him again.

An entire new shade of crimson washed over me for good measure.

"Um, yeah. I mean, it kinda all happened so fast last time. It blew my mind a little, you know. Like, all of it." I paused, blinking at the thought of the sensory overload of my last visit. "Sorry I left so abruptly. But, you know, um, I just didn't really know what to do." My head shook as I made a mess of my words.

"Yeah. We can have that effect on people. Certainly not the first time I had a girl run away from me." He forced a chuckle, then dropped the hot poker into a bucket of water. "Ya kinda get used to it after a while."

"Shut up. It wasn't like that. And you know it." My face burned hotter. "I guess I just never realized there were more people like me. Besides one other, anyway." My eyes fell to the floor.

"Another?" He stopped moving.

Shit. I probably shouldn't talk about that right now. There was no way to explain Maeve without sounding totally crazy.

"A good friend of mine. She had strange visions too. I guess it was a kind of second sight." My shoulders lifted. "I suppose."

"Had?" he prodded.

"I don't know." I shook my head in an attempt to reset the conversation to a clean slate. "What's that?" I pointed to a curled spiral piece on the table.

His eyes moved to the piece but were back on me in an instant.

"I'm not that easily distracted." He huffed. "But it's fine if you don't want to talk about it." He stepped to the table and picked up the curled piece of metal. "It's a garden stake. For decoration. They sell really well, too."

"I can see why. Very Celtic-feel to it, with the ancient spiral effect." I reached for it and he handed it to me.

The weight of it made my arm drop at first, and I pulled it back up for a closer look. His metal work was rough but that was what made it beautiful. It was all clearly hand-made but with the skill of a master craftsman.

I looked up and caught him gazing at me with a slight lift at the edges of his mouth.

"What?" I blushed again.

"Um." He looked away for a second. "No, I haven't had any other girl in here before."

"What! Crap!" My eyes bulged at him. "That's crazy! Don't do that!"

Oh my god. He'd read my thoughts in that split second.

"I'm sorry. I can't help it. It's only when I have contact with you, I promise. When I passed the spiral to you, it, well, yeah." He shook his head.

"That's so embarrassing! I can't!" I looked to the door, ready to run again, but this time in pure embarrassment. But something in me kept me there. His honesty, maybe. And it was almost like I didn't really mind that he could see what I was thinking. "It's okay. I guess." I looked down to avoid his eyes.

He grinned. "No really. I forget sometimes. I spend so much time alone, I forget what it's like to touch someone else. It's just how it's had to be around here." He shrugged. "So, sorry. I'll try to be more careful. But, seriously, no, girls don't come here. Ever."

"I was only wondering." I turned the spiral stake in my hand.

"I know." He reached for the stake to put it back.

"Hell no!" I pulled it away from his reach. "I got it." And I brought it back to the table, keeping a squinted eye on him.

"Hmph. I see how it is then." He grinned. "Come on. Let's get out of here. I saw porpoises at the beach earlier today."

I followed him out of the shed and watched his broad shoulders turn toward the sea. My eyes trailed down the length of him, to his perfectly fitted jeans, and I pulled them away before my face reddened again.

But I couldn't help wanting to stare at him, to try to figure him out. He was complicated, like me. And I knew I could learn so much from him. I chewed on my bottom lip.

If anything, he might be able to help me learn to control my unstable visions, for starters. Or maybe he could see things in me that could help.

My pulse quickened at the thought of allowing him to look into the depths of my soul, for answers. My protective wall shot up on its own. But maybe we could help each other.

We wandered down the narrow road toward the beach that was just at the end. Galway Bay opened up before us as we rounded the bend of hedgerows. Large boulders bordered the edge of the rocky beach and a huge pile of them towered above us.

Ryan pointed to the tall mountain of boulders. "That's where yer gran found the sword."

I glanced at the pyramid of enormous stones, the top one jet black, and wondered how they ever created that formation. Then we scrambled over more rocks and made our way to the smoother sand. I looked across the bay at the rolling green hills of County Clare.

"Wow, you can see so far today, right across. I can nearly make out some houses." I squinted to try to see more.

"Yeah." He pointed to the right. "Check out the Aran Islands out the way. Clear as day now that the mist has gone."

My eyes moved across the water and out toward the open Atlantic where the Aran Islands guarded Galway Bay since the beginning of time.

I walked closer to the lapping waves, searching for marine life or anything of interest.

"So, really. What made you come back here today?" he asked out of the blue.

My breath sucked in. If he wasn't so cute, I wouldn't feel so awkward about it. But he was so distracting that I couldn't even understand my own actions fully. Ugh, I hated myself.

Focus, Izzy. Stay focused.

"I guess I just feel like I need to learn more about this stuff," I started. "I mean, I've been stumbling through my own life. Like, led by these visions. Never able to do normal things without people noticing or thinking I'm weird. It's no way to live. Ya know." I reached for a cool black stone. "So, maybe, I can learn more about it, how to control it, from you and Mother Maureen."

He watched me and looked at the stone in my hand, then nodded.

"There's more though." He picked up his own rock and chucked it into the water, skipping it several times.

"Yeah, okay. So I might have a side agenda as well. Doesn't everyone?" I grinned.

"Not everyone's agenda includes time travel." He looked at me through his lush lashes. "I did see something about that when you were here last time." He paused. "I know it's none of my business. But shit."

I stumbled across loose rocks, moving along the edge of the water to avoid his close scrutiny. I mean, seriously, he must think I was a freak. But he was *here*, so...

I stared out at the water and then back at him as I considered my next words. Telling him more might be unwise. But maybe he already knew a lot, and more would just clarify things better. But maybe not.

No matter how I worded it, it was going to sound crazy. But

Maeve did it, time-travel. I knew she did. But she got lost somewhere in the vortex and didn't come back. And it was the unknown of what became of her, and what might become of me, that led me on this quest.

I turned to Ryan and walked back to him, feeling braver about telling him and praying he wouldn't judge me too harshly. And I figured, if I was going to tell anyone, it made sense to tell someone who believed in these sorts of things.

He stepped closer to me as I approached him and his eyebrows lifted, ready for whatever it was I about to say. My mouth opened to speak the first words that came to mind, but I bit my lip, slipping on a loose stone and stumbled forward. Just as the taste of blood tingled my tongue, Ryan's hand grabbed my arm to stop me from face planting in the jagged rocks.

His firm grasp steadied me and I lifted my gaze to meet his. As if in slow motion, I began to thank him for saving me from further humiliation but the frozen, horrified look in his eyes forced my head to turn in the direction of his stare.

I looked back toward the bay where the waves lapped at the sandy beach. But this time, the gentle lull of the waves against the coast turned to the sound of desperate wails on the wind. Lost souls searching for peace.

My hands went to my ears to block the terrifying sound, leaving my unshielded eyes exposed to the numerous bodies that bobbed in the waves and rolled up onto the beach with the tide.

Ragged-clothed, skin-and-bone bodies littered the beach and clogged the waves.

Lifeless. Gone.

I turned to Ryan in horror. "What's happening?"

He jolted back from the gruesome sight and pulled on my arm. "Come on. We need to get out of here."

"But they need our help!" Desperation grew in me that left me no choice but to try to do something for these poor souls.

"They're gone. There's nothing you can do for them. Let's go." He pulled on me again. "Isobel!"

His tug and desperate pleas for me to leave made no difference. I couldn't leave them. I wouldn't.

One final yank on my arm to get me to move and he stumbled back on the wobbling stones. He staggered a few paces to catch his balance and then launched back to me. But before he grabbed hold of me again, he stopped and froze.

His hands rubbed across his eyes and through his hair as he blinked into the clarity of the day. I watched his tight grimace relax in relief and I spun around again to the gruesome scene. The beach was clean now. Fresh waves lapped at the sand and a group of porpoises glided past in the depths.

"What the fook was that?" He exhaled every last bit of his held breath.

I thought about the ragged, starved people. The ones from my visions of the Great Hunger. They had plagued me my entire life, reaching to me for help.

"My vision," I stated.

"You *see* that shit?" His face twisted in shock. "Like, often?"

"Yes. All the time." My eyes fell to the sand.

"And you want to *go* there?" He kept an examining eye on me.

"Yes."

Apparently, I *was* crazy enough to want to travel through my visions to the horrific time of the Irish Famine. And the shocked look on Ryan's face proved it was beyond nuts. But something had been calling to me my entire life from that time in history and I just had to find out what it was.

Maybe learning about the source of the visions would ultimately be what put them to an end. That thought was actually too wonderful to even truly consider, in case it wasn't true. I couldn't put myself through the disappointment if it wasn't possible to end them.

Then my thoughts returned to Maeve. This was exactly what she had attempted as well. To figure out the source of her visions and end them. And now she was gone.

My mind flip-flopped back and forth, from being terrified of my visions to wanting to confront them and end them. It made me dizzy.

There was a small voice in me that wished I would just walk away and continue hiding, like Ryan. But deep in my soul, I knew what I had to do. It just wasn't going to be easy. And maybe even not safe.

I rubbed my eyes and blinked them clear as I looked at Ryan.

He stood with slumped shoulders, still recovering from the terrifying sight of all those lost souls strewn across the beach.

"I'm sorry. I didn't mean for that to happen to you." I stepped up the beach a few paces in the direction of his cottage. "Come on. Let's get back to the shed."

He nodded and followed me in silence.

"Are you okay?" I asked. "I'm really sorry. I didn't have a chance to warn you about, well, about how scary it can be." I looked into his face again to search for any clues of how he was feeling.

His eyes gazed straight into mine, searching for something.

"Seeing those poor people. Yeah. That was unpleasant. Not gonna lie." He paused. "But *being* there with them. Like, *with* them. That feckin' scared the shit out of me." He held up a ragged piece of rough fabric. "Shreds of their garments littered the beach." He stared at the cloth as it flapped between his fingers in the wind. "I was there, Isobel. *With* you."

A loud gasp escaped my lips before my hand could stifle it. My jaw fell open.

"Where did you *get* that?" I moved to him and stared at the material in his hand. It was the same as the shreds that blew across the beach around the emaciated bodies.

"From your vision," he stated.

"Shit!" My hand smacked across my mouth and I turned toward the cottage. My feet moved fast across the knocking stones and faltered little in their determination to take me back to the cottage. "We need to see Mother Maureen."

"Wait!" He slowed behind me. "I just don't understand. Why in hell would you ever want to go there? Like, travel back to that time?" He paused holding his hands up. "It's the most brutal time in Irish history. Like, genocide." He stood frozen, waiting for an explanation.

He was right. It seemed irrational to want to go to such a dark time. But it had been haunting me my whole life. It called to me.

I knew there was nothing I could do to change the wretched course of history, to save those poor souls, but if I could somehow influence the course of events, or even just help one person, or one family, it would be worth it.

There was something there for me to do. I was sure of it. And when I did it, I could finally be free of the visions.

"I know." My hands pushed my hair back from my face. "It's a frightening time. I don't understand it, but somehow I have a part in it. And I need to find out what. That's why I want to go back there." My empty words blew away on the wind, leaving Ryan with nothing.

"No. There's more you're not telling me. It has to do with the other gifted one you know. Right?" he prodded.

Yes. He *was* right. If it weren't for Maeve, I would probably just live with my visions as if they were only a nuisance, like a health condition that needed to be dealt with on a regular basis. But Maeve proved to me that it was all connected somehow. It was all...real.

"Um, actually, yes." I paused and he moved closer. "Maeve was my friend. She had visions just like me." I exhaled, resigning myself to telling him everything. "They were like dreams that took her back to medieval Ireland and she was able to like, live there and interact with the people. She was able to help them." I struggled to find my words without sounding too insane.

"What makes you so sure it was real? I mean, some people might have a condition where they, you know, hallucinate." His eyes trailed away from mine.

I restrained myself from smacking him. His train of thought was similar to that of the general public and I was shocked at him for not assuming it was part of her gift.

"Right. That's what everyone thinks. That's why we're always hospitalized or medicated." My tone was firm and curt as I turned to walk toward the cottage.

"No, wait. I'm just playing devil's advocate. You need to expect that," he snapped at me. "What made her visions so real to you? Like, what made you believe she could actually travel through time?" he pressed.

I took a deep breath and on the inhale decided to take a chance and trust him fully. "She came back with artifacts from that time, just like the fabric you're holding. And she conjured the spirits of her ancestors. Others saw the apparitions, too."

"Did you?" His eyes studied mine.

"Yes. Right before she went away." I stopped as my throat constricted, remembering the day Maeve disappeared and never returned. "The Original Three, she called them. Three people from her village, from five hundred years earlier. They came for her." I cleared my throat to loosen my words. "And she went with them."

A loud crack from the shrubbery at the edge of the beach broke the tension and pulled our eyes for a moment to its sound.

He turned back to me after a moment. "What? How?" His eyebrows pinched together.

"I don't know," I murmured. "The wind and mist swirled all around us. Her friends called for her and fought through the gusts. But when the chaos died down, she was gone. And the Original Three, gone. We haven't seen her since." I looked down at the stones under my feet and watched a tear fall from my face and splotch onto the surface of a flat rock.

"It sounds so unreal." His head shook. "I don't not believe you. I just can't get my head around it. Who were her friends?"

"Declan and Michelle. She was the one who dropped me here earlier. And then Paul and Rory. Paul was her lover, like destined-to-be-together lover. And Rory was, well, he loved her too actually, but they were more like rivals." I took a deep breath, remembering them. "Paul broke that day. I'll never forget the pain in his cries." More tears fell from my eyes.

Ryan's head shook. "Jesus. Did you call the Gards?"

"No. There was no doubt in our minds what had happened. She travelled through time, to a time she was meant to live in. She was a warrior."

"How can you be so sure?" His eyes remained fixed on me, unblinking.

"I know how crazy this sounds, but the castle ruin where this happened, it was barely standing in crumbled, battle-worn condition. But when I went back the next time, after Maeve had disappeared, it stood in its full glory, all four walls intact. Maeve was able to stop the decimation of the stronghold. Somehow. For her clan."

"Shit. Are you serious?" His chin pulled back. "Which castle?"

"Doona. At Ballycroy." I pictured it clearly in my mind as I wondered if Maeve was still trying to get back there.

He swallowed hard. "Come on. Let's find Maureen. She might know something about this sort of thing."

The sharp snap of a twig made both our heads turn and we scanned the shrubbery along the edge of the beach. We froze as our eyes and ears homed in on any other sound or movement.

Nothing.

As we turned to head back to the cottage, a rustle and another snap came from the same location.

Our last nerves made us jump as a squeal escaped my lips and we ran all the way to the cottage without looking back.

Mother Maureen barreled toward us as soon as she caught a glimpse of our rattled condition. She'd been tending her herb garden when we hopped off the road into the yard.

Our ashen expressions were probably enough to rile her up, but she also likely knew we shouldn't spend too much time out in the open. Fear of raising suspicion with the nosy neighbors seemed to be the main worry.

"Sure, ya look like yeh've seen the divil himself," she blathered as her arms wrangled us into the cottage. "Git now, inside wit' ya."

"It's okay, Shanny. We're fine. Stop fussing." Ryan played it cool.

"Oh, I know fine when I see fine. And ye lot are far from it." She pushed back at him. "What happened?"

I listened without breathing or blinking, hoping to not miss a single detail of his personal account of the freakish story for Maureen. He filtered the most intense parts and avoided the haunting piece of fabric altogether. And no mention of Maeve. So, basically, he left out the dangerous bits while giving her the important information she would need in order to help us.

I wasn't sure why he gave Maureen the vanilla version. He probably didn't want to worry her. But more than likely, he was protecting her somehow.

Maureen looked into his eyes without blinking, then turned to me with a slow, mindful gaze.

"So, Izzy, will you be sharing the real story now? Ryan seems reluctant to dispense all the details." She looked back at Ryan as her lips pressed together in dismay.

My eyes darted to Ryan's. He nodded and rolled his eyes in defeat, giving me the go-ahead to embellish.

By the time I'd finished the story from the beach with all its eerie details, as well as the backstory of my visions, Maureen had a fresh pot of tea on the table and luscious scones with homemade strawberry-rhubarb jam. But through it all, I'd left out the story of Maeve. I just wasn't ready to share that again.

Ryan and I dove on the scones and ate them with a voracity that was unexpected, and it would have been vulgar under any other circumstances. Something about our experience had drained us though, leaving us famished and parched.

Maureen chuckled as she watched us and her bosom rose in satisfaction.

"I'm delighted ya came back to us, Izzy. We've a lot in common and I believe, from the depths of me heart, we were meant to all be together with our gifts. Not apart." She nodded at me. Then at Ryan.

"You know it's dangerous, Shan. They keep a close eye on our numbers. To be sure we don't expand." Ryan's voice took a firm, serious tone that straightened my spine.

"Feck 'em, Ryan," She blurted out. "Who do they think they are anyway? Controlling us the way they do. I'm tired of it. And Izzy here, she's awakened a glow in me that has been dead for years." She turned to me. "Thank you for that. I hadn't realized I'd let my light fade to such a dull flicker."

I pressed my thumb nail to my teeth. "Who keeps a close eye on your numbers?" My eyes darted from Maureen to Ryan.

Maureen gazed at the tea pot. "They all do."

Ryan brushed crumbs from his hand onto his plate. "The church ladies mostly. Well, that's what they like to think of themselves as, but they're far from women of God, if you ask me. Never minding their own business. Always on a witch hunt."

"Why?" I asked. "Why should they care?"

Maureen leaned in to me. "Any time someone is threatened, dear, they lash out." Her eyes bore into mine, bringing unease into my gut.

My eyes moved back and forth between them. I prayed I wasn't going to be responsible for something terrible happening to these good people. They'd kept themselves safe and quiet for so long, then I showed up. Whatever happened now, it couldn't be good.

"I should probably go." I placed my empty cup on the table.

Ryan's chair scraped the floor as he stood up in haste. "No." He steadied his chair. "Please. Stay just a bit longer."

"I really think I should be going. Just to let things settle a bit. Then I'll come back when you want me to." I sent a weak smile to Maureen, then turned back to Ryan. "Can you take me back to town? Now?" My heart rate quickened as I hoped for an easy exit.

"Yeah. Sure." He rubbed his brow like he had a headache.

Maureen fumbled through a trinket bowl in the kitchen and pulled out keys. She threw them to Ryan.

"I hope we'll be seeing you soon again, Izzy. You've brightened up the place more than you know." Maureen waved me off as I left the cottage with Ryan.

He went along the side of the house and turned back to me with his hand up. "Wait there."

A moment later, the engine revved with a boom and he backed a powerful black pickup truck into view. Its shine pushed through the mud splattered along its sides, and the edge of my mouth lifted in approval. My eyes moved along its strong lines and landed on a blue oval in the center of the grill broadcasting the Ford name——like an American vehicle on holiday.

I hopped in like a giddy child excited for a ride at the park. I'd actually never ridden in a truck like this and chuckled, feeling like I was in a cowboy movie or something. Ryan noticed my amusement and shook his head.

"Well, could be worse, ya know. At least the bed's only seen seaweed in its midst. Could'a been used at the cow fields for fertilizin' instead." He huffed at the unpleasant idea of hauling manure in his truck rather than seaweed.

"No, I like it. Really. I've just seen these trucks my entire life but never actually rode in one before. It's cool." I nodded my approval.

As we pulled out onto the main road, the engine hummed and I lowered my window to get the sea breeze. Wind moved through the cab, blowing my hair, and I turned to Ryan to see if he was enjoying the ride as much as I was.

He focused on the road, his face relaxed, and I caught the hint of a slight smile. I couldn't help but stare at his mouth. It expressed his feelings to the same degree as his eyes, with its subtle movements and hint of wetness. Then my gaze moved along his jaw line and through his chestnut brown hair, short on the sides but longer on the top. My stomach fluttered and I nearly twitched from it.

"Do you hang out with anyone other than James?" My question flew past my lips before I could censor it.

I just really wanted to know if he had a girlfriend. He said he didn't have girls come to his shed, so that was good. But it didn't mean he didn't have a girlfriend. I bit the inside of my cheek and my eyelids fell in shame at my direct questioning.

"I don't have a girlfriend. If that's what you mean," he replied without a flinch.

Shit! He could freakin' read my mind without touching me. I was sure of it.

"Oh, no, just wondering what you do for fun. You know. When you get bored." I picked at my cuticles and avoided eye contact, waiting for his next response.

"I've kind of grown used to my own company. A loner, basically." He kept his eyes on the road.

"Have you ever had, you know, friends?"

"No. Never." His hands tightened on the wheel. "At least, not once they noticed I was different."

My heart sank for him. He'd never had real friends which meant he'd probably never had a girlfriend either. I gazed out the window as I realized I had a similar situation.

"Yeah, same. It's good you have Maureen. And James, I guess." I huffed, teasing him with my first impression of James. "I have Declan and Michelle. And Gram. I guess it just works best that way for us."

His eyes flicked over to me then back to the road. "Gets lonely sometimes though."

I exhaled, knowing he was right. The loneliness carried pain with it, physical discomfort that couldn't be soothed. I knew too well.

But I couldn't help fixating on the fact that he never had a girlfriend. Holy crap. He was at least nineteen. I mean, that was still young, but most guys would have had a first kiss of some form by then.

He pulled the truck up along the front sidewalk of Gram's house. In my wandering thoughts, I hadn't even given him directions to where I lived.

"You knew the one?" I asked.

"I've dropped Maureen here a buncha times before."

My eyebrows lifted in surprise. "Funny I never met her until now. I mean, I'd heard stories of her, but had no clue she was here so much."

A twinge of resentment shot through my core for Gram keeping such a secret from me.

He nodded. "Seems like yer gran made sure of hidin' it from ya. Didn't want you influenced by the village witch, maybe." He chuffed. "You were probably in school most of those times, anyway."

I smirked. "Maybe most, but not all." I chuckled at my incessant habit of missing school as I opened my door. "Well, thank you for the lift. I'll…"

He interrupted my parting words. "I'd like to see you again, Isobel." He paused. "Soon."

My breath sucked in and I prayed he didn't hear it. I wanted to see him again too and the jitters that ran through me, lighting up my insides, proved it.

"Me too. Thanks." I stepped away from the truck onto the curb.

"And I think we should try again some time," he added.

"Try what?"

"A vision. Together. You know. To the past." He paused. "It almost seems like we're supposed to. I don't know." His shoulder lifted. "I just have this feeling that combined, our, you know, gifts, could be stronger. I don't know."

He looked at his hands on the wheel and then back at me. My words wouldn't form no matter how hard I forced them. The idea blew my mind.

Together, our gifts could be something more.

We had to try it.

CHAPTER 8

The second I entered the house, Gram's Wi-Fi kicked in and my phone lit up with fifty text messages from Michelle.

My eyes fixed on onto my screen:
u back yet
what happened
hes so cute
how long did you stay
answer meeeeeee
omg hes so gorgeous
u r killing me

I blushed as I read through her texts but the Snaps were even better. Every shot of her face was up close, up the nose, morphed. She was hilarious.

Michelle's communications dropped my shoulders from my ears and eased my tension. I hadn't realized I was clamped tight like a vice until her antics relaxed me.

I texted back:
home safe
it was good
kinda weird and stuff but ok
thanks for taking me there

I looked out the window, half hoping his truck would still be there. I already wanted to see him again. It was the first time since Maeve that someone actually understood me, the real me, in any way.

My chest warmed as I thought of him and a tingling sensation ran through my body. I shook it off, trying not to raise my hopes. But I couldn't help it. It had been years since Maeve left and my loneliness had become my normal. But Ryan awakened something in me, something that showed me it *wasn't* normal. And it wasn't okay to be so alone.

The idea scared me though, after so many years of building my defense against the isolation. It left me vulnerable because maybe I would always be alone and I needed that defense. But I couldn't stop thinking about him. Not even for a second.

"Isobel." Gram's voice snapped me to attention. "Is that you, dear?"

"Yes, Gram." I walked down the hall to the kitchen.

"Where've ya been, loov? Ya need to tell me where yer goin' so I don't worry. You've been gone half the day." Her tone held annoyance but worry overshadowed it.

"Sorry. I didn't realize I'd be gone for so long." My filters sieved through how much I should tell her. But of course, Maureen would probably mention it. Or would she?

I wasn't sure now where the line was drawn. But something told me it stopped before Gram. Maureen would want to protect her from needless worry. And she would want me to keep coming back, and being reported to Gram every time would surely derail that.

"I took a walk along the prom and went a lot further than I had planned. They're starting renovation work at Black Rock, you know." I attempted to distract her with trivia.

"Ach, sure, finally. The Corporation's been discussing renovation for years. About time, really." She clanged cups and plates as she unloaded the dishwasher.

I pulled out the silverware tray and sorted it into the drawer while thinking of my early days at Black Rock. Gram had brought me numerous times so I could jump off the high platforms into the sea with the other kids. I sighed at the thought of all the attempts to keep me normal. I'd never jumped, though.

But I was ready to now.

"Gram." I hesitated on my words but for the life of me couldn't stop them.

"Mm?"

"Tell me more about Ryan." Her head picked up in an instant. "And Mother Maureen." I did my best to distract her from my keen interest in Ryan but it was too late.

Her smile spread across her face.

"Gram, stop! I'm just curious about him," I whined.

"He's a looker, no?"

"Gram!"

She chuckled then added, "He's a fine lad. Maureen dotes on him. She adores him." She hesitated. "Poor chap doesn't get on well with his peers though. She homeschools him. I think the isolation hasn't been great for him."

Interesting. Gram didn't seem to know about Ryan's gift, or his curse--whatever I should call it. Maybe that was a good thing. She knew Maureen was special though and that was why she brought me to her.

"Yeah. I know what you mean. He's a little different." My eyes moved to the ceiling as I thought about him. "He doesn't even have a cell phone," I blurted out.

Gram laughed out loud.

"Sure, that's the least of it," she teased. "But in his defense, he does a great job with his craft. He keeps them afloat with his metalwork.

People travel great distances for his art. They're happy to buy what they want while turning a blind eye to the fact that he and Maureen have been outcast. Disgusting carryon if you ask me." She clanged plates into a stack, louder than necessary.

Outcast?

She was right. That was exactly what had happened to them. The townsfolk treated Maureen like she was mentally ill and unfit to care for Ryan. They were out for her. It was probably either jealousy or greed. They envied her special skill and they wanted her prized piece of land. It was despicable how they treated her.

And Ryan too. The school. His peers. They pushed him aside as well. It was so sad.

It was just like me, actually. Only Gram had been able to protect me from a lot of it, as far as the town went. There was no witch hunt for us, thank goodness. But my peers, she had no control over that part and I just had to learn to live with their cruelty.

My heart swelled as I yearned to be with Ryan again. To let him know he wasn't a freak and wasn't alone. That he could have a normal existence too. That we could be friends. Or more.

I bit my bottom lip as I thought about spending more time with him. But then my anxiety returned, fading my sunshine to black with negative thoughts. What if he didn't feel the same way? What if he preferred his quiet, lonely existence?

My eyebrows scrunched together as I realized I'd been fantasizing about something that was impossible. No one had ever wanted to get close to me. I was weird. I was...

"You're special, Isobel," Gram said. "I know this now and I want you to take some time to get to know yourself in a better light. It's time for you to blossom." Gram shook water of a silver bowl as she watched me.

Special? Great. No one wants to be called special anymore. It meant different. My eyes fell to the floor.

But I was glad Gram opened her mind to what was going on with me. She had spent so many years stifling me and hiding the truth from herself even, so now it seemed she was at least open to understanding me better. It was clear though that her guard remained up at full mast.

"Thanks Gram. I think I want to take another walk. I just need the air today. And open space. I'm tired of being locked away in my room all the time." A lump in my throat grew larger, threatening to choke me as I fought the isolation that begged for me from my room.

But it also proved I felt something. Anything.

"It'll do you good, dear. A walk into town maybe. A cup of coffee in Griffin's?" Gram couldn't help but plan my every move.

"Yeah, that sounds good. Thanks."

I grabbed my jacket and stood at the entryway mirror. Blinking at my reflection, I noticed color in my cheeks that hadn't been there for years. A delicate glow. And my long wispy white strands actually looked pretty for the first time ever. I'd always hated my thin, baby-like hair, but today, it suited me. It made me look like a sprite or woods fairy, and I liked it.

I stepped out into the afternoon mist and allowed it to coat my face, waking me further to a new level of self-awareness. It felt good.

Turning onto the sidewalk around our thick hedgerow, I looked in both directions to decide which way to go. Left, I glanced toward the sea and considered walking the prom for real this time and then right, down Dr. Mannix Road toward town and Griffin's Bakery. Then a gasp escaped my lips as shock jolted through me.

My body went rigid and I stopped short. Ryan's truck was parked two doors down and the sight of it sent adrenaline pumping through my veins.

Oh my god. He was still here.

My heart rate accelerated to the point I could feel it in my ears. Heat rose up my neck and hit my face in an instant as my breathing grew heavier.

Was it another panic attack? The familiar rapid heartbeat, the hot flash that reddened my face, the shallow breathing. But it was different this time. I didn't want to run away from it or escape the situation. I wanted more.

And my feet moved me toward Ryan's truck in search of more.

Approaching the passenger's side, I stood back and peered in. Ryan's silhouette gazed forward, holding the wheel as if contemplating pulling out. His head dropped then and his eyes appeared to be closed.

I tapped gently on the glass.

His head popped up and he turned to me with surprise splashed across his face. Without hesitation, he reached across the console and pushed the door open.

"Shit. You scared the crap out of me." He huffed.

"Sorry. I didn't mean to." I searched for more words while staring into his anxious face, but they wouldn't come.

"Get in. Outta the wet." He pushed the door further open and I climbed right in.

"What happened? Why are you still here?" I asked.

He pulled his eyes off me and looked out his window. Then he turned back to me. "I don't know. I just wasn't ready to leave." His deep blue eyes gazed into mine, showing me his true self as he waited for a reply.

"I didn't want you to leave." My words surprised me. They were raw and left my lips without filter. I couldn't stop them. I didn't want to.

He exhaled like he'd been holding his breath for hours. He reached for my hand but then pulled back in caution.

I pulled myself onto my knees and leaned in to him.

"It's okay. You can touch me. I don't mind." My mind exploded in the excitement of his hand on mine. I craved any form of contact with him like it was my oxygen.

"I can't. I want to. But I can't. It's not fair to you." His eyes fell.

"Please, Ryan. I have nothing to hide from you." Desperation rose in me as I understood the reality of our situation. He would never touch me. He wouldn't want to violate me or compromise anything between us.

"Isobel." He reached his hand to my face and moved it along my hair, just out of reach.

I held his warm eyes in mine as his jaw clenched with his internal struggle. His hand shook as he pulled it away.

My shoulders slumped and I dropped my head.

"It's okay," I said. "I'm just glad you're here."

His hands gripped the wheel again and he looked away.

"Want to go for a drive?" he asked, peering at me from the corner of his eye.

"Yeah." I twisted in my seat and settled in. "Duh."

He chuckled. "Where to? Anywhere you want."

Anywhere was good with me.

"Up the coast maybe?" I suggested.

He nodded. "Yeah. Perfect."

And it *was* perfect. Our conversation flowed like a river, moving from one topic to another, the two of us cracking each other up with our ridiculous stories of trying to fit into a world that didn't understand us.

"No, the worst is when you have an episode and as soon as you come out of it, everyone is staring." I shook my head. "And of course, the mean girls are snickering and pointing. Talk about awkward." I rambled about the social suicide my visions caused at every turn.

"Same. But guys have a different way of showing their distaste for the odd. They just beat the shit out of you," he added. "Maureen finally yanked me after my third hospital visit with broken ribs and bruises." He huffed.

"Oh my god. That's insane. A-holes." I punched the air like it was their faces.

I didn't know what was worse—the social exclusion from the girls, or the physical beatings from the boys.

Ryan laughed. "It doesn't matter anymore. I'm over it. Took a while. But I finally figured out I was different and that was it. I found my own path then."

"Yeah. I guess. Me too. But why does it feel so bad? Like, being outcast is a miserable feeling. Like torture actually. It's a sick form of pain that hits so deep." I grimaced at the reminder of the hurt I'd endured. "It's brought me to a very dark place on more than one occasion."

I'd never spoken words like these out loud before and I watched him through my lashes for his response, worrying he might judge me for being weak.

"Same," he stated with flat affect.

I fell silent, understanding he knew the pain too. The kind that made you feel there was no escape from it. No reason to keep fighting.

We drove in silence for a few miles and I watched the beauty of the Irish landscape unfold before us. The rolling green hills spilled into the bright blue sea as stone walls and white sheep carved and speckled the landscape.

I recognized the route to every last detail. This was the way I took whenever I visited Doona Castle.

My eyes shot wide.

Doona!

I twisted in my seat to face him. "Wanna see the castle where Maeve went missing?" I clamped down on my bottom lip with my teeth.

"Um, ya," he stated without hesitation.

I giggled as a warm light glowed inside me. For the first time ever, I looked forward to going there. To showing him everything.

Excitement rose in me like Christmas morning and my knees bounced in eager anticipation.

Then a strange feeling brewed in my gut, causing me to bite on my thumb nail. Sometimes I hated my gut because it was always right. And that annoyed me. But maybe this time it was just nerves. Or butterflies. Maybe it had nothing to do with my bringing Ryan to such a volatile place.

My stomach twisted again, sending warnings to my brain.

Damn it.

By the time Ryan turned onto the inlet leading to Doona, my stomach was practically in my mouth. I'd spent the last leg of the journey swallowing hard, trying to press it back down. But it hadn't worked.

Before long, the old cemetery came into view and the ruin of its church stood proud in its timeless purpose. The crumbling walls allowed me to see right inside to the ancient stone altar.

"Someone's here." Ryan's voice broke the silence making me jump.

"What?" I looked in the cemetery, half expecting to see a zombie.

"Over there." He nodded toward the grassy patch behind the stone wall surrounding the graveyard. The back end of a hidden car poked out from behind the stones.

I looked all around for the owner of the sedan but found no one in sight. "Maybe a local. Walking the headlands?"

"Yeah, probably." He took one final look around and then pulled into an open area past the cemetery, closer to Doona. "That must be it?" He pointed to the ancient ramparts that broke the horizon.

Doona rose up from its hidden seclusion within the rolling hills of Ballycroy.

"Yeah. Come on!" I hopped out of the truck and released the anxiety that had built in my stomach. It dissipated into the fresh air as I filled my lungs with excitement. I couldn't wait to show the castle to Ryan.

We walked along a path that led along the incline that surrounded the south side of Doona. Once we made it to the top, the castle came into full view and I stared in amazement like it was my first time seeing it. Every time, this got me.

The west side of the castle opened onto fields that sloped down to the sea and the rest was surrounded by the protection of the hills. I glanced up along the slope that led to the clearing. As soon as my eyes landed on the site, my gut twisted again and I pulled my eyes away.

"What is it?" Ryan caught the fleeting flash of panic in my gaze, but I blinked it away with a shake of my head.

"Nothing. It's just crazy to be here." I took a step closer to the castle.

"So, show me around. Like, where did all the shit go down?" He looked around for any remaining evidence of the six-year-old legend.

I walked toward the well-preserved castle ruin. Every part was intact from the outside, but the inside had been gutted either by fire or time, or both. The stronghold stood proud though with solid walls, jagged ramparts along the top just like in fairy tales, and a large, brooding black door at the entry.

Doona always looked much different than the first time I'd seen it. When Maeve brought me here.

"I was almost twelve. When it happened." I paused, remembering the story like it was yesterday. "Doona was a derelict ruin. Only one corner remained. The rest was just...gone. Lost to brutal battles and time." My eyes moved across the miraculous sight of the castle in its entirety. "Maeve said it had been decimated by her clan. The O'Malley's. Led by their chieftain, Grace O'Malley."

His eyes widened. "I studied her in my history books. The pirate queen."

"Exactly! The only female chieftain of her time in the sixteenth century." I looked out to the sea that Grace O'Malley had ruled with her army of over two hundred men. "Well, Maeve was a descendent of Grace O'Malley. Her visions were from that time, five hundred years ago, when Gaelic Ireland was under attack from the British. She was determined to travel back through her visions, to change the course of history. To stop the battle of the clans and unite them against Britain."

My head shook as I heard my own words and understood the enormity of what Maeve set out to do.

I was so young at the time it all happened, it just seemed normal to me. But now, hearing myself tell the story out loud to someone who'd never heard any of it before, I realized it sounded outrageous. Maybe I was crazy.

But I wasn't.

I looked up the castle walls. It was only after Maeve disappeared that the castle took on its full form.

She had changed the course of history. I was certain of it.

And I couldn't help but think I was meant to do the same. Somehow.

My visions of the famine haunted me, just as Maeve's visions of the pirate queen had haunted her. The similarities couldn't be ignored and Maeve was able to act on hers. The changed condition of the castle was proof of it.

"We all came here with Maeve," I continued. "So she could conjure one of her visions. She was convinced she could use them to make a difference." I took a deep breath. "It seemed like a fine idea at the time. But then it all went to hell."

I closed my eyes, remembering the heart-stopping vision of the Original Three approaching Maeve. The ghostly figures moved across the field as if their feet didn't even touch the ground.

They came for her. They knew her.

My story poured out to Ryan with little room for breathing.

"The Original Three told her it was time for her to return. Mist whirled around us and heavy gusts blasted in every direction. Paul and Rory were closest to it all but they lost sight of her. Their shouting voices broke through the wind just as it died down." I exhaled for miles. "And she was gone."

Ryan's eyebrows scrunched together as he looked at me.

"Just...gone?"

"Yeah." The blood drained from my head as the questioning tone in his voice rattled me. "You don't believe me."

"It's not that I don't believe you. It's just, it doesn't make sense." He stared out toward the castle.

"Obviously. I know that. But it happened. You should—"

He interrupted me with his hand in the air. "Don't get defensive. You have to admit, it sounds a little, you know, unbelievable. And you didn't call the Gards?"

My heart sank. No we didn't call the Gards. My internal voice squeaked out each word in the most annoying, mocking way possible.

My irritation turned to fury in a matter of milli-seconds and I turned on my heels. My legs charged toward the truck as I spoke familiar self-loathing criticism to myself. *"What made you think he would believe you, anyway? Freak. Did you hear yourself? Jesus. You idiot."*

"Isobel. Stop." Ryan's footsteps followed close behind me. "Please. Give me a break. I just need a chance to absorb this."

His words made me slow a bit. He was probably right. I couldn't expect him to just buy every word of this so easily.

"Maeve..." A low, hollow voice echoed and wailed across the hills, filling me with pure terror.

My eyes widened and I turned to Ryan, launching myself at him. I wrapped my arms around his waist like a frightened child and his arms held onto me as he scanned the hills for the source of the eerie sound.

"Maeve..." The broken voice trailed off along the swaying grass, scattering out to sea.

My bulging eyes looked up to Ryan's face, searching for an explanation of the ghostly cries, but all I saw was his blank, frozen death stare.

CHAPTER 9

I shook Ryan as hard as I could to snap him out of his trance. His empty eyes gazed at nothing and his face remained frozen and lifeless.

"Ryan!" I pushed his shoulders again, then stepped back and shoved him. The jolt of my hit sent him stumbling back and light returned to his eyes as he gasped for a breath.

"What the hell? Are you okay?" I stepped toward him, examining his expression.

He stepped back like I was a threat to him.

"Don't touch me." His words commanded me to halt and stung like poison at the same time.

My hands fell by my sides and I froze in confusion.

"No. When you held me...I—" He hesitated, searching for words. "I saw your mind." He pulled his eyes away from mine. "I'm sorry. I can't control it."

Oh my god. I forgot. When I grabbed him, I didn't realize I would set him off.

When I grabbed him? The eerie echo of the wailing voice returned to my mind and I stepped closer to Ryan, looking back over my shoulder at the hills.

"What was that creepy sound?" I whispered. "It was a voice." I glance around again.

"I know. I heard it too." He stepped around me. "Let's go back to the truck."

"Wait. I want to see if it will happen again." I paused, having no idea where my courage came from, and turned an ear toward the hills.

A steady breeze moved around us, carrying the briny scent of the sea mixed with damp earth. We waited in silence, hoping for it to happen again. Or maybe hoping it wouldn't.

"You saw my mind?" I broke the silence. "Tell me. It's only fair," I whispered, as if someone else might hear.

Ryan raised his eyebrows scanning the hills, as if this conversation could wait.

But it couldn't. I needed to know what he saw.

He looked back at Doona, then at me. "I saw your memory of Doona. In broken ruin. Only the far corner stood. The rest was gone."

"I told you!" I jumped at him. "What else?"

"That's kind of it. There was wind. A lot of wind. And shouting." His eyes squinted, like he tried to see the memory better, or maybe tried to filter what he shared with me. I couldn't be sure.

"Shouting? Like what?" I pressed.

"Like, searching, and—" His voice cut short.

"Maeve…" The haunting voice echoed through the hills again as if traveling across centuries.

I jumped and moved closer to Ryan. He stepped back with precision to miss my reflexive grasp.

"Jeez. It came from up there." I pointed along a stream that led up into the hills. I'd traversed it many times. "From the clearing."

"Where?" He followed my finger as I motioned up the slope.

"The clearing. It's a flat area up there surrounded by boulders. They used to take prisoners there, to a whipping post. It's a historical site now." I took a step forward as if drawn by a magnet. "I've been there before. Many times." I looked back at Ryan and hesitated before speaking my next words. "Strange things have happened there."

His face fell as he reluctantly glanced toward the clearing. "What kind of strange things?"

"It's hard to explain." I remembered his uncertain response to my story about Maeve and considered filtering from here forward.

I certainly wasn't about to tell him about the mystical possession that happened there once. To Rory. When something had taken him over and he went after Maeve with murderous intent. Which made no sense. Because he loved her.

Paul loved her too.

They were both there that day when she went away. It was their desperate voices calling to her that Ryan heard in my mind. I would never be able to erase or dull the sounds of their harrowing cries as they realized they had lost her.

"No, tell me. What kind of strange things?" he pushed.

Chewing the inside of my cheek, I considered my words. "Mystical stuff. Like a connection to souls from the past. It's a portal, maybe." I paused after hearing the word portal. It was strangely accurate.

Ryan's feet planted firmly beneath him and he looked back toward the truck.

"Please," I pressed. "Can we just have a quick look? I always go up there when I come here." I gave him my best puppy eyes.

"This is messed up." His hand ran through his hair. "I feel like we're asking for trouble. I mean, do we really want to stir things up?" He lifted his hands into the air like he just didn't get it.

I thought about my life of running. Running from who I really was. Running from the uncertainty of it all. I wanted to be more like Maeve now, and face my fear. Take on whatever it was that haunted me my entire life.

I was ready.

But Ryan wasn't.

He had demons too. I wasn't so sure he was ready to face them yet. But he was here, willing to explore. So that was a start.

"Please. Let's just have a quick look." I took two steps forward and nudged my chin in the direction of the clearing. "Just a little one."

He smirked and rolled his eyes. "Fine."

We moved along the trickling stream as we rose up into the hills. I thought about my last time at the clearing and the strange flower bundles I found wedged into a cavernous space between two boulders. Some were brown and brittle from age, others still held a hint of color in their wilted petals.

As we made it to the top of the last ridge, I slowed and looked back at Ryan. His rosy cheeks celebrated the open-air exertion of the climb but his wide eyes exposed his rising alarm.

"It's just over this ridge." I waved for him to catch up so we could enter the clearing together.

Walking beside me, he continued to scan all around us. Then we moved up the final incline together.

The boulders surrounding the perimeter of the clearing came into view first and I shot a smile at Ryan.

"Isn't it cool? It's ancient. Like a ritual space or someth—" My instincts shut me up and I crouched, signaling Ryan to duck as well.

A figure moved inside the clearing along the edge of the rocks. Pacing. Head in hands. Pacing more. Head falling back, gazing into the sky.

"Holy shit. Who is that?" Ryan whispered.

"It's gotta be the owner of the car, from the cemetery," I squeaked back at him. "Damn it. I wanted to be alone here." My disappointment laced my voice as I watched the intruder in our adventure.

My first response was to turn and go, but we'd come so far. We were here.

I looked at Ryan for a cue on what to do next. His firm stance proved he had no intention of leaving, so that was good.

"I guess we can just wait. Give him space to explore, then..." My spine straightened like I'd been hit by a bolt of lightning as my name resonated through my skull.

"Izzy?"

My head snapped toward the opening in the boulders and my eyes locked with the stranger in the clearing.

Paul.

~

My heart stopped as I stared at Paul standing motionless in the middle of the clearing. The gasp of air that sucked into me was audible as I comprehended the layers of what was happening.

I wasn't the only one remembering Maeve, to the point of never giving up hope. Paul was here too. Searching for her.

My legs carried me to him like he was my salvation—the one thing that proved my sanity.

"Paul! What are you doing here?" My simple words flew out, allowing room for more complex processing.

"Wow, Izzy. You're so grown up. I knew it was you in an instant though." He reached for me and gave me a hug like I was his long-lost baby sister. "My god. I can't believe you're here."

"Yeah." I blinked in disbelief. "I come here a lot, actually. I just, you know." One shoulder shrugged up to my ear.

"Me too." His gaze dropped to the ground.

My eyes pulled across the clearing to a bright yellow bundle in the grass. Then my head snapped back to him.

"You? You're the one leaving the flowers?" My jaw fell open.

He looked back at the bouquet and nodded.

"Oh my god." I pictured the stash of flowers wedged in the boulders and the amount of visits it would have taken to create such a hoard. "I'm so sorry." My eyes fell from his as echoes of his grieving wails returned from my memory.

"I just can't let her go." His hands wrung and he cracked his knuckles.

I nodded. "Yeah. Me too."

Movement behind me snapped me out of the intense moment as Ryan approached us.

"So, you two know each other?" he commented as he joined us.

I half-smiled. Yeah. We knew each other. We experienced the type of thing that bonds you to someone else for life. We would always be connected. By Maeve.

"Ryan, this is Paul. He was Maeve's...Maeve's..." I struggled for the right words, to not belittle the otherworldly bond they shared with trivial modern terms.

"Paul McGratt." He extended his hand to Ryan.

I caught Ryan's immediate flinch, but only because I anticipated it. He would have to touch Paul and I wondered how he would handle the interaction.

Before I could finish my thought, Ryan's hand reached out for Paul's and shook it. "Ryan O'Shaughnessy."

As the words passed from Ryan to Paul, so did an enlightened gaze as Ryan connected with Paul's mind for a brief moment. Their hands released and Ryan looked straight into my eyes, as if to say, "*I have so much to tell you.*"

Paul sent a calculated nod to Ryan. Paul was a researcher of Celtic history—a celebrated professor at the university in Galway—and never dropped that identity, ever.

"Where ya from, Ryan?" Paul fished for details straight away.

"Spiddal," he stated. "And you? Is that a hint of a Dublin accent I hear?"

Paul huffed. "Yeah. Closer to Wicklow." His words held no tone or emotion, as they were simply fill for the conversation. Paul's attention was back on me in an instant, not Ryan.

"Izzy, are ya keepin' well?" His eyes searched mine to the point where I looked away.

He knew I had the visions too and I could practically hear the questions in his thoughts that he was dying to ask me. And the small talk wasn't going to fly.

"You're here. For Maeve?" I asked him.

His back straightened and he shifted his weight. I'd hit a raw nerve.

He hesitated, as if calculating his response, and his eyes focused on me like a missile homing in on its target.

"You too?" His eyes narrowed. "Have you ever been able to make contact?" He stepped closer to me, like I suddenly had value or special worth to him.

Ryan closed in by my side, picking up on Paul's anxious response to me.

"Well, no. I don't...I don't know." My eyes dropped to the ground to avoid his desperate stare.

"You must. Please. Can you try?" Desperation rose in his voice and he reached for me like a lifeline. "You have the visions too. Maybe you can find her. You must!"

Ryan stepped between us. "I beg your pardon. I don't mean to be rude." He lifted his hand to stop Paul's anxious advance toward me. "But you're a little intense right now, McGratt. Can we take it down a notch?"

Rage clouded Paul's eyes, causing his handsome face to twist and shift into something more sinister. He glared at Ryan as if he were a roadblock to his source for finding Maeve: me.

A chill shuddered through me as Paul's response confirmed what I had always suspected. Maybe I did hold the power to find Maeve.

"Come on, Isobel. It's time we head back." Ryan gestured for me to move out as he held firm eye contact with Paul.

"No, wait." Paul's voice cracked in fear. "Please. If there's anything you can tell me. Anything. Please."

His shoulders fell limp. Then he pulled his hands through his hair, as if he'd yank it right out. His angst seeped from his every movement. It was obvious he'd been tortured with unanswered questions for years and the deep worry lines in his brow and around his eyes proved it.

His unnerved, battered condition actually frightened me. He used to be so, so together. Smart. Handsome. Adventurous. But now, he was thin, pale, and broken. Grief had a wicked way of taking a strong person down and Paul was living proof.

He was worse than that though. A deep desperation gnawed at his core, like he was a caged animal waiting to pounce. Waiting for any scrap of meat.

And that scrap was me.

It was as if I was the one who held the key to his survival now and it was too late to convince him otherwise.

I took a step away from him, pulling my eyes from his wide glare. "If I learn anything, I'll let you know. You're still at the university, right?" I feigned quick follow-up as a means of getting him to allow me to leave.

I wanted to help him though. I really did. I just had no idea how. I'd been considering the same things as him, using my visions to find her, but I just didn't know where to begin yet. And I definitely didn't feel comfortable exploring the idea under his intense pressure.

His eyes darkened. "No. Please. Don't go yet. You need to try. Use your vision. Now. Right here. It's bound to work." His eyes begged mine. "Conjure her, Izzy. Please!"

He launched for me as if he could stop me from leaving and somehow force me to generate a vision.

I gasped as he moved toward me and I was yanked out of his direct line of approach by Ryan.

He shoved Paul hard and knocked him off course. Paul stumbled and then turned back to me with heightened focus. He straightened his shirt and ran his hand through his hair to settle it, as if trying to take on the appearance of a sane person. Then he moved for me again.

"Stay, Izzy." His voice cracked as he reached for my arm. "You must—"

Ryan swung his arm, knocking Paul's grab away from me. "Stop, man. You're outta line." He pushed Paul backward knocking him off balance, sending him staggering toward a boulder.

My eyes flew wide in shock at Ryan's defense of me.

Before I could say anything, Ryan grabbed my arm without thinking and pulled me along with him toward the exit of the clearing. He twisted his wrist, then shook it out.

"Shit, that hurt." He looked at his bruising forearm as I sailed along with him, trying to keep up with his speed. "But he had it coming. Dude's a mess."

My vision clouded for a moment, causing me to stumble, then a thick fog surrounded us making it even harder to navigate the uneven terrain.

Ryan pulled me along faster and he looked back to be sure Paul wasn't following us. "Quickly. A storm's rolling in!" he shouted as the wind picked up.

His grasp trailed down my arm and found my hand. His fingers interlaced with mine and he squeezed as he pulled me along even faster.

His intimate touch sent my mind spiraling as I ran with him. The wind whipped through my hair, creating a sensation of weightlessness. Our feet barely touched the ground as we ran for the truck.

Then I realized.

It was my vision.

It was coming.

And we were touching.

"Ryan! My vision!" I screamed. "It's happening!" My voice blew away in the violent bursts.

"Keep running! I feel it too! Run faster!" The panic in his voice rang loud.

He didn't want this. I heard his resistance in his voice. He wasn't ready for it. But his firm grasp proved he refused to let go of me.

Then everything went calm.

The wind settled around us and the mist dissipated. We blinked into the clear view around us.

Ryan squeezed my hand. "We're okay. It's okay."

He exhaled, looking around to be sure we were safe. My eyes moved with his and widened as I took in our strange surroundings.

He turned to me with a lost gaze. "Wait. Where are we?"

CHAPTER 10

The comforting presence and majesty of Doona Castle had disappeared, leaving us in unfamiliar territory. The disturbance of the brooding clearing, gone too. Eerie silence surrounded us with its shocking twist on our heightened senses.

Ryan and I stood motionless, hands still clamped together, as we stared all around us. Spongy, damp grass underfoot had turned to a hard dirt road that drew our eyes out across a massive lake, black as night.

"What the hell?" Ryan looked into my eyes with anxious apology lining his forehead. He dropped my hand like it had burned him and pulled away to create distance between us. "I shouldn't have touched you." His voice rose in alarm. "I made this happen."

I glanced around us and stepped closer to Ryan, keeping the space between us to a minimum for fear of somehow being separated.

His rising angst sent my nerves sparking but I closed my eyes and took a long inhale, reminding myself that this was all a part of the process—us, doing this together. It just so happened to occur when we didn't expect it to.

"No, Ryan. It's not your fault. This is what happens. All the time." I glanced all around us without alarm to show him it was something I was familiar with. "The only weird part...Okay, there are a lot of weird parts. But the only thing new is that you're here with me. Again." I stared into his eyes in disbelief. "How is that even possible?"

As he looked into my eyes, his anxious brow slowly fell, and his breathing returned to a steadier pace. It seemed he was accepting the situation as it became more real to him. I nodded back in a silent pact that we would do this, together.

Strangely, the typical fear and anxiety of my visions hadn't hit me yet. My usual flight response hadn't exploded within me, jarring me to run from the situation.

My head tipped while looking into Ryan's comforting face. With him here, I felt almost...brave. Like I could take a minute to look around, rather than trying to escape or finding a way to end the vision as quickly as possible.

I glanced up and down the road with a quick jerk of my head, making sure we were alone. Memories of my earlier visions flooded me with images of ragged, starved people searching for help. I prayed we wouldn't encounter anything like that here but the subtle gnawing in my gut suggested otherwise.

And where was *here* anyway?

My eyes fixed on the highest mountain along the horizon and Ryan followed my gaze behind him.

"Crough Patrick," we said in unison, establishing our location.

"The holy mountain. We're still in Mayo. But somewhere near Westport," Ryan calculated. "The black lake, then, it must be Doolough." He gazed at the dark water and a shudder ran through him as he spoke the name.

"Doolough?" I shook my head, watching his nervous reaction to the lake. "What's that?"

With a deep inhale, his eyes closed for a moment. "It's the site of the historical death march of 1849. Ireland's bleakest hour of the Great Famine." He hung his head. "Six hundred innocent people. They walked over fifteen miles in search of help. And no one came to their assistance." His voice trailed off in remembrance of the lost souls.

"Oh my god." I closed my eyes, as I imagined the horror and then saw flashes of it in my memory. "I think I've seen part of the death march in my visions. The last survivors make it to Westport House in search of food."

Ryan nodded and looked all around us for perspective.

"Westport House would be that way." He pointed down the road, using Crough Patrick as his compass, and turned his body in its direction.

I inhaled loudly as my chest rose, pulling in the courage to take the next step. Ryan's strong posture proved he was willing to partake in whatever we embarked upon. Instead of trying to end it and getting back to the truck, he egged me to move forward with him. My eyes brightened at the thought of not being alone, for the first time ever.

Biting my bottom lip, I let my head fall back as I summoned the strength to move ahead. This time with Ryan by my side.

"Okay. Let's do this. Let's go toward Westport House and see what's there," I said.

Ryan moved with me like there was no other option in the world and our keen focus remained fixed ahead of us.

We walked the historical trail with the strange knowledge that it wasn't yet historical. Instead, it was current, and the foresight of knowing what was to come made it all the more terrifying.

We were merely observers of a horrific time that once was and the thought of not being able to change it tore at my gut.

As we moved together in somber silence, the trail began to display signs of its tragic past. First one, then two, then ten. We stumbled upon lifeless body after ragged body of the death marchers, some with grass in their mouths in a final attempt at gaining life-giving sustenance.

The trail took on the feel of a minefield, littered with bodies, and we wove around them to not disturb their final rest. The stench of death clung heavy in the air, coating our throats, and our pace picked up as panic mounted within us.

Women. Children. Men. All ages. Scattered everywhere.

Tears stung my eyes as I clung to Ryan. "Get me out of here," I begged. "I've seen enough." I choked on my wretched words.

But nothing made it stop. The horror continued, frozen forever in the desperate faces of its helpless victims.

There was no turning back. We had to keep marching through the despair.

For miles.

I couldn't fathom the thought of there being any survivors after passing so many deceased. These people marched toward something powerful. They believed in something strongly enough to get them to leave their homes with their families in emaciated condition to travel to Westport House.

It was hope.

I remembered the huge caldron on the front terrace of Westport House. The starving people must have got word that there was relief. Food for their hungry families. The hope of salvation led them on this ominous journey, now remembered as the Death March of Doolough.

Staying close together, we charged along the trail, desperate to get to something new. We held each other's eyes as much as possible, clinging to our sanity within our tight gaze. Finally, we caught sight of those still standing ahead—staggering toward their destination with sunken eyes and hollow moans.

Our own health and vigor allowed us to quickly move to the front of the march toward the strongest members of the group. The band of filthy, skeletal villagers shuffled behind us toward the gated entrance to Westport House, loyally following their leaders.

Ryan moved alongside one of the taller men who appeared in somewhat better condition than the others—with enough energy to lead the pack, slightly less emaciated but starving never-the-less.

"What will we find here? What are you seeking?" Ryan asked him.

The man turned in slow-motion and gazed at us. His weathered skin and sunken features made him look like he must be seventy, but whatever strength he had left in him made it clear he was likely in his thirties. He blinked his eyes at us like he was dreaming.

"Are ye angels?" he asked, peering into my face.

Ryan and I stared at each other in shock. The man could interact with us—just like we were actually there.

"No. We're not angels," I answered as Ryan shot a puzzled glance my way. "But we've come to help. What are you searching for?"

"The virtuous Lady Sligo has sent word of assistance. From England. The lords have come to take count. To send word back to the queen. They've brought rations for us all." He panted from the effort of speaking.

I knew of Lady Sligo. Her handwritten letters from the 1800's were encased and preserved on display in the Westport House museum. She wrote of failed crops. Growing numbers of those fighting the hunger. She saw it coming and wrote for help. Help that never came.

But these people thought help had arrived. They marched for it. They used their last ounces of energy and many their last breath to get to it.

"Oh my god, Ryan. There's nothing there for them." My voice broke as it left my mouth. I coughed to get the sounds out of my constricted throat. "Come on. We must get in there to help. There must be something we can do."

I pulled him along to race ahead of the group toward the manor.

We hurried up the long drive that led to Westport House, getting far ahead of the dragging, starving villagers. As we turned the final bend, the regal manor came into view, standing proudly with its floor-to-ceiling windows, stately columns, and topiary landscaping carved to perfection. We paused at the contradiction of such wealth and surplus versus such poverty and suffering. Our faces grimaced as it turned our stomachs.

We flew across the tiled terrace and jumped two or three steps at a time to the first level lawn. An enormous black caldron sat in the grass, bigger than a clothes washer. We barreled toward it and grabbed onto the rim as we bent to look inside.

It was bone dry and cruelly empty. Chipping sides and a rusting interior gave the famine pot the appearance that it hadn't been used in months, or maybe even years.

I pressed my eyes shut, trying to remember my history lessons about the famine. It occurred in the 1840's and I thought it lasted around 5 years. Over a million Irish died of starvation and disease. Another million emigrated. It was the largest scale disaster Ireland, and the 19th century, had ever seen.

I lifted my haunted gaze from the bottom of the empty pot to meet Ryan's sorrowful eyes. His face held the same devastating disbelief as my own. How could this even be possible? Why was no one helping?

We turned to the enormous double doors of the grand entryway to the manor and charged up the final set of perfectly sculpted granite steps. Moving along the stone patio past large containers of decorative shrubbery, we peeked into the enormous windows as we moved to the entryway doors.

I stopped short as I caught a glimpse into the elaborate dining room. There were walls covered in portraits and tapestries and an intricately carved oak table that ran the length of the room with at least twenty chairs. A fire roared in the massive hearth and the detailed craftsmanship of the mantle glowed and flaunted its European appeal.

Two uniformed officers sat at the far end of the table, lost in discussion, while they licked their fingers and dropped chewed bones onto their plates. They pulled bread from an overflowing basket and ripped it, swiping the drippings from their plates and filling their mouths. Cups overflowed with red wine which they drank in gulps, wiping their mouths with the backs of their hands.

My face contorted with the contradiction of information before my eyes. I stared at Ryan with my mouth agape, lost in utter confusion. He balled his fists as he struggled to discern the reprehensible information.

"The British officials," he stated through his tight jaw. "They've come for a report for the queen."

"Well did they bring any help?" I blasted. "Why are there no preparations being made for the starving people? They'll be here in a matter of minutes." My eyes darted down the drive as my voice rose to shrill. "We have to do something!"

Ryan followed my gaze back along the road to see if the first suffering villagers had appeared yet. Only silence filled the landscape.

In an instant, I moved to the huge doors and reached for the heavy iron knocker. I lifted it and dropped it back on the door with a loud bang. I lifted it again and this time held on, smashing it again and again onto the reverberating door.

Ryan's spine straightened as his face turned white and he jumped like a skittish animal. "What the hell are you doing? Shit, Isobel." He stepped back, like contemplating running away. "Jesus! You don't fuck with the British. Not at a time like this."

"But I have to do something! Did you see them stuffing their faces like pigs? While people all around them are dying of starvation. What is going on here?" I reached for the knocker and pounded again.

This time, just as the knocker hit down on its target, the door creaked open.

A woman in a black and white servant's uniform held the door, peering out at us. Behind her, the two British officers stood tall with inquisitive pinched brows while picking at their teeth. Another woman, dressed in the highest fashion of the time, meticulously coiffed, lingered further behind, examining us up and down.

Before we could speak, the taller officer with squinty eyes blasted at us in a harsh tone, "State yer business." As the words left his mouth he stepped closer, inspecting our clothing and our condition with a skeptical eye. "Where are you from? Who sent you?"

I looked to Ryan as I considered my reply, but the paranoid insecurity in the officer's tone wasn't lost on me. He was on high alert, like he had something to defend, or something to hide, and his anxious response to us spoke volumes.

Preparing to respond to him, my words stuck in my throat as I stared at Ryan's jeans and machine woven button-up jersey with a concert t-shirt poking out at the neck. His clothing, and mine, must have appeared wildly foreign to these people, making it impossible to place us as friend or foe.

"We've come up from Galway, from the university." I broke the silence that seemed to stretch for centuries, remembering the plaque at NUIG's gothic quadrangle; "Founded 1845"—four years ago. "To help," I stuttered. "We've come to help."

"And how da ye children intend to help a starving nation?" The sarcasm in the officer's voice made my hairs bristle and sparked an anger that had been brewing deep within me.

My top lip curled as I drew in the smells of their bountiful meal. My eyes moved around the great foyer and immediately locked on a large pile of sacks stacked to the ceiling at the far end of the wide entrance hall. The hemp bags displayed stamps of blotched ink of varying colors but the words were clear enough to understand the contents without question. Grain; Barley, rice, and oats.

Oh my god. It was enough to feed these people. For weeks. Or months.

"We can help distribute the food. We're strong and healthy. We'll fill the caldron and serve the hungry. We'll work until it's done." I took a step forward, anticipating a welcoming invitation in—open arms receiving us as angels of mercy.

But the door began to close as one of the officers commanded the servant to do so.

The smaller officer with a lazy eye had less self-restraint and couldn't help but chastise us. "Have you no idea the value in those sacks, girl? They're more valuable than gold. And it's a price we're willin' to charge."

The first officer jabbed him in the ribs. "What's wrong with ya? We've no idea who these people are." He looked at us again with one eye pinched in a scrutinizing glare.

But it was too late. My temper had popped my head off and there was nothing left to control my actions. I pushed the door open with my full body weight and entered the foyer. Ryan pressed his way in with me, likely feeling the same fury.

I bounded toward a sack of grain and grabbed the corner of it. "Just one bag. The people are coming. They're dying! They need this!"

Ryan stood tall between me and the officers.

The stately woman at the back stepped toward me. She helped me tug at the sack to pull it from the pile.

"Release it, woman!" an officer's voice boomed.

She dropped the corner of the sack and shuffled back toward the wall in a cowering response while I continued to pull.

In the same instant, the officers flew into an aggressive rage that seemed far too intense and unnecessary for the situation. Voices shouting, commands flying, their teetering volatility further exposing their dishonest agenda as well as their oppression of the lady of the house.

In an exaggerated gesture of authority, the higher officer commanded the loose-lipped one, "Seize them!"

My eyes widened as the blood drained from my head. The officer's commands to stop us filled my heart with terror. My mind whirled in confusion over how they couldn't want to help these starving people. I stared into the eyes of the woman of the house who had helped me with the sack. Her helpless gaze proved it was not within her control.

"Lady Sligo!" the servant woman called to her. "Please. Step back!"

Lady Sligo slinked along the wall and moved to her house maid's side. She stood back and watched the officers take on a larger than life persona against us.

"You are under arrest!" The head officer's voice boomed through the foyer, bouncing off the marble walls. "Disloyalty to the crown. Attempting to steal from the queen herself."

I stared at him in disbelief. Was he making it up as he went along?

"What are you talking about?" I shouted back with a tone that must have stung like a slap.

Ryan's hand shot up to stop me. "Isobel. No."

But it was too late. My words hit the officer's pride in its deepest, most vulnerable core and he lost his mind to his volatile rage. A growl started low in his throat and grew as his words formed.

Spit flew as he launched for me, shouting words like 'treasonous witch' and 'rotting in dungeons'.

Ryan jumped and pulled me out of the officer's line of attack. Frozen by the utter shock of being treated like a criminal by the officers, I would have been flattened if Ryan hadn't yanked me out of the way.

I clung to Ryan's arm for stability and looked back only to see the second officer regaining his balance and taking another aim at me. The steel in his eyes exposed his unwavering determination to get his frustrated hands on me.

Ryan pulled me into his chest as he commanded the officer to stop. But just as his words left his mouth, they were lost in the blurring haze. Mist swirled all around us, making us lose sight of the officers and the women of the house. The manor faded out as blasts of wind whipped around us.

Ryan wrapped his arms tighter on me and we crouched through the tempest. Our trembling bodies quaked as we gave in to our fears and the danger that had threatened us.

Tears poured from my eyes. Tears of frustration for not being able to help. Tears of heartbreak for the lost souls. Tears for the despair of Ireland during the Great Famine.

A heavy silence like the vacuum of space surrounded us, making my ears pop and with a blast of bright light, the mist faded. I looked up into Ryan's face and reached for it.

"We're okay?" I checked him for any damage. "I think we're back."

His arms remained firm around me as he checked our surroundings for any danger. The rolling green hills and the lull of the waves lapping the coast confirmed we were back in Ballycroy. Safe. The shadow of Doona Castle lumbered over us as we crouched by Ryan's truck.

"Jesus." Ryan's head fell back as more shivers twitched out of him.

"Yeah." I shook with massive quakes, allowing the safety of the present to sink in.

We'd escaped in the nick of time, avoiding the clutches of the British officers. Their wrath soured my mouth, poisoning me from within. Their bully tactics were familiar to me but their aggression was beyond anything I'd encountered before. I shuddered at the thought of the second in command getting his filthy hands on me.

But the people. They were starving. And the bags of grain were just out of their reach. The thought made me sick to my stomach and my eyes squinted to clear the images burned into my mind.

From behind us, the sound of crunching gravel shot our heads around and my heart accelerated to its maximum.

Paul leaned back against Ryan's truck, arms crossed, and watched us while nodding his head in affirmation.

"Thought so," Paul spoke at me with flat affect while rubbing his jaw. "I'm not gonna press you any further this time. I apologize for my earlier, rather gruff, approach. But I'm desperate." He hesitated, tipping his head. "But now, thanks to you two, I'm feeling better. Particularly because you've confirmed this to me." He smirked and waved his hand at our crouched, shaking condition. "You still have the visions."

CHAPTER 11

P aul paced with fidgeting impatience, but coming back from that vision to full functioning was proving to be more difficult than usual. Heavy fatigue settled deep within my bones and my body resisted any attempts at moving.

Wasted and spent, Ryan and I pulled away from each other to break our intense contact. Just as we separated, his stealth gaze into my eyes weakened, like he'd lost something needed for survival. Our connection, and the vision, had bonded us somehow, and separating actually caused physical discomfort.

Pushing ourselves up to standing, we shuffled to the side of the truck. Ryan pulled opened the passenger door and reached in for a water bottle. He opened it and handed it to me, then motioned for me to climb in.

I sank into the comfort of the seat and drank deeply.

Ryan turned to Paul.

"I'm taking her home now. She's not ready for this conversation with you." He spoke in a direct tone, leaving no room for negotiation.

Paul studied Ryan's face. "I've heard of the O'Shaughnessy's from Spiddal," he said out of nowhere, remembering Ryan's introduction. His voice held critical judgment, causing Ryan's shoulders to square up. "Something tells me there may be some truth to the stories I've heard, no?"

"You talkin' fairy tales, McGratt?" Ryan replied with a hint of sharp annoyance.

Paul shifted in surprise, moving his weight from one foot to another. "I think we might be able to help each other."

"I'm not so sure of that," Ryan replied, moving around to the driver's side.

"Well, I am. Meet me at the university. Both of you. Monday." He held my eyes with his. "Please." And he turned and walked away toward his car.

Ryan's eyebrows pressed together and he looked at me with an expression of *"who the hell does that guy think he is?"*

I just shook my head, unable to generate a proper reply as I sank deeper into my seat. But I couldn't help hearing Paul's words repeating in my mind. He knew something of Ryan's family curse and he definitely knew all about mine. And he wanted to work with us.

The more I thought about it, the more it seemed to make perfect sense. Too bad he had become an obsessive, crazed lunatic, though.

I paused. Who was I to judge?

Ryan drove us back to town in no great hurry. We were traumatized and needed the extra time to process what had happened.

"I can't believe we interacted with those people. All of them." My words were simple compared to the complex reality of the enormous experience.

"Those officers were feckin' assholes," Ryan blasted.

I giggled at his outburst. I couldn't help but laugh at his passionate remark. Our nerves were shot and swearing was basically the simplest attempt at catharsis.

He fired a harsh look at me for snickering, but it quickly faded and he started laughing too. "Feckin' assholes," he said again. And we laughed until tears rolled down my cheeks.

"We need to go back," I stated. "They need our help."

The words popped out of me before I had a chance to even deliberate on them. Going back to help those starving people and to stop the corruption of the British officers at Westport House wasn't a debate, it was a necessity.

"Are you shittin' me?" Ryan barked. "We nearly got ourselves royally drawn and quartered." His eyes scrunched in annoyance.

"No. We'll figure out a better approach. Not so forceful, ya know." I bit my bottom lip, contemplating returning to that horrific scene. "Lady Sligo will help us."

"I don't know, Isobel. We have no idea of what they're capable of in your visions. It all seemed real enough to me. I wouldn't fook wit' it, if I were you." His shoulders twitched, sending a shudder up to his head. "I could use a pint. Calm me nerves."

"Seriously?" I gawked at him in feigned wide-eyed judgment.

"Hell yeah. Want one?"

I never really liked beer much, it just made me tired and I didn't have much opportunity for it anyway. But something about his playful expression and the rebellion of it encouraged me to partake.

"Umm. Okay." I smirked.

He pulled onto the side of the road outside a small pub and hopped out. "I'll be right back."

He went inside for a couple minutes and came out with a brown bag. "Sold me a few cans," he said with a sinister smile. "We can hang out in my shed, if you want."

I nodded and he took us along the coast road toward Spiddal. Spending time with him in his shed sounded perfect. We just needed a chance to talk about everything that happened and what we would do next. But, really, I was just happy to have the chance to be with him a little longer. I only hoped the twisting in my gut was residual stress from the visions and not its usual nagging.

As he took the turn onto the green road that led to the cottage, he slowed down to navigate past a few cars parked along the side. The lane was already narrow and the unexpected vehicles made it nearly impossible to pass. He squeezed the truck through and then pulled it off the road into the yard.

He hopped out, pissed off by the jam the cars created on what he felt was his road. And I guess he was right.

"Hang on," he said without looking back to me.

He barreled toward the front door in search of Maureen. It didn't seem like her to have company, particularly that much.

Just as he approached the stoop, the door flew open and a large man in a dark suit lumbered out. Ryan stepped back by instinct and then walked straight up to him.

"Who are you?" Ryan asked, wasting no time on pleasantries.

"Town surveyor. And you are?" Arrogance dripped from the man's flat tone and detached demeanor.

Ryan pushed past the man and went inside. I stayed in the truck, not knowing what to do. So, I waited.

After several minutes, another gentleman and two women left the cottage. They walked past the truck, not noticing me inside, and spoke freely.

One woman said, "She's not fit to stay here alone. And the boy, he's just not right."

My chin pulled back in disgust at her callous comments.

The man nodded in agreement and as he passed by the truck, I noticed the white collar poking out of his jacket. He was a priest.

My hand covered my mouth as my eyes widened. It was like they were organizing something against the O'Shaughnessy's—looking for excuses to meddle in their business.

My eyes moved across the lawn and past the shed, along the road that led to the sea. At the edge of the yard, I noticed someone lingering. Watching. Then they moved out of my view. The darkness of evening settled around me, causing me to second guess what I'd seen.

Then, like an explosion of thunder, the truck door flew open and Ryan jumped in. A small scream left my mouth as I nearly jumped out of my skin. He'd scared me half to death.

"It's a feckin' witch hunt," he blasted. "They're trying to convince Maureen to sell the place. That she's not well enough to keep it. They're threatening to have her sent to a home for the elderly. It's ridiculous! They just want our land for a new development of holiday homes. It's so obvious. Total shite!" He slammed his hands on the steering wheel.

"They can't do that." I shook my head in disbelief.

"Oh, they can. And they will." He turned to me. "There are enough stories of our 'odd' behaviors that can be used against us for years. The church ladies have already started a log of people's stories. Totally blown out of proportion, one sided. Total bullshit."

He paused and stared out the window. His furious expression fell and turned to something more harrowing.

"I need to get you out of here. The last thing I want is for them to target you, too." He roared the engine and pulled out of the yard. "I gotta drop you home and get back to Maureen. She's a nervous wreck."

"I can get a ride, Ryan. You need to stay here with Maureen." I dug for my phone to call Michelle.

As I lifted my hips to reach into my back pocket, my eyes moved out the side window down toward the sea. A shadow lurked at the bend. The spying stranger.

"Ryan. There's someone there." I pointed down the road. "They were there watching earlier too."

"Shit." Ryan gunned it, causing dirt and pebbles to shoot out behind the truck. "It's Ol' Lady Flannery. Nosy feckin' neighbor. I'd swear she's the start of all this."

I shuddered from the creepiness of her spying.

"What's *her* problem?" I cringed at the number of people who had it out for the O'Shaughnessy's.

"Jealousy. Greed. Always is." He huffed. "She claimed to have the gift. Fer years. Took many a fool's money too. 'Twas only when Maureen's true gift was discovered and the people worshipped 'er for it, that they called Flannery a fraud. Laughed 'er out of the social circles. She's hated Maureen ever since." He knocked the truck into gear. "Can't help but think she started the witch hunt, bit by bit, years ago. Twistin' the truth. Makin' Maureen and me out ta be freaks."

A shiver ran through me as I thought back to the beach, when Ryan and I had our vision of the ragged bodies washing up on shore. I got that creepy feeling you get when you think you're being watched. And then I'd heard the rustling in the shrubs.

"I think she was watching us when we were on the beach. I heard her in the brush." I swallowed hard.

"I know. Me too." He fixed his eyes back on the road, determined to take me home safely. "This is getting big, fast. I think we are going to need some help."

He was right. We needed help. Things were flaring up and it felt like the attention of the entire village was on us.

"But who?" I asked, knowing the situation was escalating by the minute.

Ryan's head shook.

I added, "We need someone who understands us. Who believes in what we can do without wanting to exploit us."

I bit the inside of my cheek in thought. It was obvious who we needed. His knowledge and firsthand experience of mysticism was one thing, but his depth of understanding of Irish history and folklore was a critical other. But he also was a threat at exploiting us. We had to tread cautiously.

I nodded, knowing I was right, and spoke the words.

"We need Paul."

On the drive back to Gram's, Ryan's silence filled the truck with deafening anxiety. His concern for Maureen pulled his face down and dulled the light in his eyes, causing my worry to compound.

I twisted in my seat to face him. "What can I do?" I shrank in defeat, powerless. "I feel like I brought this attention on you guys. It's best I stay away for a while." I shook my head in regret.

"No." His curt tone cut my words short. "I don't want you to stay away." He took his eyes off the road and looked at me. His stern gaze appeared angry at first but then I saw it was something else. Fear, maybe.

"Can you meet me at NUIG on Monday?" My eyebrows lifted. "We could look for Paul. He'd be surprised we actually followed up on his invitation."

Ryan nodded and put his blinker on for the turn to my house. We both knew Sunday would be long and lonely, but neither of us wanted to admit it was best to leave it for now.

I reached to unbuckle my seatbelt and while my next words formed, they got stuck in my throat as we pulled up to Gram's. A strange car sat out front, one I'd never seen before, and a chill of warning ran up the back of my neck. My eyes rolled, annoyed at another complication, no matter how trivial it may be.

"Company?" Ryan parked behind the black sedan.

I let my seatbelt snap back into its holder absentmindedly. "I don't know. I've never seen it before. Maybe it's for our neighbor."

"So, Monday? The university?" he reminded me. "See you then?"

"Yeah. After school. Okay?"

"Yup." He reached for my hand, but stopped just before touching it.

My fingers walked closer, nearly touching his, and I looked into his wide pupils. Deep pools in his eyes pulled me in and held me there. His chest rose with a heavy inhale and his lips parted to allow the breath to flow out. I wanted to just crawl over to him and curl into his arms—to feel his strength around me. I ached for him to touch me.

Then he pulled his hand away.

I lingered, allowing the moment to settle into my memory, then forced myself to move away from it. I climbed out of the truck and smiled.

"See you Monday," I said. And every step toward my front door added weight to my already burdened soul.

He swung around in a U-turn and drove back toward his home. His focus had to be on Maureen now. She needed him.

My throat constricted as he left my sight. I wanted to stay with him, to spend more time with him. We still had so much to talk about. So much.

Thoughts of his shed and the cans of beer distracted me and my heart plummeted in my chest. It was first time I yearned to be...with a friend.

Then the front door burst open and Gram's voice trailed out on the heels of an older woman with a slight build, dressed head to toe in navy blue.

"I appreciate the concern, Sister Margaret, but I've heard enough fer one day." Gram's tone held no warmth.

"I mean no harm, dear. Ya know I've only the best intentions fer ye. Yeh've had yer hands full now, and I'm merely offerin' a bit o' guidance to ya." Sister Margaret resisted Gram's closing door. "Ya just need ta know, there's talk, is all. She's raisin' concern, ya see, tamperin' in things unholy. And now the boy."

Gram continued to close the door, ignoring her last words. "Good day, Sister Margaret." And Gram gave a final tug on the door and then at the last moment caught a glimpse of me standing at the end of the driveway.

Sister Margaret whirled around in affronted disgust and nearly smacked right into me. Looking me up and down, her glare displayed every judgmental thought and she couldn't hide her disdain.

"Isobel." She stated my name like a formal greeting.

"Sister Margaret." I stated her name back with the same tone and tipped my head slightly, inviting her to take a swing. Daring her.

She flinched at my disrespectful retort, likely thinking she had me rightly figured out. And she scampered to her car with tiny little steps that filled the neighborhood with annoying tapping.

Gram threw open the door to let me in. Her lips pressed into a white line as she glared at me. Okay, maybe I'd crossed a line, but that woman was asking for it.

"Word travels fast, I guess?" I looked into Gram's eyes anticipating a reprimand.

"Small village." Gram nodded.

I slipped past her into the entryway. "What did she want anyway?"

I continued to the kitchen and flicked on the kettle. Gram followed with thunderous steps like she was about to send me off to the nunnery.

"One of the church ladies saw you with Ryan," she said. "Says the two of you were dabblin' in black magic. Somethin' like that. She's got the biddies all wound up, thinkin' yer some modern-day Jezebel."

"Fer crying out loud, Gram. They're such prudes." I grabbed a tea bag and threw it into my mug. "You can't be bothered by them. They've got nothing better to do than judge the unruly, unholy youth of today. It's ridiculous."

I did my best to make light of it, teasing their Bible-thumping ways. Anything to keep the focus off what was really happening. People were starting to talk about my curse again. That was obvious. I'd laid low with it for a while, trying to keep it under wraps, but now, if that nosy neighbor Flannery saw Ryan and me on the beach, she could be saying anything.

"I *am* bothered, Izzy. I don't want them speakin' of you that way." Gram smacked her hand on the counter. "Their words can cause permanent harm to yer reputation. To our family."

"But they're just a bunch of bored, rigid..." I struggled for names I could call them. "Gossiping..."

"No. They're right." She interrupted my rant. "They know you're different and these God-fearing women do not like *different*. They see it as their mission to control you. We need to lay low for a while."

Oh my god. They sounded just like the mean girls at my school. Did it ever go away? Women bullied each other just as much as girls. It was mind boggling.

"Control me? What the hell does that mean?" My voice climbed three octaves.

"Isobel. You must listen." Her voice lowered to nearly a whisper. "These women have been watching you for years. I've done every-thing in my power to show them you weren't..." She stumbled on her words and hesitated.

"That I wasn't what? Cursed?" I spat the words.

"They don't understand it. They think you belong locked away." Her voice tightened and squeaked out of her.

Jesus! What?

"Let them think that then!" I snarled. "Who cares what they think."

"They have more power than you realize, Isobel. They've got the power of the church behind them. If they can prove, even a little, that you have visions or are gifted in any way, they will have you sent away for heresy." Gram's eyes shone with tears as her words remained forceful.

My sharp inhale filled the kitchen with its desperate sound.

"My dear, this is…" She shook her head. "This is why I put you through so much, all these years, with the hospitals and the treatments. To prove to these women you weren't cursed. To show them it was a medical condition instead. I did my best to believe it myself as well." She dropped into a chair with a heavy thud.

"What?" My shock resonated through the kitchen with the only word left in my vocabulary.

I pushed my mug away and stared out the window into the back garden.

"It's getting bigger than I can handle now, Izzy." She rocked in her chair. "They don't believe me anymore. They think you're some kind of witch." Her eyes lifted to meet mine. "Sister Margaret said they'll be making a formal complaint to the school and city council. To have you sectioned."

"What the hell does that mean?" I stared at Gram in wide-eyed panic.

"Evaluated, psychologically. And if you're found unstable, they will have you institutionalized. State-mandated."

"State mandated?" I scratched my head.

"Against your will."

My hand flew to my mouth. "Why would they do that? Why do they even care?"

"Why do people ever care? It's a mystery." Gram reached for a tissue on the side table. "But it's become their mission to take us down and they spend every waking moment conspiring against us. It's sport to them."

My body twitched with anxiety as I contemplated the power they had over us.

"But don't they know this would hurt you, Gram? Why would they want to hurt you?" The irrational thought infuriated me.

"It goes back many years, loov. A grudge can be a powerful thing. And Sister Margaret holds one over me." She stood and flicked the kettle on again. "One that blames me for taking her man and forcing her into the call to the church. Her life's mission is not for God at all, but for bringing me pain in disguise."

I fidgeted, having never considered Gram's earlier life and the drama she may have lived through. She'd crossed the wrong person and was being forced to pay now. It was harassment at its finest and no law to stand behind.

I had to protect Gram from this and I had to protect myself. If they had the power to take my freedom, I needed to keep far away from them and lay low. The idea of it twisted my stomach in a knot. Laying low meant only one thing and it was something I wasn't willing to give up.

Ryan.

"What can I do, Gram? Tell me. I'll do whatever you think." My eyes begged her for a rational solution.

"They can't see any evidence of your episodes. You must contain it. At least until they find a new focus for their meddling knitting circle." Sarcasm laced Gram's last comment.

"Okay. So I need to be more careful and stay out of their view. Everyone's view." I prayed I wouldn't have any public episodes, staring into space, or worse. "That's doable, I guess." I bit my bottom lip, knowing I had no control over disguising it, particularly if I was in school, surrounded by twenty other students. "So I just have to hide away for a while?" My voice trailed off as I absorbed the full scope of my prison sentence.

With one final comment, Gram threw away the key.

"And you can't see Ryan anymore. It's too risky."

My hands smacked down on the counter as Gram's ultimatum poisoned me. There was no way she was stopping me from seeing Ryan again. My temper heated my face and threatened to pop my head off.

"You can't do that, Gram. Ryan's too important to me right now." My strong words shocked me.

But it was true. Ryan meant a lot to me. He believed in me. He saw straight into my soul and didn't run. Together, we were whole. I knew it was all happening fast. It was still all so new. But there was no doubt in my mind: we fit.

I shook my head in self judgment. I'd only just met him, practically. How could I be falling for him so quickly? It didn't make sense. I wrung my hands together. But it *did* make sense. We needed each other.

"You don't even know the boy. Have ya lost yer senses completely? Leave him be in Spiddal. Get back to yer studies and focus on what ya need be doin'."

Her words sent alarm to the deepest parts of my being, like my actual existence was being threatened. My flight response kicked in and I made a move to exit the kitchen.

Gram was quick and stepped in my path, blocking my way.

"Gram, move." My stern tone turned my stomach as soon as I heard it.

I loved my grandmother. She was only trying to protect me. But I wasn't a little girl anymore. She couldn't control me the way she used to.

I turned and bolted for the laundry room. There was a door in there that led out to the side yard.

I pulled the door open and flew out, slamming it behind me. I moved past the recycling bins, heading for the gate to the front of the house. My adrenalin hit full flight-mode and my only focus was to get out of there and keep my freedom.

Just as I reached for the latch, a figure came around from the front of the house and blocked the gate.

I looked up in utter shock as my eyes met his.

"Declan!" I gasped.

"Izzy. Stop." He held the gate firm. "Just stop."

"Oh my god! You're in on this too?" I accused him with a tone of utter betrayal. "What are you doing here?"

"Gram called me. She knew she'd need my help." He steadied the gate against my pushing.

"Declan, you guys can't hold me prisoner. I'll run." My threatening words allowed me to feel some form of control in the situation.

"No, Izzy. You'll run straight into trouble. You need to lay low for a couple days." His tone remained steady and I stopped pushing on the gate, knowing he was right.

And in that moment, my newly expanded world closed back in on me and familiar darkness crept back into my insidious thoughts.

I laid on my bed well into the next day, behind my closed door barricaded with the top of my chair wedged under the doorknob.

Prisoner.

Trapped in my darkness. Brewing in my methodical self-loathing.

But then I sat up. I blinked into the brightness out my window and filled my lungs to full capacity. New energy moved through me as I pushed away the darkness and its poisonous treachery. I had power within me. I had the ability to shape my destiny and in that moment, I decided to take back the control.

I pushed the darkness away and followed the light.

I grabbed my journal and wrote about the vision with Ryan. I wrote every detail of the events at Doolough and Westport House. Then I grabbed my laptop to research everything written about the Great Famine and the death march. Everything about the British involvement and neglect. I researched the gift of second sight and all that was known of seers throughout the centuries. I followed every link until exhaustion took me to the suspended bliss of restful sleep.

My alarm jolted me back to the reality of Monday morning. And school.

Dragging myself through my early morning routine, I purposefully ignored Gram, avoiding her as best I could. I just couldn't have this conversation with her anymore. Enough had been said and it only stressed me out to talk about it anyway.

Gram picked up on my blatant avoidance and didn't push the issue. But that didn't stop her from giving me my orders and expectations for the day.

"Straight home after school. Ya must keep yer grades up if yer to pass the exams," she stated.

I crammed a piece of dry toast in my mouth and slung my pack over my shoulder.

"Mhmm." And I walked out the door into the morning mist.

The further I got from my house, the lighter my steps became. My school was just at the top of the road, but the walk was enough to fill my lungs with fresh air and new strength.

I had plans to meet Ryan at NUIG later and I had no intention of missing that—no matter how much trouble it got me in with Gram.

I spent the day dodging bitchy glares from the girls in my classes and enduring the constant feeling of being ignored, like I didn't exist at all. The feeling used to make me want to die. But today, for the first time ever, I understood it wasn't real.

I *did* exist. Larger than life, even. And these assholes knew it. They needed to shut me down for fear I might one day be better than them. It was a game. A vicious, nasty game. And I quit.

I'd set my sights on things much bigger and better than these trivial social games. While they all spent their energy on building their social collateral by stealing it from others, I focused on the final bell and getting to what really mattered.

Ryan.

And our strange and complicated quest.

The final minutes in the school day dragged, killing me with the slow tick of the second hand. And then the final bell launched me from my seat.

I flew out of the school and set my sights on the bus stop at the corner. The bus came every fifteen minutes and I prayed the next one was due to arrive any second. If I'd just missed it, the wait for the next one would be enough to start Gram wondering where I was.

I looked up the road for any sign of the next bus. As I turned back toward the stop, I smacked right into Declan again.

"Shit!" I barked. "What are you doing here?"

"Gram told me you might avoid coming home." He looked at my close vicinity to the bus stop. "She was right, so."

"Declan, please. You don't understand. So much is happening right now. I'm figuring out my visions and I've found people who can help me and..." He cut me off.

"It's too dangerous." His voice remained rigid. "I won't lose you the way we lost..." He hesitated. "You know." He reached for my arm. "It's up to me to protect you. Come on. Let's get you home."

I yanked my arm away from him.

"No. I know you want to protect me, but I'm not a little kid anymore. You and Gram can't hide me away. It's too late. Can't you see that? You've already lost me. And I won't stop now. Not for anything."

He reeled back like I'd knocked the air out of him. So I kept going, to finish him off.

"Don't you see it, Declan? I'm on my own path now. And if you try to stop me, I'll find another way. Every time." My words made me stand taller as he shrank.

"I'm scared for you." His voice cracked.

"I know." I hesitated as my heart broke for him.

It must have been difficult for him to see his little sister grow up right in front of his eyes as we stood at the bus stop of my escape route.

"Help me, then," I begged.

CHAPTER 12

D eclan crumbled before my eyes. He battled his loyalty to Gram, carrying out her wishes of protecting me and getting me home safe. He fought his big brother need to shelter me from the world and keep me unharmed. But he knew in his heart I had outgrown these efforts and needed to be set free.

"Can you take me to NUIG?" I asked him. "We're meeting Paul there."

"McGratt?" Declan took a step back.

"Yes. I think he can help. He has so much knowledge of Irish history and he knows all about the visions because of—" I hesitated, knowing Declan didn't like to speak of it, but then I let it out. "Maeve."

He flinched like I'd burned him. "Fuck."

I smirked, well aware of his inner turmoil, but I could tell he was with me now.

"So, you'll take me?" I pressed.

He directed me toward his car. "Get in."

He dropped me in front of the archaeology building on campus and I looked at the large granite steps leading up to the entrance. Ryan wasn't there yet. I hopped out anyway.

"Thanks, Declan. I'm all set. I'm gonna meet Ryan here before I go in." I waved him on.

"Text me if you need a ride home."

"Thanks." I smiled at him. "What are you gonna tell Gram?"

"I'll figure that out when I get there." He scowled and drove off.

I watched his car until it went out of sight, then I turned to the empty granite steps. With no sign of Ryan, I walked across the concourse into the Liberal Arts building where Smokey Joe's was.

I grabbed a coffee in the college cafe and then made my way back to the granite stairs and walked halfway up them. I sat on the steps and sipped my coffee, watching students pass by, each wrapped up in their own lives and their own phones.

I thought of my own life and its complex layers and I smiled. For the first time ever, I kind of liked it.

Staring into the bottom of my coffee cup, I grew impatient waiting for Ryan. The more time that passed, the more I questioned if he was even coming. A sick feeling crept into my gut but I swatted it down.

I stood up and walked into the building—half-hoping to distract myself from the insecure feelings that poked at me. No matter how good I might be feeling, the darkness was always waiting right under the surface.

Maybe Ryan was already inside. I hadn't considered that option yet.

I looked around for any sign of him and pressed through the musty smell of the empty lobby as my footsteps echoed off the marble floor. I followed my nose down the main corridor and read the various names of professors on the glass windows of each office door I passed. At the very end of the hall, I found it.

Paul McGratt, PhD. Celtic History

The gold lettering decorated his door with a regal feel. It made me stand taller and take notice of my manners.

I reached up and tapped on the glass.

"Come on in," his voice called from the other side of the door.

I turned the brass knob and pushed.

As he looked up from his desk, his eyes shot wide in surprise.

"Izzy." He stood, placing his hands on his desk for stability.

"Hi. Is this a bad time?" I inched my way in.

"No. I mean, I just didn't expect to see you here. I'm a bit shocked." He gestured for me to sit. "Please."

I looked around the office, hoping Ryan would materialize.

He didn't.

Paul stared at me, speechless.

"Um. I guess we have a lot to talk about," I mumbled.

"Izzy," he interjected. "Please accept my apology about the other day. I wasn't right in the head, from exhaustion and just, well, I'm sorry." He paused in thought. "When I go there...it really takes a toll on me. But, for some reason, I just can't stop going."

"It's okay. I understand." I half smiled. "It's hard for me too."

He smiled back and we sat across from each other in awkward silence.

"So, yeah, I guess small talk's not really an option. Do you want to tell me why you came?" He sat back like he had all the time in the world.

"Well, it's kind of a lot." I started. "I still have my visions. As you know. And now, I've met Ryan and well, he, he..." I stumbled already.

"He has a gift, too," Paul finished for me.

I did a double-take and he continued.

"I've heard of the O'Shaughnessy's of Spiddal. They're a gifted family. It's brought them some troubles along the way." He tipped his head.

"Right." I nodded, glad to know he knew something about it. "Well, yeah, Ryan and I, we can—I don't know. We can..."

"Tell me, Izzy," he pressed with impatience.

"We can travel through my visions, together."

There. I said it. Out loud.

Paul jumped to his feet again and leaned across his desk, staring into my face.

"Jesus. I thought so!" He ran his hands through his hair. "I knew it!" He pushed off the desk and paced behind it. "Jesus!"

His intensity fueled my own. He wanted this just as badly as I did.

"I want to find a way to stop my visions or at least to control them, but I also want to...to help find Maeve." My voice grew stronger. "To find out what happened to her. Basically, to be sure the same thing doesn't happen to me."

Paul ran his hands through his hair again, this time pulling hard on it.

"I can't..." His voice cracked and he cleared his throat. "I can't believe it. We have a chance." His eyes misted as he moved to the window and stared out.

He actually *did* believe I had the power to do this.

To find Maeve.

He thought it might be possible. That meant, in my mind, that maybe I had the power to help at Doolough as well. For this fleeting moment, Paul made me believe in myself. In my visions. And the vast power they held.

My hand went to my mouth and I bit on my nails.

"What is it?" Paul asked, looking back at me.

I stopped biting and gazed at him, then at my chewed nails.

"It's just that, Ryan's supposed to be here right now. And he's not." I pulled a final jagged piece of nail off with my teeth. "There's a lot going on at his house and I, I don't know."

Paul's faith in me intrigued my every fiber but I still couldn't stop wondering where Ryan could be. It didn't make sense for him to not be here.

"Like what?" Paul came back to his desk. "What's going on at his house?" His eyes narrowed.

I was sure he knew all too well about the types of disruptions that went down at the O'Shaugnessy's.

"Like, they're under attack again by the locals. They want them silenced. And they want their land," I explained. "It's a witch hunt, basically," I mumbled.

Paul pulled his top drawer open and grabbed his keys. "Come on. Let's go find him."

❧

Flashing lights caught my attention first. Then, Paul's inability to pull down the blocked drive to Ryan's cottage. It was jammed with police cars and other random vehicles. One of the Gards left the lights flashing on his patrol vehicle, which only brought more unwanted attention to the scene.

"Just pull over here," I yelped at Paul and threw my door open before the car had fully stopped.

I flew down the road, weaving through the cars with Paul on my tail. Just as we got close enough to see what was going on, an officer stopped us.

"That's close enough. We need ta keep the public back." He held his arm up to create a barrier to us.

"Fine job keepin' them back." Paul pointed to the townsfolk who gathered at the stone wall bordering the yard. His sarcasm wasn't lost on the Gard.

"Sure, they're the ones who called us," he retorted.

The gawkers at the wall grew loud with excitement as sudden movement came from the cottage. I pressed deeper toward the corner of the property for a better look.

In a flash, I caught a glimpse of Ryan stumbling out of the cottage as an angry officer pushed him to the ground and pressed his knee into Ryan's back. He pulled Ryan's arms behind him, causing a wince of pain to cross his face. Then he reached for his cuffs and whacked them onto Ryan's wrists in an overly dramatic effort.

Raucous gossip lit up the onlookers and the cackling rose to a crescendo.

"Ryan!" I shrieked.

Paul grabbed me and pulled me back. But it was too late. Every head turned in my direction and all eyes froze on me.

In a slow-motion haze of horror, Ryan was pulled up off the grass by his cuffed wrists and pushed into one of the squad cars like a hardened criminal.

"Nothing more ta see now, people. Back ta yer homes with ya now." The officer near us waved his arms to get the crowd to break.

One by one, people lost interest and walked back up the lane toward the village. Each and every one gave me a good stare as they passed but I remained unaffected by their judgment and cared only for what was happening to my friends.

Word would get back to Gram though. Swiftly, I could be sure. And Sister Margaret would have one more line item for her log of my offenses.

As soon as the officer near us became distracted, I sneaked with Paul around the perimeter of the yard, hopped the wall and went to the back. The rear door to the kitchen was unlocked and I could see Maureen inside, sitting at the table with several people around her.

I pushed in without thinking of any consequences, wanting only to get to Maureen to be sure she was okay.

As I entered the cottage, all heads turned and the closest person to the door lunged forward to shove me out.

"Leave her be!" Maureen interjected. "She's family." Her tone left no room for negotiation as Paul and I entered the cottage.

"Maureen! What's happening?" I raced to her side and checked on her nervous condition. "Why'd they take Ryan?"

"Fer the love o' Christ, it's hysteria, Isobel," she cried. "They've all gone stark ravin' mad." She stared down the people in her cottage as if they were unwelcome strangers, which most were. "A loon of an officer dared put his hands on me, threatening to take me to the home. Sure, Ryan was only defending me from his unethical ways." She choked at the memory. "'Twas no way to treat an elderly woman." Her voice cracked as she spat the words at every person around her. "They all witnessed it and sure, they did nothin'."

I bent down and hugged her as her body quaked with nervous jitters.

"Leave now! All of you. Can't you see you've upset her?" I waved my arms to shoo the people from her home. "Have you no decency?"

"Isobel, hang on." Paul came up next to me and whispered to Maureen and me. "The captain of the Garda is here, with the head of the County Council. I think we need to hear from them about what's happening."

I watched Maureen and she nodded in agreement.

"Ciaran and Ned. Ye stay. The rest of ye, out!" Maureen pointed to the door.

As the final official spectator left the cottage, the door closed behind him, allowing the dust to settle and a sense of control to return.

"Now," Paul started with a steady, low tone. "Would you mind explaining yourselves?" he asked the men.

"We're in no position to discuss details of our investig..." The police chief's words were cut short.

"Ah, quit yer load o' shite, Ned," Maureen interrupted. "We can all speak freely in my home. Sure, don't act like I didn't beat your ear on the playground in our kinder years." She huffed.

Ned dropped his eyes to the floor, like he'd been scolded and was back on his ear in the play yard.

"Isobel," she added. "Will ya please introduce yer friend to us?"

"Sorry. This is Dr. Paul McGratt, history professor from NUIG. An old friend." I spoke quickly before the shake in my voice could be detected.

"Perfect. Thank you, dear," she said. "You're welcome Paul. We could use someone here who understands how history works. How it mockingly repeats itself, over and over again." Maureen winked at him. Then she turned back to Ciaran and Ned. "Now gentlemen, would you mind explaining the basis for such a witch hunt? And Ciaran, mind you, we go way back too, so don't try actin' like ya don't know me. Got it?"

Ciaran straighten his waist coat in an attempt to appear like he held a position of power. And I guess you could say the head of the County Council did just that.

"Ta be frank with ya, Maureen, the townsfolk are talkin'. Sayin' yer up ta no good. And Ryan too. They don't take kindly ta yer, yer..."

"Our what?" Maureen narrowed her eyes at him.

"Yer ways wit' the divil," he spat as quick as he could.

Maureen reeled back in her seat with a hearty guffaw. "Fer the love o' Christ. Are ya all trapped in the stone ages? Fer feck sake." She shook her head at them like they were daft.

"They want you gone. Off the land. Ryan too." Ciaran spoke the words without looking her in the eye.

"And *yer* in on this too." She glared at Ciaran without blinking. "How much you aimin' to make from the deal? Loads, I'd say." She smacked the table in disgust.

"It's not worth the fight, Maureen. You'll lose. You'll lose everything," Ned added.

Maureen pushed her seat back, causing everyone to jump. She stood and moved around the table to where Ciaran and Ned hovered. Stepping right into their personal space, she glared into their faces.

"Yeh've both conspired against me. After all these years." She turned her head to look away from them, disgusted. "You get my grandson back here. You've one hour. And if a single hair on his head is out of place, I'll have yer jobs in me back pocket. I'll sue yer arses to kingdom come," she spat. "Ya cowardly bastards haven't changed a bit in all these years. Out of me house, swine. You've betrayed me to my core." The hurt that tightened her voice couldn't be masked by her badass approach and it wasn't lost on anyone.

Ciaran and Ned moved toward the door, nearly bumping into each other. They stood tall, but their furrowed brows proved they knew they'd let her down. Ned looked back and hesitated.

"Clock's tickin' lads!" she hollered at them and they hurried out of the cottage with their tails between their legs.

Before the hour was up, an undercover squad car delivered Ryan to the edge of the property. As soon as the door closed behind him, the car backed down the lane and disappeared from sight.

I ran out to meet him and tore across the lawn to where he stood. Watching me, his eyes brightened and he opened his arms as if to catch me.

I stopped short before colliding into him and panted just out of his reach. We stared into each other's eyes, desperate to embrace. I inched closer as I absorbed his every wonderful feature. His warm eyes and tanned skin. The angles of his cheeks and jawline. The little scar over his left eyebrow and the subtle lines where his mouth turned up when he smiled.

His mouth.

His lips parted like he was going to speak, but he sucked in a breath instead. The veins in his neck pulsed as his heart rate accelerated along with mine.

I inched closer still. Close enough that I could feel his breath on my face.

I gazed into his eyes. "Ryan," I whispered.

We reached for each other at the same time. Not thinking. Not planning. Just doing.

His hands ran across my face and into my hair as mine moved around the back of his neck and pulled him to me. His trembling lips found mine in an instant and he kissed me with every ounce of his being. He pulled away for a moment, uncertain of what might happen from our contact, but then kissed me again like nothing else in the world mattered.

I pulled him into me, kissing him back with all the welled-up desperation of needing him, wanting him. His magical touch sent warm light through my mind and body. It whirled through me with a wave of mind-numbing bliss.

I allowed him into my mind freely and jolted with the shock of seeing into *his* soul too. He yearned for me as much as I longed for him. His thoughts were filled with me just as mine were of him.

I pulled back in shock.

As I stared into his eyes, his wide pupils confirmed he also knew our minds had connected.

"Oh my god," I breathed.

"Holy shit." He gasped.

His arms closed tighter around me as he pulled me into him and lifted me off my feet in a joyous embrace.

He lowered me down then and gazed into my eyes.

"You like me." He smiled a sinister grin.

I blushed and shrugged one shoulder. "And you like me."

"Yeah. I do." He took my hand and the connection lit up again between us.

My mind swam with his and my head fell back in the thrill of it. His thoughts wanted to know me better. He had so many questions he wanted to ask me and things he wanted to show me. He wanted to touch me—to be close to me. And I was sure he saw the same things in my mind and I sheltered none of it from him.

What I couldn't believe was the fact that our touch didn't generate a vision or blast us to the past. Maybe, when my mind was so focused on him, our connection remained on only us. But if I was in a vision-state, like before, and we touched, that would cause him to have the vision too. I couldn't be sure. But it seemed to be a possible explanation and if it were true, I'd be crazy excited.

As we moved closer to the cottage, he loosened his grip on my hand and let it go. The swirling light in my mind faded to normal and the energized shivers that raced through my body dissipated.

"I need to check on Maureen," he said. He smiled at me, like a guilty church-going boy who'd just had his first kiss, and I smiled back. Equally as guilty.

Inside, Maureen and Paul sat at the table waiting for us.

"Well, ya needn't take all night ta get in here," Maureen teased.

"Are ya okay, Shanny? I could'a killed that asshole fer puttin' his filthy hands on ya." Ryan's jaw clenched at the memory.

"Just as well ya didn't, or they'd have yer guts fer garters." She huffed.

Ryan nodded, knowing Maureen was right.

"How ya, McGratt." Ryan acknowledged Paul— though I knew he was not yet sure where they stood after the altercation in Ballycroy.

"Ryan," Paul replied. "Glad to see ya home safe."

"Good ta be home." He looked from Paul to me. "Thanks fer mindin' Isobel while I was...detained."

Paul nodded at Ryan then turned back to Maureen. His comfortable expression changed in an instant to wide-eyed alarm.

"Maureen. Are you okay?" he asked as we all turned to her.

Her focus on us faded in and out as beads of sweat formed on her brow. Her head wobbled like she was about to pass out. Ryan reached for her and lifted her up, moving her to the couch as her feet shuffled along the floor.

"Call an ambulance," Ryan commanded.

Paul dialed his phone while I ran to the sink and soaked a kitchen towel with cold water. I placed it across Maureen's brow. Foam gathered at the sides of her mouth as she gurgled nonsensical words.

"Jesus! I think she's having a stroke," Ryan called out. "Those fuckin' bastards!"

CHAPTER 13

The silence of the yard held a surreal quality after the chaos that had ensued earlier. Ryan pulled the truck onto the cottage lawn and put it into park with his last ounce of energy. The glow of the midnight moon cast shimmering light on the cottage, adding a beautiful, ethereal feel to it.

Maureen's condition had stabilized at the hospital but our level of worry wasn't so lucky. Permanent damage from the stroke was always a possibility and Maureen's absence from the cottage allowed opportunity for the snakes to position themselves more strategically.

I twisted in my seat and looked at Ryan. Heavy sadness slumped his shoulders.

"She'll be okay," I said. "They know what to do." I gave a weak smile, hoping my words were true.

He rubbed his forehead in a slow, deliberate manner.

"I hope so," he whispered. "It's the bastards I'm worried about now. Ciaran's selfish motives were written all over his greedy face."

"What does he want anyway? He's already head of the County Council." But I already knew the truth. It was greed that drove him.

"Elections, campaign contributions, popularity. I don't know." Ryan shrugged. "Maureen always said he was the runt of the litter.

Now's his chance at payback, even at the expense of a peaceful old woman who'd spent her life helping others."

"That's disgusting. How can he even sleep at night?"

"He's set to make millions if the developers get our land. He'll sleep just fine on that." Ryan gazed out the window with a blank stare. "How do ya fight that?"

My gaze wandered along the cottage and across the land to the sea. The beauty of it all belonged on the cover of a coffee table book of Ireland. My stomach twisted in knots at the thought of it being leveled to make way for cookie-cutter holiday homes. All just to line someone's pockets.

"Did Declan get word to your grandmother?" Ryan's voice jolted me back to him.

"Ya. She'll be there first thing in the morning. I don't know how much she's heard about everything, but pretty sure she'll have every detail by the time she gets there." I could only imagine what version she would hear first, depending on the source. "She thinks I'm at Declan's right now. So that's good."

He nodded. "Coffee?"

"Yup."

When we dragged ourselves out of the truck, our exhaustion revealed its heavy hold in our slumps. Within minutes, we collapsed on the couch and sank into the cushions, warming our hands on our cups.

After a moment of quiet, Ryan sat up taller and looked at me.

"So, what happened with Paul?" His voice awakened. "I missed that entire chapter of the day."

Pulling myself up, I leaned my elbows on my knees and smirked. "Yeah, you were kinda hauled away in cuffs at that point, if I recall correctly."

He huffed. "I can be a little dramatic sometimes. So I've been told, anyway. My apologies."

I smiled into my coffee cup, well aware of the fact that if I didn't laugh about it, I would cry instead.

"I told him. About our visions together." I watched Ryan for his reaction to my honesty with Paul, not sure how he would feel about it. Paul had seen us during the vision of Doolough, so, well, there wasn't much to hide at this point.

"And?"

"He thinks the visions are his chance at finding Maeve. He's kind of desperate for us to help him," I added.

Ryan nodded without a flinch about Paul knowing his secret. "Thought so. No surprise. People always want a piece of this when it satisfies their own self-interest." His tone sharpened. "Finding Maeve is all he thinks about."

I sat up higher. "How do you know that?"

"I saw it in his thoughts. When we met in the clearing that first time. He shook my hand..."

My jaw fell open as I remembered the interaction. "Oh my god. That's right. I forgot about that." My eyes grew wide as I waited for details.

"It was a brief handshake, but an enormous surge of energy burst out of him. He's been holding it all in, you see, with no one to talk to about it." He sipped his coffee. "He seeks Maeve. He loves her still. His effort hasn't waned in six years. It's only become stronger."

I watched Ryan as he spoke, soaking in every detail. My hand covered my open mouth as I imagined Paul's grief, enough to keep him searching all this time. Then I remembered the blonde girl.

"I thought he had a wife now or something," I mumbled, trying to picture her face. But I'd met her a long time ago.

"I don't know. I didn't get any of that. Probably because the rest of the information took center stage." He enticed me.

"Okay...what else?" I leaned in further.

"I saw his final memory of Maeve. When she disappeared." He took a deep breath. "Something happened and he plays it over and over in his mind. Endlessly. But he misses the very detail that continues to present itself to him. He misses it, every time, in the extreme emotions of the moment."

I shimmied to the edge of the couch, studying his every word.

"As she was drawn to the Original Three, the wind created a

vortex that pulled on her. His vision was blurred from the gusts and from his panic but the details could still be seen in his memory." He paused. "Her ring flew off her hand, Isobel. She grabbed for it as it sailed away on the powerful surge, out of her reach. And then she was gone."

I stared at him as my jaw dropped. My hand moved to my mouth as I considered his words. Her ring flew off her hand before she disappeared.

My breath sucked in with a gasp. Oh my god.

"So the ring is still there," I stated.

He nodded. "Yes. Unless somebody's found it since. It must be."

I sat back with a thud as I pressed into the couch, staring into the air.

The ring of the pirate queen. Lost at Doona Castle. Waiting to be found.

"We need to go back and find it." My mind exploded into action.

The ancient ring of the pirate queen, Maeve's ancestor from the 1500's, sat waiting for us. The ring had been passed to Maeve through a mystical encounter with her medieval clan chieftain, Grace O'Malley, that transcended centuries.

"It could be the missing link to all of this," Ryan added.

My head nodded as my mind scrambled with the possibilities. The ring of the pirate queen, it could be the piece that made the hope of finding Maeve possible.

Somewhere, hidden in the grass at Doona Castle, was the key to unlocking the mystery of the visions.

Sneaking into the house like a mouse, avoiding the creaky floorboards that waited eagerly to sound their alarms, I crept to my room. Dealing with Gram's interrogation at this point would be the death of me. Bypassing her heavy guard, I fell into bed without interruption and my mind swam with the enormity of the day.

"Isobel..." Gram's voice travelled up to my room and jolted me from my blissful sleep. "Time for school..." The drawn out syllables of her message made me cringe.

Morning already, I dragged myself down the stairs to the kitchen and propped myself on the door jamb.

"Gram. There's no way I can go to school today. Please. I feel like crap." I pushed my hair out of my face.

"Yeh've missed enough school already," she snapped. "They'll send the warden after me for failing ta get ya a proper education." She rubbed the counters with her tea towel, avoiding eye contact.

"I want to see Maureen. Please, Gram. I wouldn't be able to concentrate in school anyway. There's too much going on right now."

Gram stopped her incessant wiping and looked at me. Her lips pressed into a white line.

"Ya went against my wishes. I know you went to see him."

My head fell. "I'm sorry. I didn't mean to disobey you. It's just that..."

"No. Stop. It's not a game. I warned you about Sister Margaret." Her tone slapped me in the face.

Tears stung my eyes. Gram never spoke to me so harshly before.

"I'm sorry, I..."

"It's too late for that now, Isobel. You've placed the power right onto their laps." She threw her rag into the sink. "I've heard all about yer carry on. The phone rang off the hook last night with all the excitement. The biddies haven't had this much fun in quite some time."

My face reddened as my heart rate accelerated.

"Stop, Gram. I don't care what they say about me. I'm done hiding. And the O'Shaugnessy's need our help. Now." I pushed back on her intimidation.

Gram stood taller and stared me down.

"You've no idea what these women can do to you. Sister Margaret will have you sent to an institution and will throw away the key. Her power infiltrates every corner of the city and no one has the courage to stop her toxic manipulation."

"I haven't broken any laws."

"In the eyes of the church, you have." Gram paused, giving me a chance to absorb her words. "And the church of Ireland holds power supreme." She covered her eyes with her hand and rubbed her temples.

My stomach tightened. I seriously had no idea the church even mattered anymore. I'd ignored it most of my life. But looking back through my history lessons, it was pretty clear it ruled everything.

I remembered the laundries run by the Magdelene Sisters. They scared the crap out of me. Wayward girls were sent there, never to be seen again—institutionalized for being promiscuous or even simply misunderstood. It was a living hell for any of the survivors brave enough to tell their stories.

My body shuddered at the thought of being sent to a modern-day version of the laundries, disguised under the acceptable term of 'wellness program'.

I attempted a fix. "I'll prove them wrong. They'll see that we mean no harm."

"We?" she interjected.

"Yes. Maureen and Ryan. And me. They're targeting all of us. And Maureen's in the hospital because of it. She needs our help right now. Please." My voice cracked.

Gram went silent and rubbed her chin.

"Yer right." Her lips quivered. "Maureen should be our focus for the day."

I sighed in huge relief. "Thank you."

Gram's jaw clenched in silent resignation, as if she knew things had shifted further from her control.

"So, you'll come to the hospital with me?" she asked.

I nodded. "Yes. I'd like that."

"Well, come on then. No need wastin' time." She reached for her coat. "I just don't know how to keep you safe anymore, Isobel. That's the piece I just don't know."

～

Wandering the hospital corridors, my hair still wet from my speed shower, we counted down the room numbers until we found the right one. The door was propped slightly ajar, so we pushed our way in without making a sound.

Over Gram's shoulder, Maureen slept with a peaceful look on her face. I gazed at her resting expression, surprised at how she could look so content after the assault on her family just the night before. As my eyes moved toward the window, they widened in surprise. Ryan slouched in a hard vinyl armchair with his eyes closed and head tipped onto his shoulder.

He slept with his hands folded across his stomach and his legs splayed out in front of him. I couldn't help but notice how handsome his resting face was and how good his jeans looked on him. His messy hair sealed the deal and I had to suppress my inappropriate urges, but all I wanted to do was to climb onto him and have his arms wrap around me.

I stared at his lashes, willing his eyes to open but also enjoying the chance to soak in all his features without his knowing.

Gram tidied the empty cups and folded the stiff white blanket at the end of Maureen's bed. A curious nurse poked in and asked, "Family?"

"Yes," Gram replied.

Ryan's hands twitched and his eyes opened. He sat up and looked at me through groggy eyes.

"Mornin'," he said, rubbing his face.

I smiled at him.

"Hello Ryan," Gram said. "I'm so sorry about Maureen." Her words sounded too formal and made my lip turn up. "Have you any news of her condition?"

Way to let him wake up, Gram. Pounce all over him for information.

"Give him a chance to wake up, Gram. Jeez," I couldn't help myself from interjecting.

She sent me a firm glare and looked back to Ryan. I watched the wheels in her mind turning as she saw the two of us together in the same room. Maybe it wasn't such a good idea to have come.

"I'll find you some coffee," I said to Ryan and stepped out of the room to avoid any further scrutiny from Gram.

By the time I got back, medical staff was in the room checking on Maureen and discussing her condition with Ryan and Gram. They said her prognosis was good considering how quickly she was taken in for medical support. They said the stroke was likely brought on from stress and that she would need to return home to a stress-free environment to ensure a full recovery.

Ryan and I looked at each other with skepticism, knowing how impossible that expectation was.

"Nothing but rest for her now, son," the doctor told Ryan. "We'll keep her in medical-induced sleep for a couple days more. 'Tis good for her healing."

"Come then, Izzy. We'll head home. I'll make some meals for Ryan. You can help me." Gram started to gather her things.

I looked at Ryan like my heart was being ripped out. I wanted to stay with him. Every cell in my body yearned to be with him as he worried for his grandmother and their future.

"It's still early enough, Gram. Maybe I should just go to school," I suggested as we approached the car.

"You're askin' me ta take you to school?" She pulled her chin back in shock. "Well, it's not a bad idea. Shall I ring them?"

"No." My response was too quick. I had to be more careful. "No need. I'll tell them I had a doctor's appointment. Maybe you could just write me a note." I pulled paper and pen from my bag and she scribbled her message on it then signed it.

She dropped me at the front entrance of the school and I sauntered toward the doors waiting for her to drive off, but she waited, watching my every move. As I got closer to the door, my heart sank with the realization that I would actually have to go in.

I looked back at Gram's car one last time, accepting my fate, and caught her reading a text message. Taking advantage of her distraction, I hopped behind tall bushes by the school entrance. After a few moments of hiding, I peered out and watched her car drive away.

Before I came out from behind the bushes, another car pulled in to her exact spot and parked. I huffed, trapped for another moment while the visitor passed me. Holding my breath, I followed the woman's form as her shoes clomped in quick beats across the paved walkway.

As she passed by my hiding spot, I glimpsed her navy blue uniform and my jaw fell open.

Sister Margaret.

The moment she was in the building and out of sight, I jumped out from my cover and flew to the bus stop. Looking back over my shoulder, pacing and wishing for the bus to hurry up, I prayed she wouldn't come back out and see me. Finally, after an eternity, I glimpsed the bus up the road at a red light. My feet tapped as I counted the seconds.

The bus pulled up and my head fell back in relief, like it was my transport to safety. Or maybe even sanity. A small smile lifted the edges of my mouth as I took one last look back at the school.

To my horror, my eyes hit directly onto Sister Margaret's. She stared at me like she saw pure evil in human form. The shock of her foul judgment sent stinging poison through my veins and I turned and jumped into the safety of public transportation.

Shit. I was dead meat now. My hands ran over my face while my heart rate shot out of my chest. What the hell? She was the evil one, not me! And now she would tell Gram and...I looked back down the road where my school was and my spine stiffened. What was she doing at my school anyway?

Flying through the hospital corridors, desperate to get back to Ryan, I counted the room numbers out loud as I got closer to Maureen's room. Once I found it, I slowed and took a deep breath, calming my elevated anxiety. Pressing through her door, I poked my head in without making a sound.

She slept through the steady rhythm of beeping machines around her, but the rest of the room was empty. Ryan had left.

My heart plummeted to the floor. I'd risked everything to get back to him and now Sister Margaret was hot on my trail. My hand covered my eyes and rubbed them. Everything was a mess.

My eyes fell closed in disappointment and I turned to leave, uncertain of where I would go.

"I expected as much." Ryan's voice burst my heart open. His head shook and a smirk covered his face. "Figured you'd find a way to come back." He reached for my hair but refrained from actually touching me.

I gasped in shock. "Oh, I thought you left."

"Nah. Just freshening up. You wanna get out of here?" His eyebrows lifted.

"Yes! Pleeeeease!"

He turned and walked, leaving me no choice but to follow him. "I'm not a fan of you ditching school, though." His tone took on the sound of a slight reprimand but his eyes still twinkled. "You need to stay focused these last few weeks so they don't kick you out or something." He glanced at me sideways to be sure he wasn't right.

I took a huge inhale. "Actually, it *is* getting a little weird. There's this nun who's made it her mission to expose me." I paused and pressed on my temples. "I don't know."

"What nun? Like, she knows about your visions?" He stopped short, waiting for more information.

"Sort of. My Gram's been warning me about her. Like she has the power to send me away or something. She thinks I'm a, you know, witch, I guess." My words turned into mumbles as I grew self-conscious about the accusation.

"Sister Margaret?" he asked.

My eyes flew wide.

"Shit," he blasted. "She's been spear-heading the witch hunt for Maureen all these years. Shit, Isobel." His hands ran through his hair. "She's a fuckin' loon."

I stared at him as fear permeated my bones. For the first time, I felt true terror from the woman.

"She went to my school today, Ryan. She saw me leave and get on the bus. It's like she's after me." My lips pressed together.

"Okay. Don't worry. She's got nothing on you. We just need to get her off your trail." He stared into the sky in thought.

Biting my nails, I imagined her in my school speaking with the head master, filling her up with lies. I had to get out of that school and all its negativity. No one supported me there. I needed out.

I turned to Ryan as my eyes brightened with an idea.

"Paul needs us," I said to Ryan. "Well, guess what. I need him too. I need him to become my tutor. To sign off as my educational mentor."

"Is that even a thing?" Ryan asked.

"I think so. My school allows final year students to do internships. And Dr. McGratt happens to be highly respected around here, so no one would second guess him."

Ryan paced for a minute then said, "Are you sure you want to get wrapped up with him to that level? I mean, he seems a bit unwound these days. Just sayin'."

I hesitated, knowing he was right. But I just didn't see any better options.

"I don't think I have a choice at this point," I said.

Ryan's head nodded in thought. "And not to sound too pushy but he won't really be able to say no. I mean, he needs you. I guess he'd call refer to it as 'field study'."

I smiled. He was right. Whatever lay ahead of us with Paul could easily be defended as research—to the untrained eye anyway.

A huge smile crossed my face as the relief of finishing school outside of its crushing walls soaked into my bones. A deep sense of peace emerged within me, one that had been blocked by the routine action of placing myself in harm's way, day after day, year after year.

Our pace picked up to match our enthusiasm, but just as we rounded the bend to where Ryan's truck was parked, my euphoria broke like shattering glass.

Parked next to Ryan's truck was Gram's car. And she stood next to it, arms crossed, staring at me with a tight scowl.

Shit! My stomach dropped to the floor as Gram glared at me, as I walked with Ryan toward her.

"Get in." Her stern tone curled my toe nails.

I froze like a child caught with her hand in the cookie jar. But then, something turned in me. Shifted.

"I'm sorry I deceived you, Gram. I just had to come back here to see Ryan." I stood taller. "I know you don't understand, but things are changing quickly. Things are different now." I stepped closer to her as Ryan went to his truck to give us privacy.

"Get in." Her face remained unflinching, matching her monotone.

"No," I stated back to her.

We stared at each other, each waiting for the other's next move.

Her lost expression proved she needed more from me. An explanation. Something to let her know I knew what I was doing.

"I have a plan for finishing school, Gram. I'll fill you in once I confirm it. It's a solid plan. I promise." I took a deep breath. "And I'm with Ryan now. He's an important part of my life and I won't be kept from him." I watched Gram's eyebrows pull together in annoyance but didn't let her wall stop me. "And I love you. More than words can say."

I stepped away from her and went to Ryan's truck.

He climbed in and started the engine.

Gram didn't move from her spot.

"I'll text you, Gram. So you know I'm okay. I'll be at NUIG working out the details of finishing my education. Okay? I'm sure I'll see Declan and Michelle there too." I waited but she remained frozen. I couldn't tell if she was even breathing.

I closed my door. "Let's go," I said to Ryan. "She'll be okay. She knows I'm safe."

Ryan lowered his window and reached his head out to see Gram. Her eyes moved to his and he waited. He waited for her permission to take me. After what felt like an eternity, she finally gave him a nod and he pulled out.

I exhaled for miles.

I'd never confronted Gram so hardcore before. I mean, it had been coming. Step by step. But wow. It was terrifying. Breaking free.

But I knew Gram would come around. She was just scared. Scared of my growing up. Scared of my curse. Scared for how I would be judged and sentenced without proper trial. Letting go was probably the hardest thing she ever had to do.

At least she knew she was letting me go with Ryan. She trusted him. And that was what likely helped her through this.

I sank in my seat and allowed a small smile to cross my face. I was going to be okay. I felt it in my bones.

"So, I'm an important part of your life now?" Ryan smirked, teasing me with my earlier words that he must have overheard.

"Shut up!" I swatted at him.

He pulled the truck over to the side of the road along the sea. "You're an important part of my life now, too." He looked at me and swallowed hard. "When I first saw you, I didn't know what to do. I couldn't remember how to breathe. And now you're here. With me." He reached for my hand but stopped just before touching me. "It's good."

My heart rate sped up and I wished for him to be able to touch me whenever he wanted. It was torture not knowing what would happen. Maybe, if we were careful...or maybe if we focused like when we had kissed before, it would be okay.

"Take me to the cottage," I said without pause. "I want to try something." My breathing sped up to match my heart rate.

"What?" Ryan's eyes widened.

"I want to try being close with you again. But more." I smiled a wicked grin. I couldn't help it, I wanted his hands on me. I wanted to hold him and touch him. The feelings were so new and overwhelming.

Ryan's air sucked in as his brows shot up, lining his forehead with worry.

"We at least have to try," I encouraged him.

It didn't take much more encouragement before the engine roared to life and we flew down the coast road toward Spiddal.

Butterflies took flight in my stomach as I fantasized about being close to him. Being held by him. Kissed. The anticipation was magical and lit me up inside. I watched him as he drove and he smiled under my gaze.

He skidded to a stop on the lawn of the cottage and we jumped out at the same time. We flew through the front door and tossed our jackets on the couch. He led me to a door off the back of the kitchen and stopped with his hand on the knob.

"This is my room," he said as he watched me for a reaction.

"Let me see it." I nudged at him to open the door.

He took a deep breath and pushed the door open.

I stepped past him and entered the small room. Two windows let in pools of light that danced across the messy sheets on his bed. The comfortable space smelled of him—fresh air, the sea, oak. I smiled as his personal space filled me with joy.

I reached for his hands and pulled him further into the room. Our touch sent bright light through me and tingles awakened every part of my body. I prayed our touch wouldn't cause a vision and hoped the intimate nature of it would create its own kind of event. Like our first kiss, it hadn't launched us into a vision yet, so maybe it would be okay again.

Ryan lifted his hands to my face and looked into my eyes. I swam into his gaze and got lost in his mind. He thought I was beautiful. He couldn't believe I was here with him, in his room. He wanted to touch my soft skin and hold me against his chest.

"Are you sure?" His words were carried on his heavy breathing.

I tilted my face closer to his. "Yes."

He lifted my chin and leaned down to kiss me. His full lips found mine with a sweet hunger that sent my mind spiraling. His breath quickened as his kiss grew stronger. A slight whimper escaped his throat as his arms pulled me closer.

My mind raced with excitement and I craved more of him. I wanted to feel his skin on mine. To be as close to him as possible.

He stopped and pulled his face away from mine. "You're killing me, Isobel," he gasped. "Your thoughts are making me wild. I won't be able to control myself." He panted. "It's too much."

I pulled him back to me and ran my hand down the front of his t-shirt along his chest and stomach. His muscles twitched beneath my touch and his head fell back. "Isobel," he whispered.

The sound of my name on his lips sent me over the edge and I grabbed the bottom of his shirt and pulled it up over his head. His shirtless form made me gasp and I yearned to touch him more. He watched me as I reached for his chest and he swallowed hard.

As I touched and explored him, his thoughts filled my mind as he raged with the effort of self-restraint. He wanted to throw me on his bed. He wanted to kiss me everywhere and feel my body on his. He was on the verge of explosion.

He grabbed my wrists from his chest.

"Isobel. Stop. Please." He choked on the words as he pressed at his crotch to relieve the pressure that was threatening to explode. He gasped. "You're so fucking beautiful. I want this with you right now. Jesus Christ." He stepped back and rubbed his hand through his hair. "I want you, Isobel. You know that. You can see it." He exhaled. "I just don't want to fuck it up."

He was falling in love with me.

I saw it in his thoughts and in his eyes. With every fiber of his being. And I was falling for him too. I was sure he knew.

But why did he have to be so sensible? The feel of his skin under my fingers drove me to a wild place. I wanted his body on mine. I wanted him to touch me everywhere.

What the hell was wrong with me? I didn't even recognize this part of myself. This crazy-ass wild woman who wanted to make love to this freakin' hot man. Was this even okay? I wasn't even sure how to do this or what to do next but knew I wanted to try it with him.

Bang! Bang! Bang!

The smashing nearly made me jump out of my skin.

"Ryan! Ya in there?" a voice boomed through the walls.

"Shit. It's James," Ryan growled.

CHAPTER 14

The pounding continued as Ryan pulled his shirt on over his head. He held my shoulders and kissed me.

"I'm sorry. I have to see what he knows." He watched my face for my reaction.

"I know. Go." I pushed him toward the door and then sat back on his bed to catch my breath.

I ran my hands through his sheets and pulled them up to my face. I took a deep inhale and my mind filled with him again.

"*Oh my god.*" The words escaped my lips in a whisper but held so much significance. He had consumed me completely and I wanted to lower all defenses, release my insecurities, and let him in.

A smile spread across my face as I straightened my hair and fixed my rumpled shirt. I shook as leftover chills coursed through me and I imagined what almost happened—what I hoped would happen in the future.

I listened at the door for the rumble of their voices, and the front door slammed. They must have gone outside to talk, so I crept out of his room like a thief and scanned the open area. Out the window, they moved to the shed and a huge exhale of relief fell out of me, knowing I'd gone undetected.

I fumbled around the sink and stove, gathering what I needed to make coffee. The old-fashioned moka pot confused me at first but its charm was undeniable. I filled the lower chamber with water and poured grounds into the filter. Placing it on the stove top, I searched for a match to light the burner. There was no doubt in my mind this would be the best coffee ever, coming from such an authentic, well-made tool.

As I stared at the pot while it brewed my coffee, I filled my face with the aroma that wafted up at me. With a huge inhale, my senses awakened but then snapped shut as the sound of the slamming door whirled me around.

James filled the doorway and stared at me in shock. His wide stance and arrogant gaze annoyed me, like he was some rude frat boy evaluating me on a ten-point scale. A smirk spread up the side of his mouth as he looked me up and down.

"Well. Now I get it. Ryan couldn't get me out of here fast enough." He laughed and turned back toward the yard. "He's been holdin' out on me."

My head shook in disgust. What an asshole.

"You don't get much interaction with girls, I can see," I stated plainly. "For starters, it's appropriate to say hello." My head tipped to the side. "Give it a try, sometime." And I turned my back to him to fix my coffee.

"Oh, shit! Feisty," he retorted as he stepped further in.

Ryan came up behind him then in a hurry and pushed past him. "What the fuck, James. You just walk into other people's houses when they're not lookin'?" He shot his eyes to mine, trying to determine what he'd missed.

I glared at James and he fidgeted.

He turned to Ryan. "I didn't mean to interrupt."

"Shut up, James. Are you ever plannin' on growin' up?" Ryan shook his head at him like he was wasting his time.

"The town's talkin' about you two, ya know. I don't mean to be rude, but it just caught me by surprise, I guess. Seein' it was true." James looked at each of us.

Ryan deflected his comment. "This town is too small. They're always looking for something to gossip about."

"Maybe. But they say she's bad for you. She causin' ya to go weird again. Ol' Lady Flannery's tellin' stories of feckin' witchcraft and the like." He turned his gaze on me. "Know anythin' about that Isobel?"

My eyebrows scrunched together like he was talking gibberish.

"That's bullshit," Ryan interjected. "And you know it."

"Call it what you want. But they intend to make trouble fer ye both. And you know the County Council's aimin' ta build a stretch of holiday homes here. They'll make a feckin' fortune. They're just looking for any excuse to drive ye out." He paused. "And ya've not many friends in town vouching fer ya."

Ryan ran his hand through his hair as his brow tightened.

"Just warnin' ya, is all. I mean, me da has a lot ta gain from it. But I think it's only fair ya know what's goin' on."

"Yeah. Thanks James. I actually appreciate it," Ryan stated.

"Nice to get a bit o' gratitude." James' tone oozed with sarcasm. "See ya, Isobel." And he turned and left the cottage.

I brought a cup a coffee to Ryan. "He's an asshole."

"Yeah. He is," Ryan nodded. "Always has been. His father's Ciaran, head of the County Council. James is nothing but a spoiled child."

"What did he want, anyway?"

"He was actually checkin' in about Maureen. He must have a bit of a soul hidden somewhere deep in there." He huffed. "I don't know. I think he considers me a friend. He doesn't really have any, I guess."

"No wonder he's so weird about me being here. He must think I'm stealing you away from him." I laughed.

"You're probably right." Ryan laughed too. "But what's all this shit about witchcraft? Are they all stuck in the last century?" His head shook in frustration. "We've been layin' low for years. It's like they were looking for any excuse to bring it all up again."

I lowered my eyes to the floor. "Yeah. And *I'm* that excuse."

෴

Ryan moved across the room to me in an instant. His pinched brow held anger that darkened his eyes.

"Don't say that." He pressed his hand on the counter next to me and bent his head to look into my face. "I know what you are suggesting. Please stop."

"But it's true, Ryan." My eyes pulled away from his haunting glare. "My grandmother warned me. She said I should stay away from you." My lips pressed together. "I thought she was trying to protect me, or something. But now I get it." I looked back into his eyes. "She was trying to protect you and Maureen too."

I realized in that moment the danger I had brought upon them. How had I missed it before? Lost in my own selfish journey, I failed to see my influence on what was happening to them. My throat tightened as the reality hit me.

I was bad for him.

"We can take care of ourselves, Isobel." His voice grew stronger as his eyes pierced into me. "Don't let James' stories turn you from me." His voice broke at the end as his nails scraped on the counter.

But I couldn't help it. James' stories scared me. They pointed directly at me. The whole village was watching now and the final hunt had begun.

"Shit, Isobel. I can feel you closing yourself to me already. Fuck!" He pulled away from the counter and stormed to the door. He leaned on the jamb and stared out into the yard.

Holy crap. How was he able to read me so well? We weren't even touching and he picked up on all my fears. My apprehension.

I couldn't help my feelings though. I wanted to protect him. And if that meant staying away, going into hiding for a bit, that was worth it to me. For him. And for Maureen.

My feelings for him were stronger than any I'd ever known, causing a constricting ache in my heart.

I walked over to him and reached for his shoulder, just barely touching his shirt. His slumped head lifted and he stared into my eyes. His wide pupils pulled me into his desires. His need to be with me. His hope that I would love him back. His urge to devour me.

His arm reached around my waist and pulled me into him. His other hand held my chin as his fingers ran across my cheek. And he kissed me.

He kissed me with a desperate passion that filled me from head to toe. He gave everything to me and took all that I was. My head fell back with a gasp of pure delight and he lifted me up into his arms. He carried me through the cottage and pushed through his bedroom door with his back. Holding me to his chest, he lowered me onto his bed and kissed me more. His breathing grew heavy as he positioned me beneath him.

"I can't control myself around you, Isobel," he panted in my ear.

His thoughts raced around the fact that I was there with him, allowing him to do this with me, and not knowing for sure how to proceed. He was new at this. And so was I. But we would figure it out.

"Then don't," I replied as I pulled his shirt off a second time.

I laid in his arms as my body quaked from the bliss that coursed through it. He'd loved me so completely. With his soul and open heart. A lump grew in my throat, nearly choking me, as I relived each intimate moment: some clumsy and fumbling, but all genuine. I had given my full self to him and he took great care with my gift.

He ran his lips along the side of my face and breathed in. "You are my heart, Isobel."

I turned to him and looked into his warm, vulnerable eyes. "You are mine."

And it was done. We had committed ourselves to each other.

It was raw and new. He became the other half of me, necessary for breathing. It was scary. And it was real.

I pulled up to sitting and gazed at his strong body. He was perfection and I craved more of him.

He smiled as he saw my intent. He reached his arms around me and pulled me close to him. In a strange blast, light flashed in a bolt, sending images of the death march into my mind.

Ryan released me in an instant and pushed himself back.

"Shit." He sat up. "Are you okay?"

"Yeah." I sat up tall, blinking away the images. "I figured that would happen again."

His head shook. "It's always lurking just beneath the surface. Like it wants us in some way." He climbed off the bed and pulled his jeans on.

I crawled along the sheets and reached for him. He stepped out of range and flashed a wide grin.

"Well, at least it gave us a chance to be together," I said as my arm fell in disappointment at not touching him again.

"Thank Christ," he blurted out. And we both laughed. "Come on. I'm starving. Let's get out of here."

I got ready in slow motion, not wanting to leave the comfort and bliss of his room. I could easily stay there forever—have food and water delivered and just be with him the whole time. I smiled to myself and wrapped my arms around my own shoulders. I actually hugged myself. And it felt amazing.

We tripped over ourselves in the cottage, fumbling to get ready to head out into the day. It was like our bodies were sapped of all energy and we giggled at our ridiculous condition.

"Let's go to that coffee shop in Barna," I said. "They have the best soup and scones."

He grabbed the keys and led me out the door. "Anywhere works for me. I just want..." And his words were cut short as we both stopped in our tracks.

Ol' Lady Flannery stood in the road, leaning with her elbows on the stone wall at the front of the cottage. Her pinched face and sharp glare startled me and Ryan stepped in front to shield me from her judgment.

"Whore," she spat over the wall. "Cheap whore."

Holy crap. Her words cut me.

Ryan sent me toward the truck. "Get in," he commanded. Then he walked over to the vile woman.

"I'll kindly ask ya to get off my property, Ms. Flannery. Your words mean nothing to us here. And your intentions have been nothing but foul toward us for years. Remove yourself and take your misguided name-calling with you."

"It's not proper!" she interjected.

"No. You are not proper. Calling yerself a god-fearing woman but going out of your way to cause harm to others. Take a look at yerself for once and leave us be." He turned toward the truck and then hesitated. He looked back at her again. "Don't you ever call Isobel a whore again." He narrowed his eyes at her and stared until she pulled her gaze away. "Ever."

And he hopped into the truck with a slam of the door and drove right past her without easing up at all.

"I've had it with her harassment. It's got to stop. Now." He shook his head, looking in the rear view mirror for her silhouette. "I'm sorry you had to hear that. She's not right in the head."

"It's okay." I hid the sting to my soul behind my eyes. No matter who said it, those words cut deep.

"No. It's not," he interrupted. "Don't let her cheapen what we have." He turned to me and made me look at him. "Don't give her that power."

I nodded.

He slammed the brakes and pulled to the side of the road. "Isobel. You just changed my life. You know that right? You own my heart. There's nothing cheap about that. Nothin'. Okay?"

I took a deep breath and allowed his words to soak in. And I smiled. "Yes."

"Good." And he pulled back onto the road, heading toward Barna.

His words healed my wound and instead of allowing her hate to pull me down, I allowed his love to build me up. It was a powerful shift, as it had always been much easier for me to believe the negative. But he'd convinced me of the opposite. And I believed him.

Inhaling every morsel of food and then ordering more, we giggled our way through the meal as we looked at each other, silently giving reminders of favorite parts of our intimate connection earlier. We didn't take our eyes off one another the entire time.

As we climbed back into the truck, Ryan said, "I'd like to go check on Maureen. Ta see if there's any change. You want to come?" Then he added, "And, I think we owe a visit to McGratt, you know, to discuss your education, for starters."

"Oh, do we have to get back to the real world so soon?" I whined. "I like it here with you."

He laughed. "Yeah. Me too. But if we want to be able to do this more, which I do, we need to put a few things in place first." And he turned the truck in the direction of the hospital.

With a smile, I looked down at my phone and pressed it. It glowed to life and sent a text message across my screen that stopped my breath.

They are here

It was from Gram.

CHAPTER 15

G ram's text sent my head flying in a million directions. My mind played tricks on me about who 'they' could be. Her text read only 'they are here'. What could that mean?

I grabbed the sides of my head. "What if it's the same people who want to take Maureen to the elderly home? Maybe they've come for my Gram too. Or maybe they've come for me. That's got to be it." Panic rose in my voice.

"We don't know anything. There's just not enough information. Check again. Did she get back to you yet?" He glanced at my silent phone.

"No. Nothing." My head fell back. "Ahh. I hate this." My jaw clenched. "I bet it's Sister Margaret. And my head master. I'm sure of it."

"All the more reason for us to get this squared away with McGratt. We have to get that done immediately." He exhaled through tight lips.

"I know. But Maureen first," I said.

"Yup. Maureen first," Ryan repeated.

Not long after our arrival, the staff ushered us out. "Time for some tests, you two. She's in good hands. Out wit'ya now." And we were swept away like nuisances.

Maureen remained in her suspended bliss, sleeping peacefully through all the turbulence. Just as well, really.

Ryan pulled the truck into the lot outside the archeology building at NUIG and threw it into park. He turned to me. "At least she looked comfortable. I guess she just needs time now."

"She'll be okay. She's in good hands," I assured him as my heart bled for him and Maureen. His lost stare proved she meant the world to him and I prayed all would be well.

"Come on. Let's get in there. The distraction is just what I need." He pushed himself out of the truck and came around to me.

We hopped the granite steps up to the front door of the ivy-covered academic building. I stopped and turned to Ryan. "Thanks for helping me with all this. I mean, it's kind of a mess."

"Sure." His shoulder lifted in a shrug. "It feels natural. Like it was all meant to be, somehow. Ya know?"

"That's true." I thought about how naturally we fell together. Like it had all been waiting for just the right time. And that time was now.

And the interesting thing was, it was Gram who started it all. I actually owed a lot of gratitude to her for taking such a risk in introducing me to Mother Maureen. It all began after that.

I swore in my mind to have a good long chat with Gram when I got home. She teetered on the edge of a cliff and I had the power to settle her. She would understand, once I explained things better.

Ryan pushed the door open and we entered the echoing, marble-covered foyer. My eyes pulled up to the dated clock on the wall and I wondered if it was even working right. The detailed hands looked like they were about to fall off the face of the Roman numerals but judging by their positions, they heralded the approach of four o'clock.

I pulled my phone from my back pocket and checked the time. I did a double take as the glowing numbers confirmed the clock's accuracy. Time had flown and I cringed, wishing I had more of it in the day.

We travelled down the long corridor to Paul's office and knocked.

Before long, we were engaged in the details of my tutelage and Paul's enthusiasm grew as we formulated the document for my headmaster, listing the criteria that would be covered during the intern-ship. It became quite apparent that Paul would benefit from the arrangement just as much as me. Maybe more.

"The main focus will be on archaeology and Celtic history. We'll make note of field studies and research opportunities. Sure, the head-master will love this. It's a college level experience. And beyond." Paul pecked some final notes onto the proposal.

"Yeah, and beyond," I added with a sarcastic ring to my voice and Paul glanced up.

I looked to Ryan and he nudged his chin at me to go ahead.

"Paul, I think we have our first field study in mind." I gazed at the document he was working on and his eyes shot to mine, ready to soak in every detail. "We plan to go back to Doona. To look for something."

Paul's eyes shot to Ryan's, then back to mine. "Look for what?"

"Her ring," I stated.

Paul sat back in his chair like I'd spoken blasphemy. He pushed back from the desk and placed his hands on his knees, unblinking.

"What about her ring?" The effort of keeping his voice calm caused it to shake.

Ryan said, "It might still be there, somewhere in the grass. It flew off her hand when she…"

"How do you know that?" Paul's contorted face held an intensity that looked like anger.

I interrupted. "In the visions. It looked like her ring flew off when she was pulled into the wind."

Ryan shot a quick glance at me as we made a silent pact to not disclose too much information to Paul about *his* gift yet.

Paul stood and walked to the window. His hand lifted to his mouth in heavy thought. Ryan and I waited and gave him time to process the idea. Then he turned back to us with an expression that held the weight of the world in his deep, searching eyes.

"The ring could be the connection we've been searching for," he stated as he walked back to his desk. "It was *her* connection to the past. To her ancestors and her ancient clan." He inhaled sharply. "If we could find it..." His palms pulled together as he lifted his hands to his mouth. "We might find her."

~

Tearing through my room, I packed my cinch sack with anything I could think of that would help with a modern-day treasure hunt. I barely slept the night before in anxious anticipation of our trip to Ballycroy. And my gut still clamped around the nagging conversation I had with Gram when I got home.

Her cryptic text left us both uncertain. Someone had stopped by with a message for me. Gram assumed it was to do with my new educational plan and had texted me, 'they are here.' But I knew it had nothing to do with that. She told me they just asked for me, then hearing I wasn't home, they left. Gram could only describe them as two young men dressed in plain work clothes.

Was it a random coincidence? Or was it related to everything happening? The twist in my gut sent a clear answer.

Pushing through my discomfort, I thought of the email sent by Professor McGratt to my headmaster. I smiled as I imagined her response to it. It would be impossible for her to refuse. It was a stronger proposal than any final year project I'd ever heard of.

"Mornin' Gram." My voice held a lighter chime than I was used to.

"Well, someone got up on the right side of the bed for a change," she teased me.

I buttered my toast and grabbed a cup of coffee. I poured cream into my cup and stared into the swirling promises of a good day.

"I'm still concerned about what your headmaster will say to all this. I'm sure Sister Margaret has poisoned her against us. But I 'spose yer in good hands." She paced from the counter to the fridge and back again.

"Don't worry. We went over all this last night. I know it's moving fast, but you'll see. It's all for the best." I assured her of the decision for me to do an independent study. "And Gram, you need to know you did the right thing bringing me to Mother Maureen."

Gram's eyes fell as her head shook. "I'm not so sure, dear."

"I know. But it's okay. Or, it will be." I watched the worry lines return to her brow. "I was lost. And now I'm not. I have you to thank for that. Everything you tried, everything you did, and this was the one thing that made the difference."

Gram's lips pressed together. It was hard for her. It wasn't the plan she had wanted. She'd have liked everything to be, well, normal for me. Cookie-cutter. But it wasn't. It never would be. And I think she knew that now.

We left our other worries unsaid. The strangers who looked for me yesterday, they lingered right beneath the surface, causing uncertainty for both of us.

The doorbell rang.

We both jumped and Gram went to the door as if to greet the reaper. My heart rate accelerated to triple time as I heard Ryan's low voice speaking with her.

They lingered at the entry way as I grabbed my things and joined them.

"You take good care of her now, Ryan," Gram said. "I don't know this McGratt fella, and sure, I feel better knowin' you'll be there too."

"Will do, Eileen. I won't let her out of my sight," he assured her.

"Yer a good boy." She reached for his shoulder but hovered just above it. "Always have been. Maureen gloats about ya any chance she gets."

His eyes fell as he nodded.

"Will you be visiting her in hospital today, by chance?" he asked.

"I will indeed." Gram smiled.

"Grand. I stopped by this morning already," he said. "They say no changes since last night. But I still think she knows when she has a visitor. It helps, I'm sure." He reached into his pocket for his keys. "Tell her I'll see her again tonight."

"I will. Now shoo, you two. Git." She swatted her tea towel at us as we headed out the door.

Climbing into Ryan's truck, we both noticed a clean white van parked across the street. I'd never seen it before and it stood out like a sore thumb.

Ryan pulled out and kept his eye on his mirrors while I turned fully around to watch the van. As we suspected, it pulled out at the same time and swung around in the middle of the road to head in our direction.

"Shit!" I blasted. "They're following us!" My eyes bugged out of my head as I stared at Ryan. "Is this for real?"

Ryan remained silent and reached for my seat belt, giving it a yank to tighten it. "Hang on."

His foot hit the gas and the engine roared to life. He turned down a side street that cut toward the bay and blasted down the clear road. I turned to look behind us and a shriek flew out of my mouth as the white van barreled after us.

"They're right behind us, Ryan. I don't get it. Who are they?" I tripped over my words.

"No idea. But I'll lose them in the traffic at the docks." He revved his engine and tore down the coast road.

Careening along the straightaway, he slowed at the roundabout so not to take it on two wheels. The white van caught up to us and took the roundabout at such speed the entire carriage shifted over its wheels.

"God! They're determined!" I shuddered.

The blast of a siren filled the cab of the truck and we both turned to it. Flashing lights filled our vision.

"Shit!" Ryan slowed the truck and pulled to the side of the road. "Figures."

I looked back. "No, Ryan. The Gards stopped the van! Keep going!" I squealed and laughed. "Go, go, go!"

We burst out laughing in relief as we sailed through the city center, adrenalin still pumping.

"Never a dull moment with you, Isobel Ross." He smirked.

"Nor with you, Ryan O'Shaughnessy."

We drove in silence for a ways, gathering our wits.

"Gram said two men came to the door looking for me yesterday.

Something tells me that was them." My eyes squinted in thought.

"Did she have any idea who they might be?"

"No. She assumed it was about my internship, I think. So, she was kinda taken off guard." I bit at my nails.

"I think we need to be more careful right now, like, you need to not be alone. Ever." He looked at me with raised brows. "Agreed?"

"Yes. No need to convince me of that. I got it." It wasn't safe for me right now. There were too many forces against me for some reason and I just didn't understand enough about them.

At the edge of Galway city, the roads cleared and we flew along the carriageways toward County Mayo. I lowered my window, allowing the fresh air to blow through the cabin of the truck. I inhaled the clean, damp air that carried smells of composted turf, pungent silage, and the briny sea.

Green hills travelled alongside us, spotted with distant white flecks of grazing sheep. Stone walls carved the landscape like a puzzle. I never grew bored of soaking in the beauty of the Irish countryside. It helped to reset my day.

"Did McGratt text back yet? He better have been able to get a TA to take over his classes." Ryan worried the day's plan may already have another glitch.

"Not yet. But that's probably a good sign. He's not the type to text and drive." I chuckled and looked at my phone. "We'll probably get there before him. We're on the early side."

I silently hoped we'd get there first. I craved as much alone time with Ryan as possible. Even just a chance to hold him and press against him as we waited. It was all I could think about.

Ryan pulled his eyes off the road and looked at me. "What?"

Oh my god. He'd caught me staring at him. His perfect mouth. And his jaw line cutting up toward his wavy hair that flopped over at the top, threatening to cover one of his eyes.

"You better stop that," he chuffed, "or I'll have to pull over and stop you from trying to make me lose focus." He grinned, exposing the smile lines in his cheeks that led to a subtle dimple.

"Yeah, right. I dare you." I egged him on with a flirtatious smile.

"Shit, Isobel!" And he pulled the truck over with a jerk and slammed the brakes.

His seatbelt flew off and he moved across the bench to me. He unsnapped my seatbelt and his arms went around me, pulling me onto him, in two seconds flat.

Without another word he kissed me. His hand ran through my hair and around the back of my neck. His racing thoughts filled mine with his insatiable hunger for me, his desire to hold me, and his settled heart when I was in his arms. But his thoughts also held apprehension and fear that crept in through his kisses. Flashes of danger and warning.

I pulled back and stared into his eyes.

"I can't help it. I just don't want anything bad to happen to you," he said.

I touched his lower lip with my thumb. "I know."

"It's in your thoughts too," he added. "We just need to be careful."

He reached in to kiss me once more and this time, we both pulled back like we'd been shocked by lightning.

He pushed away from me and searched my eyes to see if I'd experienced the same thing.

The flash left me panting with feelings of pain and suffering. My eyes watered from the overwhelming sense of grief.

"What the hell was that?" he said. "If that's a feckin' warning of some freakish kind, then I'm turning this truck around right now."

With nervous jitters, we drove the rest of the way to Ballycroy, wondering if we were making a grave mistake. The strange flash could have been a warning about the ring but it could also have been a flash of the death march at Doolough—like a call for help or a call to action. We weighed the possibilities until we'd exhausted them all and continued moving toward Doona Castle.

We pulled in along the ancient cemetery near the castle and I looked up toward the clearing by instinct.

"There's his car." Ryan gestured toward the old church ruin at the edge of the graveyard.

Paul's car poked out from behind it, right where he'd parked last time. I wondered how many times he'd left his car there in the past. Judging from the worn tire marks in the grass, a perfect match to his car, I surmised it had been many.

After we slammed our doors behind us, Paul appeared from just over the ridge that led to Doona. His hand lifted in greeting.

As the space between us narrowed, he called out to us. "Sorry. Couldn't help but get a head start." He smiled with guilt.

"Been here long?" Ryan asked with a tipped head.

"Nah. Just a bit. I had to have a quick look fer myself. It's just...I can't get my head around it." He glanced back toward the castle, probably to hide the truth in his betraying eyes. He'd likely been there since sun up. "Come have a look. See if anything, you know, jumps out at you."

We chuckled nervously and followed Paul's lead to the front of the castle.

"I've a bunch of gear in the boot of my car," he added. "Including a metal detector. Not sure what we might need." He grinned with a spark of worry in his anxious eyes.

His clothing proved he planned to get his hands dirty. Khaki and flannel. A Swiss Army knife hanging off his belt and a small leather pack on his back. Nothing like his university attire of pressed slacks and starched white oxford. The transformation spun my head. I could see the allure that attracted Maeve to him without any trouble and averted my eyes before exposing my wayward thoughts on my face.

Too late. Ryan's eyes glued to me as I gawked at Paul while he walked closer to the castle.

But instead of judging me, Ryan nodded with raised eyebrows, like "Okay, he's Indiana Jones. We're in good hands."

I shot a guilty smile at him and shook my head, like, "What the hell? Is this for real? Glad someone's prepared."

Ryan nudged his head to get me to follow him and stumbled along the moss-covered rocks toward the looming castle.

Paul called back to us, "This is the corner that stood in the ruin. It was all that remained, originally, of the stronghold." He stumbled over some rocks.

I nodded, remembering all that was left of the decimated castle when we first came here with Maeve. Battles and time took a heavy toll on the fortress, crumbling it to ruin. But now, after Maeve's disappearance, a full castle stood in its place.

It made no sense if the story was spoken aloud, but those of us who were there, we knew what we saw. We knew it had changed. And Maeve was the change. We just had no idea how and that was the mystery that kept us moving forward with hope.

Paul continued as he pointed toward the sea. "When it all started, we moved out past the corner wall onto the field leading down to the coast." He stepped in the direction he pointed.

We walked beyond the corner of the castle where it all began and moved into the sea grass and moss-covered stones where Maeve had greeted the Original Three. It was at that point when the wind grew fierce with blinding gusts and heavy mist all around her.

Ryan stepped forward along the bumpy terrain, surveying the area for any recognizable changes in the landscape or oddities that might guide us better. And at the same time, Paul and I planted our eyes on the ground and started searching.

The longer we searched the more I realized what a terrible idea this was. More than six years had passed since the ring flew from her hand. Six years of vegetation growth, rain, and erosion. And we expected to find a glimmering ring sitting in the grass waiting to be picked up. My shoulders sank as I looked out across the wide expanse of rolling green. The ring could be anywhere.

Paul's hand gripped his forehead and rubbed it. He looked back toward the car. "I'll get the metal detector."

I watched him walk past me and felt disappointment oozing from him. His thoughts had moved to the same dark place as mine as the excitement of the expedition faded and took on a more realistic tone.

I walked over to Ryan and stood by his side. He continued to stare out into space, then turned to me with one eye squinted in thought.

"From my view, the sea was to the left. And the ring flew off to the left as well." He looked at the ocean and then turned further left trying to find the correct vantage point. "So, it sailed in that direction." His hand cut the air to the side. "It hit down and clinked off a stone surface, then bounced into the grass. It's like I can hear the clinking sound." His hand shook by his ear for emphasis.

I scanned the area all around us, searching for any sign of it. "It's probably covered in grass and moss by now. It'll just look like a small stone. Or nothing at all." I shook my head. "And it makes no sense that it banged off something. Everything here is soft. Grass, moss, sand and dirt." I stepped through the ground with gentle footsteps, careful not to step on anything unusual.

I sidestepped past a clump of loose, mossy stones and moved to a large rock slab that beckoned for me to sit on it. I hunkered down on it, scanning the area further. Ryan walked over, placing his feet gingerly on the ground before taking each next step.

He offered a gentle smile as he approached and then he froze as his jaw dropped open.

"Isobel!" He pointed to where I was sitting. "That stone. I swear that could be what the ring hit off. It's at the right angle. The same position. It would have sent the ring..." His gaze trailed out into the loose, green carpeted stones. "That way."

I hurled myself off the flat edge of the boulder into the stones and the two of us landed on hands and knees on the damp ground. We used our hands to see, as much as our eyes, and felt all around in the grass and through the dirt, around every rock and earthy clump.

My eyes met Ryan's as we searched, both of us hopeful to find our treasure, but the more we searched, the more defeated we became.

I pushed back on my heels for a better look around. Then I pressed myself up to standing. A slow exhale left my body as I took a step forward. My foot placed itself directly on wet moss and I slid forward in a shameful, slow-motion face plant, straight into the wet grass. I exhaled in humiliation and dropped my head.

As I gazed into a lonely dark space between two stones, my eyes widened in sudden terror and my heart beat out of my chest. My bulging eyes stared in awe at what we'd been seeking. Ancient Celtic designs swirled in my vision, proving what I saw was real.

The ring of the pirate queen.

Then, like a runaway train, my voice burst out of me.

"Ryan!"

CHAPTER 16

R yan sailed over to me with his feet barely touching the ground. Falling to his knees, he stared into the crevice between the rocks where I fixed my gaze.

"Holy shit!" He pulled back as if it might bite.

It was half buried in loose sand and moss crept all around it, but there was no doubt.

It was the ring.

The ring of the pirate queen.

Its elaborate design danced with hand-crafted Celtic art and mythical beasts. A large gem sat with pride at the top as scrolls and eternity knots moved all around it. My eyes widened in awe and refused to be pulled away from it.

Stories of Grace O'Malley's ghostly visit to Maeve bounced through my mind, reminding me of the first time she'd placed the ring on Maeve's hand. It had originally been given to Grace by her lover, Hugh DeLacy. My head spun with the layers of the story. Hugh DeLacy had a direct family line to Paul, so the circle was complex.

I pulled my eyes off the ring and looked back for Paul. I caught a glimpse of him moving over the ridge toward us with his equipment. Ryan grabbed my attention then as he leaned closer to the ring.

"It's incredible," he whispered. "I didn't expect it to look so, so regal. And ancient."

I bent to gaze at it again. "I know. It's a true relic." My eyes danced with the circling designs and the lure of its history and without thinking of anything else, I reached for it.

I pulled the ring from its resting place and bounced it into my palm. The weight of it landed solidly in my hand and I slipped it onto my middle finger for security.

I looked up at Ryan as my eyes misted with tears. Joy had filled me in an instant and my heart swelled, ready to burst.

"I can't believe we..." My words choked in my throat as emotion overwhelmed me.

Tears fell from my eyes and blurred my vision. Ryan's face morphed into streaks of color that moved across the landscape, mixing with the blues and the greens all around us. As I blinked, a gust of wind blasted my face, washing the tears from my eyes, clearing my vision.

"I can't believe we—" I tried to repeat myself but had lost sight of Ryan.

I jumped to my feet as the wind blew stronger and the mist thickened. I reached for him, groping through the air, but found nothing.

"Ryan!" I shouted. "Where are you?"

"Isobel!" His voice echoed as if from miles away. "Isobel! Reach for my hand! Don't leave me!"

My arms felt heavy and limp and I struggled to fight the raging wind, but it was too powerful. It pulled on me, moving me away from him.

"Ryan!" My voice flew out of me in a terrified shriek. "Help me!"

His panicked voice shattered through my mind as he shouted, "Pull off the ring!"

The syllables of his command dragged out along time and space, taking what felt like years to pull together into true sound. Everything around me slowed to melting streams of broken vision and morphed sounds of the universe. And then it all exploded in a violent flash of intense light that thrust me like the energy of an atomic blast, landing me with a thud in the grass.

My eyes remained pressed shut as their pinched muscles refused to allow any visual information into my mind. My head shook, resisting what I knew to be true. I listened like a skittish animal, trying to gather information on my surroundings. I listened for Ryan. I prayed his voice would warm me as he helped me up to standing.

But there was only silence.

Then a slow dragging sound moved on the gentle breeze. It started out low but soon grew to a steady wail of moans and ghostly despair. My eyes shot open in terror and I scrambled backward to get away, to hide.

The sprawling lawn of Westport House opened up in front of me as I stared down the road that led to the death march. My throat constricted in fear as tears fell from my unblinking eyes. Without moving a muscle, my eyes darted all around me searching for Ryan, but I knew in my heart I was alone.

We weren't touching.

When I grabbed the ring, we weren't touching.

My head fell as my chest caved in with each shallow gasp of air. I couldn't do this without him. I didn't know what to do. I scrambled over to the famine pot and crouched behind it. If I hid long enough, maybe it would all go away. I just needed to figure out how to blast back to Doona. Back to Ryan.

I looked down at my trembling hands and my eyes shot open.

The ring.

I turned my hand and my jaw fell open as I gazed at the relic.

All I had to do was take it off.

I looked up and followed the sound of the wails on the wind. I turned then and my eyes followed the grand stairs up to the stately front door of the manor. In an instant, I knew what I needed to do.

I gazed at the ring, exploring and admiring the intricate details of its design. The pond was within throwing distance. It would sink like a stone. I grasped the ring, ready to pull it off.

But then my best chance of finding Maeve would be lost forever.

My grasp tightened around it and with a deep breath, I jammed it further onto my finger.

~

As the feel of the ring settled onto my finger, I stood taller and new air filled my lungs. A burst of energy coursed through me as I sailed up the lawn to the granite steps. Taking two at a time, I flew up the stairs to the front doorway. Without wasting a moment, I pounded on the door with all my might.

After my incessant pounding, the door finally pulled open, exposing a servant girl dressed in a black and white uniform. Without needing to look any further, I knew the British soldiers stood behind her, and further back in the shadows, Lady Sligo.

The girl's eyes pinched together as she inspected my appearance. Her confusion washed all over her face. I appeared healthy, vigorous, and well-dressed and clean. Though my clothing didn't match the century, it had the appearance of masterful craftsmanship which was the foundation of their judgment.

Before she could speak, the head officer stepped into view and barked, "State your business." He looked me up and down like I was piece of meat.

All the blood drained from my head and I felt like I was going to pee myself. But somehow, from deep within me, I grew the courage to speak.

"I've been sent up from Galway City with orders regarding a shipment of supplies for the needy." I kept direct eye contact with the officer.

His eyebrows pulled together as he studied me. "Who sent you?"

My knees trembled beneath me as I focused all energy onto keeping my face unflinching. "I'm afraid I cannot disclose the source of my orders. The direct source has actually been kept from me intentionally, but with due respect, I can assure you my orders are from the highest authority."

His head shook. "They'd send a child? A girl? To do a man's job?" His lip curled in disgust.

"Yes." I took a step forward into the house. "As a decoy. A diversion. I stirred no attention through my travels and have caused no undue alarm. Now please, we must prepare for the distribution of the rations provided by Her Majesty. My guardian will surely be looking for a report from me on numbers of rations provided. To be sure the delivery was used as intended."

The last part was what turned his face red. Then purple.

My eyes fell as I worried I'd said too much. I'd exposed his plan of keeping the rations for his own personal gain. The value of it was greater than gold and the black market was alive and well.

I lifted my gaze and it fell on the sacks of grain piled at the back of the great foyer. I realized then, far too late, that they were already prepped and ready for shipment. The British officers were likely awaiting transportation to arrive to haul the shipment away while the dirtiest deal of the century went down before my very eyes.

The shock on my face revealed my understanding and Lady Sligo gasped as the officers moved toward me. Tears misted her eyes as she fell helpless to their bullying tactics and harassing occupation of her home.

I stepped back in surprise at their arrogant move toward me. They intended to grab me. The hate in their eyes proved they couldn't be stopped. They assumed prime power in this conflict and had the backing of the British army and Queen Victoria herself behind them. No wonder their cocky arrogance filled the room with a revolting stench.

Before I could step out of reach, they were on me, tugging at me, pulling me toward the back of the hall.

"Please sirs," Lady Sligo's voice whispered from the shadows. "Allow me to take authority of her. I will send her back to Galway with a message of gratitude for their support."

The officers pushed past her like she was a loathsome nuisance and I struggled to reach her safe haven. The more I wiggled and resisted, the tighter they held me.

They laughed at my futile efforts as they dragged me through the stately halls of the elaborate home. Portraits, crossed swords and shields, and intricately carved statues filled the enormous spaces but could offer no assistance.

My heart raced out of my chest as I considered where they might be taking me. My 21st century confidence in gender equality was slapped right off my face as I realized I had no power against these men. And they knew it.

"They'll be coming for me shortly," I stated through my squirming. "They'll be awaiting word from me and when they don't hear..."

"Shut yer mouth, ya filthy wench. Sure, they'll never know yeh even arrived."

My eyes widened in terror at the truth of their words. No one knew I was here. No one would miss me. My mind grew numb with fear as panic coursed through my veins.

I worried about rape. There was no one to stop them. I worried about imprisonment. Its brutality was captured in every medieval movie I'd ever seen. My legs buckled beneath me.

My body went limp as they dragged me down a dark, damp stairway that led to cold, musty blackness. The second in command lifted me by one shoulder and held me out to the one in charge for his viewing.

"Aye, if only there was time." He flicked my hair back to have a better look at my face. "A fine lassie, she is." He licked his lips as he devoured me with his eyes. "Drop 'er. She'll just have to wait. The coach will be here any time now, we must be at the ready."

He turned and climbed the uneven stone stairs back toward the light of the upper floor. The second soldier followed him, only looking back once to throw me an evil grin. The door above slammed and a sliding bolt echoed through my darkness.

I immediately felt my way around the pitch black space toward the stairs. I moved up along the steps and pushed on the door at the top. I banged and yelled for my release. The heavy thickness of the door muffled any sound from beyond and I pressed my face against its doom.

I moved back down the stairs as my eyes strained to adjust to the darkness but were unable to make out any sense of the area. My hands slid along the far wall, feeling each rounded stone that formed the barrier from the deep earth. The chill of the damp, underground space pulled warmth from my body and shivers of cold replaced my shudders of terror.

I continued moving along the far wall until I reached the end of the room and turned in the narrow space, heading back toward where I started. Passing the base of the stairs, I explored the rest of the space through my sense of touch. Large stones made up the bumpy floor beneath my feet and smaller stones constructed the walls. Nubs of metal and clanging chains hung from various locations, confirming my fear that I was in a dungeon.

Stumbling over a pile of empty wooden crates, I fell to the hard floor, breaking one of them as it smashed against the side stones. I shimmied to the wall and pushed my back against it, dropping down in despair. My eyes blinked into the darkness and my head fell onto my knees as I cried.

Violent sobs quaked out of my body and I cried without shame. I'd wanted to do so much. To help the starving people. The fight against the injustice upon my country. I grabbed my hair and pulled on it as I screamed with indignation.

My voice bounced off the stony walls and echoed through the dungeon as if travelling for miles. I let out another roar and listened to it move throughout the space. The energy of the sound lifted me to my feet and I leaned forward, letting out another shout of resistance. It blasted back at me, widening my eyes with its force.

I was still strong. I could still do this.

I moved through the space again, feeling for every detail, searching for any tool or clue I could use for my escape. As I made my way around the entire area a second time, I exhaled in defeat. There was nothing. Just vacant emptiness. A cold death trap.

My shoulders slumped as I knocked my back off the side wall, again and again. *Think, Isobel, think.*

I rubbed my face with my hands as I pored through my knowledge of ancient history and medieval dungeons. Westport House had been built on the foundation of one of Grace O'Malley's strongholds. I gasped as my knowledge of the history of this manor came to light. The dungeon had been preserved when the manor was built over it. My eyes widened at the realization.

I was in the dungeon of Grace O'Malley. With her ring.

An idea shuddered through me as I sprang to action. I lifted myself on tip-toes and felt along the ceiling. I moved across the entire expanse of the dungeon, feeling along every part above me. And then I found it.

The murder hole.

The square opening in the ceiling was framed with wood and sealed by a solid wooden slab. I could barely reach it, but knew what it was in an instant. This was the opening where they would shoot arrows at the prisoners or pour hot tar onto them. It was called the murder hole for very specific reasons. But to me, it was my salvation.

I scrambled back to the pile of wooden crates and dragged one along the bumpy floor back to the location of the hatch. I felt around again for the hole in the ceiling and then positioned the crate beneath it. My heart beat out of my chest as I readied myself to climb onto the crate.

As I lifted myself up onto it with my knee, my eyes pulled to the far end of the dungeon to a faint glowing light. I blinked into the yellow haze and focused on its center where the light was the brightest. My eyebrows shot up and I paused.

I dropped my knee off the crate and moved toward the unusual hue sending delicate shadows along the back of the chamber. Details of the damp, glistening stones in the wall popped and the sight of the rusted shackles hanging from the side walls forced a gasp from deep inside of me. The violent restraints sent fear through me again as they made real my predicament.

I moved closer to the flickering light and as I approached, it widened and filled my eyes with color and motion. As I leaned in to see more, a form took the shape of a woman, mesmerizing as she reached for me.

I shook my head and jumped back, rubbing my eyes like I'd seen a ghost, but the apparition remained. The glowing portal invited me closer again and I stepped nearer, gazing into its sphere. The woman remained and continued reaching for me. I gazed into her familiar eyes as they latched onto mine, pulling me into her soul.

Our minds connected through our eyes and I was taken with her spirit, centuries into the past. My consciousness exploded into new realms of existence as my heart synchronized with hers. The beating in my ears took the sound of a drum that generated the rhythm of the universe in our souls. And there was peace.

"Maeve!" Her name burst from my mouth in a desperate cry. "Oh my god. Maeve!" I called to her, reaching for her long brown hair, daring to touch her.

She blanketed me in warmth and safety as she filled me with her light. "You've grown strong, Isobel. And brave. You're learning the ways of the seers. Finish now what you have set forth to do. They've been waiting for your wisdom for a very long time." Her words filled my head and whirled through my body. "Continue your quest for these souls and then we shall meet again." Her voice faded as she released me.

"Wait! Maeve! Don't go! I've been searching for you for years," I cried. "I have so many questions." I fell to my knees as the glow spread out into nothingness. Darkness.

I quaked as sobs shook out of me. How could she leave again? I needed to know more about what happened to her.

But then my shoulders settled and my spine straightened. My eyes blinked into the thick darkness and I could see. Not through the black that surrounded me, but through my mind. I had clear sight.

Maeve had never left me. She was always there, watching. Aware. I understood the feeling now—the one some people might call a 'guardian angel,' but for me, it was Maeve. We were seers and had the ability to connect to each other. I just needed to learn more about how.

And all my questions for her. Somehow, I'd always had the answers. She was never lost in the void. Doona Castle was the proof of Maeve's existence in the past, her impact on history. She was a queen.

The image of Maeve remained etched in my mind. She was different. Older. Wiser. Her long brown hair held braids throughout and a simple crown adorned the top of her head. Her long, fitted gown resembled that of a lady from a medieval fair, including chain mail at the top.

She was from another time. And she had been there for years.

A look of contentment had filled her eyes. And power. Her strength was etched in the lines of her face and the confident gaze in her stare.

She had traveled to a very specific part of the past, as she intended to do, to save her clan. To help preserve Gaelic Ireland. She was exactly where she needed to be.

And she didn't come back. She stayed in the past.

I swallowed the huge lump welling up in my throat.

Oh my god. She stayed.

Tears fell from my eyes and I scrambled back to my crate. I climbed onto it and pounded at the wooden plank sealing the hole.

It rattled.

Oh my god. She stayed.

I pounded harder until it shook loose and I pushed it aside.

Did she choose to stay? Or did she get trapped there? The question harassed my every breath, though the answer was clear in her powerful gaze.

She chose to stay.

I jumped and shot both arms through the murder hole and threw them wide to hold me, legs dangling. I wiggled and inched my way up onto the floor above until my ribs were high enough on the edge that I could pull myself up. With a grunt, I gave one last heave and dragged myself out of the dungeon's murder hole.

CHAPTER 17

I crept along a winding corridor, my hands dragging behind me on the wall as my eyes adjusted to the light and my other senses functioned at their highest levels. I listened for any sign of movement or voices, and my eyes pressed wide open without blinking as I moved toward the back of the manor.

Before long, I found the rear entrance to the home, nearly as grand and ostentatious as the front, with high ceilings, ornate fixtures, and marble architecture filling every space. A large, glass double-door leading out onto a massive patio beckoned to me, offering my freedom.

I froze and listened as my eyes remained fixed on the door. Without another wasted second, I ran for it. At full speed, my body hit against it and I clamped onto the carved-metal doorknob, turning it back and forth as it rattled in its mounting. Panic rose in me as the knob failed to release the door and I looked behind me, certain a soldier would be on top of me any second.

With a deep breath, I focused on the door again and my eyes landed on a rustic key with swirled detail on its grip, sticking out of the keyhole just above the doorknob. I twisted it and as the sound of the bolt shifting filled my ears, voices from down the hall sent a sheer frenzy through my body.

"Wait." A voice burst through my mind, shattering my escape and I pushed on the door.

"Please." Footsteps hurried toward me and I turned to see my assailant while continuing to jimmy the door.

Lady Sligo ran to me while her house maid waited behind her, keeping watch.

"Miss. Let me help ya." She lifted the door knob in its housing and cracked it to the left, popping the door open. "'Tis old," she explained. "The officers are in the parlor. You're best ta run now, that way." She pointed along the trees at the side of the manor.

I turned, ready to barrel toward my freedom, and paused.

"Lady Sligo, please, you must help us. This is your home. Take the control back. You'll have our support. The villagers are just around the bend," I begged.

She blinked into my face like I'd spoken heresy. "But how? The British rule here now."

"You must turn on them. Stop them from taking what is rightfully ours. The rations were sent for the people of Mayo. The officers are criminals. They must be brought to justice." My words widened her eyes.

"It would be treason," she stated. "We'd hang."

"It would be a fight for Ireland, Lady Sligo. A fight that must be won." I held her eyes. "You have the power to change history. Do it!"

She stepped back as her eyes studied my face. I could see her mind churning while her resisting body attempted to shut it down. Then her eyes hit mine with a direct glare. One that decided. And she turned, grabbing her house maid, and ran.

Looking back over her shoulder to me, she shouted, "Go! I know what I must do now."

I burst out the open door and sprinted onto the stone terrace, jumping down the steps without even touching them. My heart rate soared, energizing my legs to carry me at a full-flight pace. I looked back one more time, praying Lady Sligo would have the courage to face her aggressors.

I tore across the lawns and stumbled onto the gravel drive without losing speed. Looking back over my shoulder, I watched Westport House move away from me as I careened down the road in my escape.

Heaving to get air into my lungs, I slowed my pace, panting as I walked close to the side of the road for shelter. My ears remained piqued for any sound of my captives in pursuit of me—footsteps, horse hooves, shouts. But the only sound I picked up was coming from the other direction, away from the manor.

At first, I thought it was low winds, moaning through the valley and across the lake, but then my senses shifted from panicked quarry to my original intent.

The death march was coming. It was almost here.

I moved toward the sound of despair: shuffling, weeping, grieving. My pace quickened as I hurried to get to them and just as I rounded a bend, I smacked right into the leader, the same man Ryan and I had spoken with in our earlier vision. Like I had hit a bag of bones, he faltered from my bump and I reached for his shoulder to steady him.

"Oh, I'm sorry. I didn't realize you were so close..." My eyes narrowed at how silent the front of the march was, like a band of ghosts.

Standing tall again, he reached for my shoulders and looked into my eyes. "Yer an angel of mercy?" He gazed at my whisps of light blonde hair and the vibrant color in my face from my exertion. He was right. In his eyes, I looked like an angel.

"I'm no angel, sir. But I've come to help you. There are rations at the manor. Enough for everyone," I panted, looking over my shoulder for any sign of the officers.

"Then you *are* an angel." He took my hand and squeezed it with whatever energy was left in his muscles.

But he held a glimmer in his eyes. A little something more than the rest of them. I latched on to him, knowing he could help me.

"We must fight for it, though. The British are hoarding the grain, to sell it for great profit." My words narrowed his eyes as his jaw clenched.

"Nothin' changes." His head shook. "They plan ta kill us all." He looked back across his companions. "Colin. Tommy. Come here ta me." He flagged two of his men over. "We may be needin' yer assistance." He looked back at me. "This here is…"

"Isobel," I said.

"Aye. The name of an angel." He nodded. "Gentlemen, this is Isobel. She's news from the manor." He rallied the ragged men in hopes of creating a force to confront the Brits.

I dropped my head into my hands, seeing their weakened condition. They were emaciated to skin and bones. Their cheeks were hollow and their shredded clothing hung from them. But they still had light in their eyes. It was incredible. Through all the horror of loss and neglect, they still had fight in them.

"They mustn't see me with you." I waved for them to follow me. "They think I'm a traitor. I'm their…" I hesitated in shame. "Prisoner."

"Well, ya don't look like a prisoner to me. Yer as free as the rest of us out here." The leader smirked in place of an energy-draining laugh.

I smiled. "And what is your name?" I asked him.

"O'Shaughnessy. Denis O'Shaughnessy. Up from Galway," he said.

My air sucked in as my eyes flew wide. "O'Shaughnessy? I know some O'Shaughnessy's in Galway." My words caught in my throat as I thought of Ryan and Maureen.

"Is that right? We're out a fair bit. Out in the village of Spiddal." His face brightened as he spoke of his home.

My hand flew to my mouth. "Yes, I've friends there. By the sea. A small road leads to the cottage and—" My voice stopped as I realized I was speaking of a place more than a hundred and fifty years into the future.

Then I recalled the strange rock formation at the beach by the house. "Near the cottage, on the bay, there's a pyramid of boulders." I reached my arms up to show the great height of it as my eyes lifted to the sky.

Denis's eyes went up too as he added, "Like a giant had constructed his own rock castle by the sea. The top stone, black as night."

"Yes! You know it?" My excitement couldn't be tamed.

"Know it? 'Tis me home." He dropped his head with heavy sadness. "Have ya been there recently? Is anyone still there? Are they okay?" Desperation rose in his voice.

"I'm sorry. I haven't been there is quite some time. I just don't know." I dropped my eyes to the ground.

"Aye," he said. "Desperate times." He closed his eyes for a moment. "I had to leave them. Ta come here to Mayo where the hunger's hit hardest. Me sister and her family, they were sufferin' here. I had to help."

"And you *are*," I said. "You've led them to hope."

"I've led them on a death march. Ta nothin'," he spat.

His burden was enormous and my heart broke for him.

"Those who were strong enough to make it, we must pull them together like an army and face the injustice at the manor," I instructed. I glanced around me to be sure the militant words actually came out of *me*.

His eyes widened at the thought of a coordinated revolt. It must have been everything his heart desired since the beginning of the famine. Five long years now and no true assistance from England. And this region, County Mayo, had been hit the hardest.

I knew from my studies that Mayo lost eighty percent of its population, in comparison to the still staggering thirty percent of the rest of the country. Looking out across the march of villagers, it was clear to me the historical data had been correct, if not understated.

A strange sound echoed from deep within the march. People staggered to the sides of the road as if making room to allow for something to pass. Many of them fell into the brush, unable to move quickly enough as two horses came into view, pulling a covered carriage and two drivers. The horses barreled through the weakened people, leaving little time for them to find shelter at the side.

We all jumped out of the way as best we could as the carriage flew past us without slowing. The drivers kept their gazes fixed ahead, determined to avoid eye contact with any of us. Their blank stares proved they held no sympathy and focused only on their own goals.

"It's the cart to take the rations away. A sale's to be made. We must hurry!" Alarm rose in my voice.

∽

Denis stood taller as he hollered to the people, "They've come to steal what is meant for us. We cannot allow them to murder us at their doorstep. We must unite and fight for our lives. For Ireland!" His voice scratched out of him in squeaks, but held the power of a general and quickened the pace of every villager.

We marched with determination toward the gate of Westport House. We pushed through and moved along the drive until the space opened up, presenting the magnificent manor to our broken, starving army.

The cart parked just in front of the sprawling stairs and the two drivers stood near the enormous front entrance. The doors pulled open and the British officers stepped out to greet them.

In an instant, their pleasantries turned to alarm as they caught a glimpse of our steady movement toward them. I looked back and my heart swelled as I took in the force of our ragged army. Dragging and beaten, they still moved with determination and hope. Their fight hadn't left them and they pushed forward with every final ounce of energy they could muster.

Tears stung my eyes as I witnessed the will of the human spirit. The will of the Irish.

Turning back to the officers, I watched the first give orders as the second ran back into the house. He returned with two muskets and armed the higher officer with a gun and heavy ammunition bag, as well as himself. A sinister smile of arrogance crossed the face of the one in charge as he made eye contact with me. He aimed his musket straight at my heart and pretended to shoot it off, laughing as I flinched.

Denis moved himself in front of me as he watched the disgusting abuse of power play out. His rage energized his body and fueled the others as well.

"Keep moving in!" he commanded his people. "We must push them out!" He pointed to the British soldiers in their bright red coats with double rows of golden buttons.

The officers laughed at our condition and gestured for the cart drivers to step aside and watch. They moved to the edge of the high stairs and raised their muskets up to their shoulders, taking aim on us.

With two loud pops, smoke blew from their guns and musket balls whizzed past us. They reloaded and took aim again, this time crouching down and taking careful mark. Their guns pointed directly at Denis and me.

Denis pushed me behind him again and commanded the others, "Keep moving. Side to side. Sure, the bastards can't hit all of us." He laughed at the cowardice of the soldiers hiding behind their weapons.

His defiance shot anger across the officers' faces and they grimaced with murderous gazes, assuring us we wouldn't see the next day. They looked at each other and then took aim again. Just as their fingers began to squeeze the triggers, a voice burst out of the manor.

"Stop! Stop at once!" Lady Sligo flew out of the house in her aristocratic attire of formal, fitted jacket and sweeping skirts of heavy fabric. Her commanding tone jarred the officer's attention for a moment, but then they resumed their position. "I demand you stop this unlawful action." Her voice broke into a near scream.

"Back in the house, woman. You best not see this," the one in charge retorted.

"I've sent word to Victoria. My letter is halfway to England by now." She stood taller and straightened her skirts.

"What word?" The officer's voice turned sour.

"Corruption. Deceit. Lies." She spat the words at them. "It's time for it all to stop. The queen will get word of the truth now. She'll not be able to ignore it. This war on the Irish people will end. Now!" She moved to the soldiers. "Lower your weapons, or be hung for treason. Your actions against the Irish from this moment forward will be against the law of the crown."

She turned to the cart drivers. "Fetch water from the pond. Fill the caldron." Her gaze moved back to the British officers. "Help us now and I will adjust my report of your crimes to Her Majesty as I see fit."

My heart raced as I watched Lady Sligo reclaim command of her manor. And of the people of her county. Tears blurred my vison as she moved among her enemies as a commander.

The men busied themselves with setting fire beneath the huge pot and dragging bags of grain onto the terrace, while Lady Sligo walked down the lawn and approached us. Our numbers continued to grow as the endless march of villagers caught up to us. Denis and I stepped forward to greet her.

She reached for my hands. "You are our salvation. I would never have thought it possible nor have been able to find the courage to face them if not for you." She squeezed my hands. "What is your name?"

"I am Isobel Ross. And this is my friend, Denis O'Shaughnessy."

She nodded formal greeting to Denis. "Well, Isobel Ross, you are an angel sent from heaven. You've turned the tide here for us. And we thank you."

My chin pulled back. "No, it's these warriors." I pointed around me. "Never giving up. Fighting to the last breath." Their fight had been calling to me my entire life. I looked into her eyes. "And you. How did you know to send word to the queen?"

"I've been sheltered here for years, Isobel. Shielded from the truth of the blight. It was only when you arrived in your desperation that I understood fully the grave magnitude of the condition of our people." Her eyes misted.

"But the letter you sent?" My brows pulled together.

"Ah, dear. I *intend* to send that letter. I swear to you. It will hold every account of this day and details of every day that led to it. The queen will have no option but to feel responsibility for this careless extermination and to end it." She smiled at her clever trick on the officers. "Come! Let's aid your ailing people. This is *my* duty now."

She turned and sent more orders to the men at the caldron and signaled her house maid to follow her into the kitchen for cups and anything that could hold the life-giving sustenance.

I turned to Denis and caught the glimmer of hope in his eyes. It misted quickly from the grief and trauma he had experienced but it lived now somewhere deep within him. He looked into my eyes like I was the angel he believed me to be.

"You must do something for me, Isobel," he said.

I looked into his eyes. "Anything."

Gazing into Denis' deep eyes, he passed great responsibility onto me without breathing a word. I accepted whatever he was about to ask of me without waver and he saw this raw willingness within me.

"When you go back to Galway. Will you check on my family?" he asked. "Me parents and siblings. I mightn't make it back to them. It will be some time before true help arrives. And I'm committed to me sister and her family here now." He spoke as if already knowing his sentence.

I nodded in agreement, unable to speak through my constricted throat.

"There's something there, in case they would ever need it. Something I buried, ta hide from the British, before I left." He continued. "By the rock pile on the beach. You know the one."

My eyes widened as I listened to his every word.

"At the bottom, where two boulders meet. They create a gap. An opening ya can look through, straight out ta sea, to Inishmore. Under that gap, I've buried our family keepsakes in a crate. Would ya be sure the family gets it? When this is all over. When it's safe again."

"I will, Denis. I promise you." I reached for his hands. "You're a good man." My heart broke for him and his plight. Deep within me, I knew he wouldn't escape it.

I stepped away as Denis turned to Colin and Tommy. "Gather the women and children first. Move them to the front. If any elders remain standing, bring them up as well..." His orders faded in my ears as I moved further from them.

My emotions rose to the surface with force. They'd been

suppressed by adrenaline and focus until this moment when my guard lowered. Tears streamed from my eyes as heavy sobs pushed on my chest. My steps quickened and turned to a sprint as I tried to escape the despair and death all around me.

Images of Maeve returned to my mind as I passed along the pond. If she only knew the pain and hardship that was to come after her. She'd worked so hard to save her clan. To preserve Gaelic Ireland. And then this.

Maybe she did know. And she believed I could help. Maybe I did. I looked back at the starving people as they moved toward the overflowing caldron.

My hands went to my face as I sobbed. My ring hit on my tooth with a clink. The ring of the pirate queen. Maeve's ring.

I pulled it off my finger and stared at it. It held so much power, so much connection. Yet, it couldn't stop this from happening. My teeth ground in my mouth, crunching the anger like coarse gravel.

I reeled my arm back and threw the ring far out into the pond and ran.

As I gained speed, the wind blew my hair back and sent my tears streaming into it. My vision blurred from the mist of my tears and all colors streamed into one.

Then the blasts came, hurtling at me from all directions. Thunderous sonic booms sounded and a vortex pulled me into its abyss. My face contorted, pushing against the anguish of the assault. And then I landed. I smashed down on solid ground that jolted my every bone.

Pushing myself up to sitting, I gazed all around me. I recognized the clearing and its boulders instantly and jumped to my feet. My legs buckled beneath me and I fell back into the grass.

Pressing myself back up to sitting, I stood more cautiously and found my delicate balance. Weakness in my muscles was more apparent than ever. Fatigue was normal for my return from my visions, but this time it felt different. Worse.

It could have been the emotional fatigue that drained me to this level of weakness. The grief of the death march clung to my soul and weighed on me like heavy tar. I pushed through it to get back down to the castle. I had no idea how long I'd been gone and who or what I might find below.

As I staggered down the hill along the trickling stream, I looked out toward the old cemetery. Ryan's truck remained in the same spot. And Paul's car. My heart rate accelerated and my feet quickened. I stumbled along the uneven terrain and went straight toward the castle. My breathing pushed in and out of me with effort as I struggled to reach it.

I moved past the high stone walls of the stronghold and stepped into the open field that led to the sea. My eyes scanned the area, searching for Ryan and Paul. My breath shot in quick gasps as panic filled me.

Then, by the large flat boulder, my eyes locked on him. Just in the shadow of the rock, Ryan hunched over with his elbows on his knees and his face in his hands.

"Ryan!" I screamed, but no sound came. I cleared my parched throat and tried again. "Ryan!"

His head lifted and turned to me. His despair dissipated as he stood in shock. "Isobel!" His voice broke and he ran to me.

I stumbled over the rocks trying to race to him but my body rejected my commands to run. As he reached me, his desperate eyes searched me and horror washed over his face.

I looked into his eyes, ready to tell him I was okay, but all went black as I fell into his arms.

CHAPTER 18

M y head whirled, causing the whole world to spin to the point I was sure I would puke. My stomach wrenched and I sat up to stifle the purge that threatened the back of my throat. When I focused on my surroundings, the spinning slowed and I took a deep breath to calm my stomach.

"Isobel? Jesus Christ." Ryan's voice spiraled through my skull. "Say something."

I started to speak but my dry throat caught the words before they could come out and I coughed.

"Get her some water," he shouted to Paul.

My eyes moved from Paul to Ryan as they fumbled with the water bottle. It was like their jumbled nerves flashed distress signals in every direction.

Ryan held the open bottle to my lips and I sipped from it. The cool wetness filled my mouth and I reached for the bottle and tipped it higher, drinking every last drop. I gasped for air at the end of the bottle and panted.

"I'm okay," I whispered, closing my eyes against the bright daylight. "How long was I gone?"

"Couple hours, at least," Ryan started. "What the hell happened? I lost you as soon as you touched the ring."

The details tied my tongue with too many to know where to begin.

Ryan reached toward my hands and hovered over them. "Can I touch you, Isobel? I need to know what happened."

I nodded my head and lifted my hands to his.

As the heat of his palms entered me, light moved up my arms and all through my body. His mind joined with mine as he helped hold me together while taking the burden onto himself.

He responded with clenched jaw and tightened fists as he understood the struggles with the British soldiers. His head reeled back in loathing anger as he absorbed the pain and wickedness of their crimes. Once he saw Maeve's face in the shadows of the dungeon, he turned to Paul, wide-eyed.

In an instant, Paul knew. He pounced over to us. "You see her?" His voice begged Ryan for details. "Is it Maeve?"

Ryan's head nodded and Paul stepped back in shock, pacing through the stones around me.

I pulled my hands away from Ryan's as my head began to spin. I needed to clear it for a moment, to help get my bearings on my time and place.

"Give me a minute. I don't feel well." My head went woozy again. "What's wrong with me?"

I looked into Ryan's eyes as he stared with concern that added years to his face.

"Why are you looking at me like that?" I asked him.

Paul moved closer and stood next to Ryan, studying me like I was a specimen of some form.

Ryan's lip trembled. "You, you're..." He shook his head. "You're extremely thin, Isobel. Emaciated, actually. I think we need to get you to hospital." His voice morphed in and out of clarity and I allowed my head to fall against his shoulder.

My mind drifted through the faces of the starving villagers, Lady Sligo, and Denis O'Shaughnessy. Faces I would remember for the rest of my life. They were people like any other people I'd ever met, only these ones had a purpose—a life force that was stronger than anything I'd ever known. My heart broke for them as I imagined their final days and their despair.

I barely felt Ryan carrying me to the truck and the trip to the hospital passed like a gentle dream. Murmuring and poking, lifting and prodding, then sleeping. Deep sleep.

I woke to the steady beep of the machine by my bed. The bag was empty but had done its job of replenishing my body with its energy and vitality. My head cleared and I was able to separate the experience of my vision from the present moment. Relief sank deep into my bones.

My eyes fluttered open and scanned the room. Ryan slept in the chair by my bed. Dark circles under his eyes defined his level of worry and exhaustion. His leg twitched, then his eyes opened.

His flinched as he saw me watching him and he moved to the side of my bed.

"Hi," he said, bending over me with a smile.

"Hi." I smiled back.

I blinked into the bliss of the in-between space where you first wake up, before you start processing the burdens of the day.

"How long have I been sleeping?" I looked out the window to try to judge the time, the day.

"About twenty hours, I'd say. Sure, you needed it."

I rubbed my head, tampering with details that swam in it.

Apparently, the hospital staff and Gram bought the story of violent food poisoning that left me dehydrated and gaunt. Whatever they gave me in the bag of fluids brought me back to life and I was grateful.

"Maureen's next door. Sure, the two of you could have shared a room," Ryan teased.

"How is she?"

"She's awake. Asking to go home. So that's a good sign." He smiled.

"She'll need some help finding her balance again. They say she'll need to use a walker for a bit."

My eyes closed as I smiled in relief. She was a strong woman. I was sure she would recover from this. But it was important that no one bothered her again. The stress was too much.

"Ryan, there's still so much I need to tell you."

"I know. I held your hand as you slept." He reached for my hair and moved it from my face. "I wanted you to know I was here. And I needed to be sure you were okay."

I nodded. "It's okay. So you know about Denis?"

"Yes." His hand ran into his hair and held it. "It's almost too much to comprehend. I could make myself crazy running in circles to follow it all."

"It's incredible that you spoke with him in our earlier vision together. It was like it was meant to be." I shook my head.

"That's what I mean. I just...it's just...ack." He snarled. "It could make a person nuts."

"We need to dig. We need to find it." I pressed my lips together, knowing that he was well aware of Denis's claim.

He smiled. "I know. Paul's meeting us there tomorrow. He's bringing his equipment. Says it could be a delicate operation, requiring proper skill and caution."

"Are you serious?" I choked.

"Yep. If any of it is true, anyway." He took my hand and filled me with his joy that I was awake, talking, and that I was myself again. "But today, we rest and take a breather."

But I couldn't rest. My mind raced with all the details of my journey and kept landing on one piece in particular.

"I saw Maeve," I stated.

"I know."

"How much does Paul know?"

"Just that you saw a faded apparition." He paused. "I think it's best *you* tell him what you saw. It seemed the right thing."

I nodded in agreement. What I learned about Maeve would destroy Paul—the fact that she made the decision to stay in the past.

I needed time to think about what I would say to him. How I would say it. She had travelled to the past and then stayed there. But just knowing that she wasn't trapped in the void or lost on the wind forever was enough to put my mind at a level of ease that I hadn't felt for over six years. Maybe I could phrase it right for Paul so he could feel the same peace.

~

Paul fumbled in the boot of his car and pulled out a large black bag. His scruffy beard and furrowed brow showed a man who carried the weight of the world on his shoulders. Ryan and I paced with eager anticipation of our treasure hunt.

"My research partner will be here shortly," Paul commented in an authoritative tone.

His professional demeanor was off-putting but made sense at the same time. We were treading on his territory now, as far as he was concerned, in regards to disturbing a possible archaeological site.

The urge to just dig up the whole area had eaten us alive since the day before, but Ryan and I kept our heads and distracted ourselves with other things. I blushed as I looked at him and the way his jeans hung on him so perfectly. There was nothing better in the world than being in his arms. Warm, protected, loved. I smiled to myself and allowed the feeling of bliss to light me up on the inside.

As soon as Paul's surveyor friend, Murt, arrived, we went to the beach with our equipment and settled in around the large pyramid of boulders. I looked to the top and gazed at the dark rock balanced so effortlessly at the top—black as night. And I knew I gazed upon a sight that Denis once gazed upon as well and his kinship warmed the space around us.

I knelt at the crevice between the largest two boulders and looked through the space out to the Atlantic. My eyes fell on the largest of the Aran Islands, Inishmore, confirming we were looking in the right place.

As Paul and Murt moved around the area, marking it with wooden stakes and pink tape, Ryan and I began digging in the sand. We started with our hands, then reached for the shovels we had brought down from the shed. With each scoop, we looked at each other with hopeful anticipation, then scooped again. The deeper we went into the sand, the darker and more solid it became. My scooping turned to scraping, and then shaving, of the wet, compact sand.

As we mindlessly continued digging, my shovel bumped on something soft, sending an echo through the depths of our hole. My eyes widened and I looked at Ryan to be sure he heard it. He froze and stared back at me.

"I think we've hit something," he called to Paul as I tapped my shovel on the area.

We dragged our tools along the surface until softened, rotted wood revealed its splinters and sent chunks into the sand.

"It might just be driftwood or bog oak. Try to make the hole wider. Remove as much surrounding sand as possible," Paul instructed as he pulled another shovel from his huge black bag.

The three of us dug at the sand while Murt took photos of the excavation. Our silence and relentless digging proved we expected more than driftwood and I held my breath with the hope of finding Denis' family treasure.

And as we broadened the size of the hole, I reached in and dusted the loose sand off the top of the wood. My hands pressed until my finger found an edge. I removed the sand from the hard side and moved along it until I found a corner. As my hands dug around it, exposing more of the size and shape, I found another corner.

We dug further along the side as we saw the direction the crate was set and quickly uncovered the rest of it. My fingers had now brushed the sand away from all corners and edges and we stepped back as we stared at the size of the wooden chest. It reminded me of a dowry trunk that would be at the end of a woman's bed, holding all of her personal keepsakes and heirlooms.

Excitement coursed through my veins as I imagined what might be inside. No matter what it held, plates, pots, other trinkets, it would be treasure to Ryan and Maureen.

I stepped back and watched the three men dig at the edges of the crate until the entire box was uncovered. Ryan stood in the hole and brushed around the chest with caution as Paul and Murt removed larger shovel-loads of sand from the location. My hand covered my mouth as I watched them jiggle the crate loose and hoist it out of its tight, dark resting place. I stepped back to make room and looked around to see if the rest of the world was aware of the incredible discovery unfolding before us.

My tingling senses were right. We were being watched.

At the edge of her property, in the hedges, Mrs. Flannery lingered. Her squinted eyes and pinched face sent seething disapproval toward us. As soon as my eyes met hers, she turned on her heels and went straight toward her house with a stealth mission in her step.

My eyes closed and I shook my head. Was she going to call the Gards on us? She was pathetic.

I shook off her negativity and focused back on our find.

Paul began recording himself as he described the crate. He noted time and date and then rattled off the dimensions and features of the wooden chest. The box wobbled as the structure had succumbed to the degradation of moisture, erosion, and time. One short side of it was missing some panels, allowing a large amount of sand into the inner chamber, soiling whatever might be inside.

"Some contents may have escaped through this opening over time. With shifting sand, storms, and tides, movement would not be unusual." His voice remained professional, like he was making a documentary. "We'll need to excavate the entire area to search for any stray contents."

"Can we try to open the box?" I asked, losing patience.

I realized we needed to proceed with caution so as not to damage any relics, but the snail pace was killing me.

Paul looked to Ryan and nodded.

Ryan stepped to the front of the crate and waved for me to come closer. He pulled on the rusty latch to open it and the entire handle broke away from the crumbling wood. He placed the latch in the sand next to us as Murt continued to take pictures through an enormous lens.

"Get your hands under that part and we'll lift together," I instructed him.

I pressed my palms under the edge of the lid along with Ryan and we heaved. It resisted at first from its wet, corroded seal but shifted once we added more muscle. We jimmied it free and carefully removed it from the top of the crate and lowered it into the sand next to us.

Together, we gazed into the box.

Our shoulders sank as we stared into a pile of sand. My air went out of me as I watched Ryan's face drop.

We reached in and touched the wet sand. We pushed our fingers into it, causing whatever was just beneath the sand to shift and clang.

We gasped and pulled back in surprise. Then we dug back in and felt around.

Ryan grasped onto a metal handle wrapped in wet leather and pulled. As he moved back, he extracted a sword from the crate. It was similar to the one Gram had found in this very location.

"Jesus!" Paul shouted.

I reached into the wet sand again and felt around. My fingers clamped onto the edge of a plate and pulled. As I wiped it clean, a glint of light bounced off the shiny metal, exposing ancient carvings on what appeared to be a small shield or maybe a coat of arms.

"Stop!" Paul cried out. "Wait." He stepped closer and his jaw fell open. "These items are more than family heirlooms." His breathing grew rapid. "They're older. Much older." He looked at Murt for valida-tion. "I'm sorry, Ryan. Isobel. I know you want to see more, but we must follow protocol. And the first step is to quarantine this area. To mark it off as a significant historical site." He stepped back. "Basically, make it untouchable."

Paul made calls to gather a full archaeological team. The excitement of the find brought a local firm as well as a research team from the university. In a matter of hours, the site bustled with academics and round-spectacled investigators. The energy around the location was thrilling as conversation moved from the Bronze Age to medieval Irish folklore.

Ryan and I made room for the workers while keeping a close eye on the crate. The contents belonged to the O'Shaughnessy family first and foremost but the historical nature of it all rooted it deeply in Ireland's past. It belonged to her.

Yellow tape surrounded the area and tables of equipment and beeping meters were set all around. Lighting was erected attached to generators and it became clear this would be an excavation site through the night and probably weeks to come.

Ryan and I grew to trust the team, under Paul's leadership, and we took a moment to go back to the cottage.

"I'll need to have the place ready for Maureen. I'd say she'll be back in a couple days." He looked around at the chaos out front and curled his lips back, exposing his teeth. "This is not the stress-free environment I was hoping for." He chuckled.

More cars pulled down the narrow road and Ryan walked to the door for a better look.

"Ah, fer the loov o' Christ. It's feckin' Ciaran and Ned. Do they not stop for even a second?" Ryan pushed out the door and I followed right behind him, certain it was Mrs. Flannery who'd tipped them off.

"Have ya permits for this carry on?" Ned waved his arm at the commotion at the beach.

"Yes, Ned. Dr. McGratt from NUIG is in charge. His team has secured all necessary approval." Ryan remained aloof as Ned's shoulders dropped an inch.

Ciaran stepped forward and handed papers toward Ryan. "We've come with orders ta remove ye from this land. The County Council has overridden yer request to stay, as the benefit to the town is too great and squatter's rights just won't hold up against us. Ye won't be able to stop progress, lad. My apologies, O'Shaughnessy."

Ryan stepped back from the papers Ciaran handed him. His jaw tightened.

"Off my property, Ciaran. You'll not bully us from our home. The O'Shaughnessy's have lived off this land for hundreds of year. Generations. And we owe ya nothin'. We pay our taxes like everyone else." Ryan turned away from Ciaran.

I watched the faces of the two men redden with anger. They were likely used to getting their way with their harassing tactics.

Beyond the men, my eyes moved to the edge of property as Paul made his way over to us. His face was bright with new discovery.

Before he could speak a word, Ryan interjected, "Gentlemen, you remember Dr. McGratt. He's the head of the excavation project."

"Excavation?" Ciaran repeated, looking to Paul.

Paul tipped his head in greeting. "The discoveries are growing. The historical sector of the County Council is on its way. The site will be deemed as historical preservation. Nothing can ever be built here or changed in any way." Paul blinked at the men and watched them crumble before our eyes.

Holiday homes could never be built here. The Council wouldn't be able to renovate or destroy the natural beauty in any way. Like Paul had said, it was now untouchable.

The three of us turned and went into the cottage, leaving Ciaran and Ned on the lawn with their jaws wide open. Their hopes of making a fortune off the misfortune of others scattered into the briny mist that blew from the sea, for centuries upon centuries.

In the cottage, Paul directed Ryan and me to the table. "Sit, sit. You need to see this." His eyes shot wide like a child on Christmas morning.

He pulled his leather sack off his shoulder and placed it on the table.

"I wanted ye ta see this before anyone else did." He opened the bag as he spoke. "I'm not sure what's in it, but you'll see what I mean." His hands reached in and delicately removed a small wooden box and placed it on the table. "I found it in the hole where the crate was dug out. Its corner poked out from the loose sand, more shallow than the deep location of the crate, like it had been buried later. Maybe as an afterthought." He pushed the small box closer to me.

I reached for it and looked at Ryan. He nodded for me to continue. I brushed the loose sand from the carvings on the top and then gasped. I jumped back like I'd been shocked. My heart beat out of my chest as I stared at Paul and Ryan in disbelief.

The carving on the top of box held crude lettering, but it was clear enough to be understood. Our eyes stared at the top of the box which read, 'Isobel'.

My hands trembled as I fumbled with the box, looking for a way to open it. I wiggled the lid with an upward motion and it separated from the bottom. I pushed the lid to the side and looked into the box.

Strips of rotted leather filled the space within and I reached for a clump of it. Something solid nestled within the cushion of the leather packing and I shook it free. With a loud clang, a heavy piece of metal dropped onto the table.

It rolled a bit, then settled in the center. The three of us hovered over it as we focused.

In exact unison, we all jumped back from the table with a burst of surprised shouts and jittering exclamation.

"Jesus!" Paul stepped back further.

"Holy shit!" Ryan's hands pulled away from the table like he was about to be struck by a venomous snake.

"It can't be." I moved back to the table as the initial startle dissipated. "How?"

I leaned in for a closer look and my eyes lit up from the proud sparkle of the ancient relic.

It was the ring.

The ring of the pirate queen.

CHAPTER 19

I looked into the dark corner of the work bench where the small box sat hidden under a dirty cloth. Paul allowed us to keep the relic without making formal record of it. He knew the contents held significance within our stewardship and shouldn't be caged within the glass of a museum.

"I still can't believe Denis was able to retrieve the ring. I threw it far into the pond." I shook my head, remembering the emotional force behind my action. "He must have seen me do it."

"I'd say the pond's not too deep. He could probably wade out there and fish around for it," Ryan replied.

I stared at the box with a cautious gaze, certain I would never touch the ring again.

"So, he made it back to Spiddal." My head shook in disbelief. "I was certain he would die in Mayo with the others."

Ryan's lips pressed together as his shoulders lifted. "We'll never really know what happened. But he was sure you would return to find the hidden crate. That's why he buried the ring with it. But how could he have been so sure? How did he know?"

A smile lifted the sides of my mouth. "The O'Shaughnessy's are gifted. Have been for centuries. I'd say Denis was no different."

Ryan stepped back as his eyes brightened. "Ya. You could say that."

The crunch of tires on gravel alerted us to Paul's arrival and we stepped out of the shed to greet him.

"How ya," Paul called to us. He crossed the lawn with a light lift in his gait.

"How ya," Ryan called back to him. "How're things movin' along?"

"Ah, good man," Paul replied. "The site's a gold-mine of artifacts. Literally a dream come true for us archeologists."

Paul followed us into the shed out of the damp mist of the day. I sat back on my stool by the workbench and watched as Paul inspected Ryan's craftsmanship and his array of tools.

Then Paul moved closer to me.

"Have ya touched the ring, Isobel?" he asked without wasting any time with small talk.

"Hell no." I reeled back even from the thought of it.

His lips pressed together and he looked to Ryan, then back at me.

"Have you thought anymore about...about Maeve?" He watched me for a reaction.

My leaned back on my stool to move as far away from him as possible and I pulled my eyes away.

I hadn't had a chance to think much about it yet. Seeing her in the dungeon at Westport House had actually given me some solace. I was content in knowing she wasn't lost in the abyss. The revelation allowed me to breathe again.

But Paul was right. Maybe it wasn't enough. There were still so many unanswered questions. There was really no way I could be truly sure that she didn't still want to come home. Paul's desperation muddied my thinking. Was it just him that wanted her back or could she want it too?

I looked at Ryan and his eyes held familiar fear.

"It's dangerous, Paul. You saw what happened to Isobel last time she touched that ring." Ryan's voice sharpened with each word as his anger grew.

"I know," Paul said. "I don't intend to put her in harm's way. I'm merely opening dialog." His hand went up to tamper Ryan's growing anxiety.

I looked into the corner at the hidden box and pictured its contents in my mind and chewed on my bottom lip.

Paul continued. "You feel it too. I can see it in your eyes." He looked more closely into my gaze. "We need to find her again."

"Are you crazy, man!" Ryan interjected, but his anguished voice was dulled beneath my racing thoughts.

My gaze fell to the floor in deep concentration as I imagined connecting with Maeve again—understanding her journey and knowing what became of her. My heart beat faster with the thrill of uncovering more of her mystery.

In an instant, my eyes lifted and met Paul's straight on.

He stood taller and a satisfied smile spread across his face, like he knew he had me.

And he did.

Gravel crunched along the road as tires rolled over the lane by the cottage. We peered out from the shed expecting more surveyors or assistants but my eyes locked on Ned. The captain of the Gards refused to give up so easily. His pride stood in the way of all progress.

We stepped out of the shed and Ryan and Paul moved ahead to greet him.

"What is it now?" Ryan snapped at him.

Ned's arms lifted, signaling officers behind him who had been hiding out of view, and they circled us.

Paul's hands went up. "Hold on now, I've got all necessary approvals right here in my vest." He reached for it and pulled out a full set of folded papers. "Sure, Ciaran's commissioner at the County Council signed them." He chuffed at the irony.

Ned nodded at an officer close to Paul and the Gard reached for the papers, leading Paul to the side of the yard by the stone wall as if for closer inspection.

"Now!" Ned commanded his men.

Three of the officers tackled Ryan to the ground, pressing him into the dirt. His struggles made no difference against the strength of the pack and his voice burst out.

"Are you insane?" he blasted at Ned.

Ned grinned and signaled with two waving hands for a vehicle to back down the lane, closer to us.

Paul jumped toward Ryan and within a second several officers surrounded him, stopping his ability to move.

"What is the charge?" Paul shouted. "This is blatant misconduct. Abuse of the law."

"We have our orders." Ned broadcasted his voice across the yard.

He waved his hands along the stone wall and from behind it, two men dressed in all white stepped out from their crouching positions. They moved toward me and grabbed me from both sides.

"Let go of me!" I commanded in utter shock. I twisted and yanked in affronted surprise at their hostility—no different from the British officers.

They pulled me and I resisted with every ounce of energy. "What are you doing?" I shouted.

Their grip grew tighter as I was lifted off my feet and carried across the yard.

A white van backed up along the stone wall and the rear doors flew open. My eyes moved along the wall and fell on two shadows near the bushes. Mrs. Flannery. And then, stepping out from behind her, navy blue. Sister Margaret.

"Ryan!" I screamed as I struggled to break from the grasp of the two men.

"Isobel!" His voice carried horrified anguish in its wake.

Paul shouted again through his restraints, "What are you doing, Ned? She's done nothing!"

Ned squared his shoulders and took a deep breath like a preacher. "She's deemed a threat. A danger to self or others. She'll be sectioned and placed under proper care…"

His voice trailed off as I was shoved into the padded interior of the van. Just as the door slammed shut, I heard Ryan's voice call my name again.

And then only silence.

The End.

Turn the pages for a teaser of book two, Curse Raider.

AFTERWORD

I hope you enjoyed book one of the Irish Mystic Legends series, Legend Hunter. For a sneak peek at a teaser from book two, Curse Raider, click a few pages and you will find it. Be sure to visit my website for more information and buy links.

Thank you!

www.jennifcrrosemcmahon.com

To sign up for my newsletter:
https://www.subscribepage.com/f1p9w6

ACKNOWLEDGMENTS

Special thanks to Rebecca Hamilton for her one-to-one author coaching and amazing mentorship.

Thank you to Naomi Hughes for her amazing editing super powers and for supporting my growth as an author through six books, so far!

And of course, thank you to my family for all the support around what it takes to write books. Love to the McMahon Clan and the O'Malley Clan. :)

CURSE RAIDER TEASER

A nd now, I was a million miles away.
Swiping at the thick fog that blurred my vision, I stared into the perfect clarity of the bright blue sky. The smoke-like curtain parted for a brief moment, allowing me to see across the choppy Irish sea to far-off, rolling green hills but then the shroud closed again. It wasn't the weather causing the impenetrable haze though. It was my clouded, drugged mind.

Startled by my own self-awareness, I sucked in my breath as if waking from a shocking dream. I turned around to take in my surroundings and in an instant it came crashing down on me.

Lucidity.

And the haunting reality of my situation.

A glorious Irish landscape sprawled across the horizon beyond the vast stretch of sea, but looming behind me were the stark gray exterior walls of my prison. Memory of who I was flooded me while vile sickness rose in my throat. I'd been imprisoned against my will for rehabilitation—or cleansing, as some called it. I'd started to lose track of time as each day bled into the next in a morphed time warp.

I wouldn't let them drug me again. I couldn't. It was my only chance at holding on to myself and getting off this island prison.

I didn't belong here.

None of us did.

But there was no hope of changing the minds of my captors. The witch hunt led by God-fearing believers had convinced everyone I danced with the devil. Only my closest circle, the other gifted ones, knew the truth. They called it second sight.

I was a seer.

Closing my eyes, I focused on my visions—the wind, the weightlessness, and the things I saw during my episodes. But no matter how hard I concentrated, I couldn't conjure a new event—one that would transport me away from this captivity. And of all times, now was when I needed one the most.

I kicked at the sand beneath my feet, frustrated from not being able to use my gift. Looking back over my shoulder, I glanced around, fighting the feeling of being watched. My captors rarely let me out of their sight, and now they were likely searching for me.

Had I sent a note for help? Maybe more than once. Or had that been a dream? I vaguely remembered sneaking a note onto the ferry that visited the island each week, but the details floated through my head, lost in the haze.

It was the haze of my drug induced stupor. It had shut down all vision and I remained lost in the confines of this horrid, abusive corrections facility. Locked away from society for quiet reflection and prayer, it was enough to make me truly insane. Or in their minds, more insane.

It certainly wasn't difficult to see why the local superstitious folk, led by Sister Margaret and Mrs. Flannery, were intimidated by me— always staring into oblivion in random trances, rambling of time travel, and embarking on a never-ending search through castle ruins for a friend lost in the abyss. They were the ones responsible for having me sanctioned here.

But there was a lot more to their aggressive actions than concern over my mental wellbeing. They intended to stop not only me, but all of the gifted ones. And somehow, they knew I was the key to the success of their extermination crusade. I just didn't know how, or why, but I was determined to find the answers.

I stared at the solemn gray building, once a retreat for monks long ago, and a shiver ran through me. Inside it held a variety of broken teenage girls, some truly unwell and others becoming unwell from the cold-hearted treatment of the uncaring, stoic nurses within. Tired nuns ran the place, biding their time as part of their duty to 'helping others', but most seemed to have lost their souls while waiting for their transfer to the next, more glamorous, mission.

My eyes widened as the fresh air entering my lungs purged whatever haze was left in my brain and I stood taller.

Now was my chance.

This brief moment of clarity gave me the chance to escape and there was no time to second guess the unexpected gift. Scanning the edge of the lapping water and then focusing out to sea, I considered the limitations of the small island with only one building, no boat, and a single purpose.

Captivity.

Too far to swim, it would be certain death to even try. I grabbed my hair in clenched panic. Think, Izzy, think.

I scoured the beach. Driftwood. Broken crab trap. Rope.

I shook my head in doubt at the usefulness of my random scavenged bits. But there had to be something better, like a hidden boat somewhere, for emergencies. I tore around the bend of the coast for a better view in search of a secret dock or maybe a shed.

"Stop right there. Not another step!" A wicked voice shot me point-blank in my back. "Sanctions. More demerits for wanderin' beyond the approved borders of the home." Then a sickening laugh. "Keep it up, girleen, and you'll have no privileges left whatsoever."

I spun around in terror and locked eyes with Sister Francis.

She approached with a sinister smirk that sent a clear flight message through my shaking bones.

I was in real danger, and it stood right in front of me.

∿

Her eyes narrowed with each step closer, calculating what she would do with the opportunity I'd presented to her—how she might torture me this time. My death gaze made no attempt at hiding my contempt for her arrogant control over me, and likely fueled her evil planning.

"You'll have yer meals alone now. Can't be trusted. Ya shan't be given any freedoms here forward. Sure, look at ya, gazing out across the sea. Thinkin' of a swim perhaps?"

My spine straightened. "No, I, I just needed some fresh air. I didn't mean to wander so far."

The clarity in my mind forced me to remain compliant and apologetic, even though my civility caused me to grind on my molars in frustration. If I was careful enough, I'd be able to appear over-medicated, so not to raise any alarm that I might actually be thinking for myself. Drooped eyes and slow speech might help make my escape possible.

I scratched my head and looked around like I was lost. "I'm not really sure how I got out here. I think I might need a rest."

"Ya don't fool me, child." She stepped closer, peering into my eyes. "Ya look rather bright eyed ta me, like a sly fox."

Her cold words sent panic through my heart. She held no care or affection for me, or for any of us, refusing to ever call us by name and then referring to me only as 'child' or 'girleen'. It was her attempt at making me feel unimportant and needy. It was even more frustrating for me because at eighteen, I was light years ahead of most my age with what felt like lifetimes of formidable experience.

I had to get off the island before it was too late. Before I lost touch with who I was—before I got transformed into a lobotomized zombie. Or worse, had my spirit broken and became a conforming simpleton.

I also had to keep faith that Ryan would still be trying to get me out of here as well. I just had to believe that.

"Really, I think I just need a rest," I said again.

"And a rest is what you'll get. We won't be allowin' any of yer carry-on here, in a house of worship. Ya won't be conjuring the beast or speakin' with anyone in the beyond. Not while yer here under my watch."

Oh my god. She was drinking the Kool-Aid too. She believed every word of the angry mob who wanted to cleanse their town of its magic-wielding misfits. I pictured the torches and pitchforks that danced in her mind and I was shaken by her simplicity.

My visions made me misunderstood, that was for sure. They made me look like a freak to those who feared the unknown. Ryan and his grandmother, Maureen, were the same. But we meant no harm, keeping to ourselves.

Our kind once held honorable labels, like mystic and wise-ones, but that had all changed somehow. Now we were targeted for being different, like we were a threat to their rigid social order.

"Let's go!" She yanked at my arm. "Time fer yer medicine."

I stumbled along the path with her roughly tugging at my wrist. Every fiber of my being begged to pull away and run, but there was nowhere to go. And I knew my best chance was to play along and fly under the radar as just another compliant patient. The thought of being medicated again made me panic though.

"I'm sure I'll be fine once I have a nap. I really don't think I need any medicine, thank you." My voice caught in my constricting throat.

"Mmhm. Ya really think we'd have any control at all 'round here without the help of yer meds? Come on, now, girl. Ya must be smarter than that." She pushed me through the rusted metal door at the front entrance. "To the infirmary."

My mind raced, planning how I would avoid swallowing any pills she gave to me. I was certain the first check would be under my tongue, so up at my gums inside my cheek would be better. I just couldn't remember how they actually checked to be sure the meds were taken and prayed this plan would work.

We pushed through the white door into the infirmary and I caught a glimpse of Jayne—my one friend here. Well, sort of. We were both out of it most of the time but every once in a while we'd have eye contact at just the right moment and laugh our asses off at the absurdity of our situations. Kindred spirits in hell.

But at the moment, Jayne was not well. She slumped in her chair with her head propped against the wall. Drool trickled down her chin and her eyes stared off at nothing. My heart rate accelerated ten-fold.

Please God. Don't let that happen to me.

Begging for God's help was always an indicator of true fear for me. And that idea alone sent my alarm to a higher point.

"Take this." Sister Francis handed me a cup of orange juice then turned back to the nurse behind the counter. Whatever meds the nurse was collecting, I was sure they would be my doom.

My mind shot into overdrive. If I drank the juice before I got the pills, then I could put the pills in my mouth and pretend to drink them down. Fake swallows would allow me time to press the pills up between my cheek and gums. In an instant of quick thinking, I gulped down the juice.

Holding the cup with my fingers wrapped around it, I hid the fact that it was now empty and waited for the pills.

Sister Francis turned to me with her eyebrows lifted and just stared. She watched me like she was waiting for me to say something or do something.

So I asked, "Are you going to give me the medicine now?"

She chuckled and looked at the nurse with an arrogant grin. As she turned back to me, her smirk pulled up higher on her cheeks. It stretched up beyond her eyes as her face trailed into a blur of colors. Her voice morphed into a slow, sickening sound as she spoke to me.

"Sure, ya just drank it."

Chapter Two

The echoing blast of a fog horn jolted me straight up in my bed. Blinking away the sleepy haze in my eyes, I wondered if the fog horn was a dream or if it was my own subconscious attempt at tearing me from my juice-induced stupor.

I glanced across the uniform rows of metal beds—girls still sleeping, unaffected by the reverberating sound of the sunrise horn that filled every space.

All the girls were sleeping, except one. Jayne.

She remained lying down, but her eyes locked onto mine, calculating our next moves through the space between us. The wheels of her mind displayed their complex turning through her piercing eyes and she latched onto me like we were the only two scheming people on the island. And she was probably right.

Her eyes moved to the window above my head and then back to me. I scrambled to my knees and looked out. With a quick nod, I confirmed her suspicion—the arrival of the Sunday morning ferry, the one that carried the priest to the island for distribution of holy communion.

My stomach turned at the thought of taking communion. Not because I had given up on the church long ago, but more so because of the arrogant stares and pompous chagrin that laced the gazes of the staff. They believed we were sinners whose penance was measured and cleansed each Sunday by this visit. My head shook in frustrated annoyance and Jayne grinned.

Her half-smile lit up her face and her natural beauty was impossible to miss—large blue eyes, jet black shining hair and full lips. And her striking beauty was the cause of her untimely downfall.

The attention Jayne received from the boys in her village was enough to raise suspicion among the locals that they may have a harlot in their midst. Ridiculous. But, more unfortunate, Jayne attracted the attention of grown men as well, some married, and the women of her town banded together. They forced her family to send her away for rehabilitation from being a whore...or becoming one, just to be safe.

At seventeen, Jayne had never even had her first kiss and now here she was, rotting away her youth for the sins of others. My fists clenched at the absurdity and I vowed to get her out of this prison and back into the real world where she belonged. A world where she could live free again.

I pulled my covers off and dropped my bare feet on the cold tile floor. Jayne's eyebrows lifted as she watched me. We weren't supposed to rise until given permission but any time my brain was thinking for itself, I took advantage of the opportunity.

I waved my hand for Jayne to follow me.

We tiptoed across the room, careful to not disturb the other girls. Some of them had been brainwashed far enough that they actually complied with the rules and ratted out any offenders. It was like they thought they belonged here and it was good for them. Like they believed Jayne and I were the trouble-makers because we thought for ourselves, when we could. And we got punished for it on a regular basis. It wasn't much different from school as I thought about the social order more—they were teacher's pets and we were their targets, the non-conforming rebels.

"What are we doing, Izzy? You're insane," Jayne whispered.

"It's a boat. We need to see if there's any way to sneak on and hide. They'll take us back to the mainland and we can run," I whispered back, reaching for her to come closer.

I turned the knob of our dormitory door and it clunked in its housing, causing us both to freeze. Scanning the sleeping girls for any alarm blowers—one shifted but then fell silent again—we turned back to the door. Jayne chewed on her lower lip as I turned the knob again and it popped open.

Standing motionless for a moment, we stared into each other's eyes in panic of rousing any of the girls, but then, certain they remained unaffected, we snuck out into the cold corridor. Creeping along the dim, antiseptic hallway, we moved toward the door that led out to the back of the institution.

"We're dead if they catch us." Jayne jabbed at my ribs. "I swear to God, I can't spend another day in solitary, praying for forgiveness. That huge crucifix creeps me the hell out."

"It's better than having to wash miles of sheets by hand. That's exquisite torture at its finest," I blasted back at her, as quietly as I could. "I never want to see another sheet as long as I live."

She chuckled. "No shit. I swear they make us do that just to drive us crazy. I mean, who washes their sheets everyday? When I get out of here, I vow to wash my sheets like once a year!"

A laugh threatened to burst out of my mouth and I caught it in my nose, making it sound like a stifled sneeze. Both of us turned red with silent laughter that we struggled to suppress. Hands on knees, we gasped for air through our quaking shudders.

"Come on, harlot." I pulled on her. "Follow me." I pushed open the heavy door and fresh early morning air circulated around us.

She shoved me out the opening. "Who you callin' harlot, devil's bitch!"

I punched at her arm. "Someone forgot to say her rosary this morning," I murmured with a silent chuckle.

After propping the door open an inch with an oblong rock, I pointed in the direction of the boat, which was hidden from view just around the side of the home. Jayne hooked her arm around mine and we moved along the side of the building, hugging close to the wall for cover.

As we reached the front corner, we peered around it and caught a glimpse of a small group disembarking from the ferry. Three nuns in traditional dresses and full-coverage habits walked alongside the priest who stepped forward to greet the head of the facility, Sister Mary Carmel. Her pinched face and permanent scowl turned my blood cold and my flight response trembled, at the ready.

I turned back to Jayne. "Once they're inside, we can move closer for a better look. The ferryman will need to be distracted when..."

Jayne's sudden silence perplexed me and I followed her frozen line of vision in the direction we came from.

"Shit," we hissed in unison.

Meek Theresa-the-Snitch peered out from behind the propped door and in our distraction, we'd lost sight of Sister Francis, who'd been standing by Sister Mary Carmel. But not for long. Within seconds, Her Evilness barreled toward us, habit flapping behind her from the wind off the sea, vengeance hanging heavy on her brow. My stomach flipped over and I grabbed onto Jayne with all my strength.

ABOUT THE AUTHOR

Jennifer Rose Mcmahon is a USA Today Bestselling Author who has been creating her Pirate Queen series and Irish Mystic Legends series since her college days abroad in Ireland. Her passion for Irish legends, ancient cemeteries, and medieval ghost stories has fueled her adventurous story telling, while her husband's decadent brogue carries her imagination through the centuries. When she's not in her own world writing about castles and curses, she can be found near Boston in the local coffee shop, yoga studio, or at the beach…most often answering to the name 'Mom' by her fab children four.

www.jenniferrosemcmahon.com
info@jenniferrosemcmahon.com

BOOKS BY JENNIFER ROSE MCMAHON

Pirate Queen Series

Bohermore

Inish Clare

Ballycroy

Rockfleet, Prequel

Irish Mystic Legends Series

Legend Hunter

Curse Raider

Truth Seer